THE STONES
OF RIVERTON

THE STONES
OF RIVERTON
Stories from a Cemetery

CLIF TRAVERS

Camden, Maine

Down East Books

An imprint of Globe Pequot, the trade division of The Rowman & Littlefield Publishing Group, Inc.

4501 Forbes Blvd., Ste. 200

Lanham, MD 20706

www.rowman.com

www.downeastbooks.com

Distributed by NATIONAL BOOK NETWORK

British Library Cataloguing in Publication Information available

Library of Congress Cataloging-in-Publication Data available

Names: Travers, Clif, author.

Title: The Stones of Riverton : Stories from a Cemetery / Clif Travers.

Description: Camden, Maine : Down East Books, [2023]

Identifiers: LCCN 2023013733 (print) | LCCN 2023013734 (ebook) | ISBN 9781684751068 (paperback ; alk. paper) | ISBN 9781684751075 (ebook)

Subjects: LCSH: Cemeteries--Maine--Fiction. | Riverton (Me.)--Fiction. | LCGFT: Linked stories.

Classification: LCC PS3620.R37476 S76 2023 (print) | LCC PS3620.R37476 (ebook) | DDC 813/.6--dc23/eng/20230331

LC record available at https://lccn.loc.gov/2023013733

LC ebook record available at https://lccn.loc.gov/2023013734

To the memory of my sister Dorothy,
a lover of art and beauty.

Contents

Acknowledgments

This collection would never have seen the light of publication without the support and encouragement of friends and cohorts. Thanks to Michael Steere and Linda Kessler, my editors at Rowman & Littlefield Publishing Group; Ellie O'Leary and the talented folks at Writerfest; my beta readers Bill Stauffer and Cindy Charles; the people of Stonecoast including Elizabeth Searle, Suzanne Strempek Shea, Aaron Hamburger, Ted Deppe, and Liz Hand; and my fellow authors Marianne Taylor, Laurie Lico Albanese, and Mary Katherine Spain.

A very special thanks to Donna and David Archambault for their support and months of dog sitting. Ollie and I appreciate it.

Prologue

THIS LAND IS NOT MAJESTIC. THE MOUNTAINS AND RIVERS DON'T inspire from afar. They're beautiful, yes, but they're humble. They grow beneath us and we grow with them. They roll and heave and dip like the living things they are, as if they're made of the same flesh as the people who live here.

If we were crows, we could fly above this valley and its twelve miles of river, get a clear sense of its lushness and simplicity. We'd see how the thin band of water winds with no apparent urgency between mountains and hills, nearly bending back on itself in places, splitting around tiny islands in others. We could see how it gathers its strength from the hundreds of streams and lesser tributaries that join its journey, flowing off green peaks and bubbling out of granite cracks. It gushes with frigid clarity from places too deep for even a crow's eye to see. There are pools of melting snow and ice that have hidden in hollows until nearly summer, eventually giving in to their nature and to the heat. They'll melt slowly and then dribble down to the mother.

From this height of a crow's flight, we would see the dozens of villages, clusters of humanity that have grown all along this river named Carrabassett—Abenaki for "One who turns quickly." Each town speckles its banks, then yields to miles of woods before the next town trickles in. The pattern repeats itself over and over before the river empties into the larger Kennebec, which will grow stronger and deeper until it surrenders to the Gulf of Maine.

But let's not linger with the clouds when there is so much below. Let's swoop down on a town, say on this town called Riverton. It's like most of the others, a village that grew from a need to be close to water and woods. There's a lumber mill down there where men and women turn entire forests—the logs of which have traveled down the river from the north—into tables and chairs that are sent to cities south. There's a post office near the center where the mail has been delivered, along with the best of the town's gossip, every day but Sunday for the past two hundred years. And a general store, the only store in town, where folks can buy anything from apples to axes, beans to boots.

Most importantly there is a cemetery, the Riverside Cemetery. This is where we will land, since all crows know that the cemetery is where any small town worth its soil keeps its history and its secrets. The stories are written between the lines of names, dates, and epitaphs. It's a narrative of a town's past, its divisions, the injustices that it sanctioned, and the questionable deaths that have gone ignored.

What follows are just a few of the secrets of Riverton—an ordinary Maine town with a buried history that has been writ in stone.

Lucy May

LUCRETIA MAY FRENCH
1692–1705
TAKEN BUT NOT FORGOTTEN

THE MOTHER CAN SEE THE TORCHES CLEARLY FROM THE kitchen window now. Six of them moving as one, like a fiery reptile up the steep switchback that ends at the settlement on the hill. There will be more than six men, of course. It sometimes takes a dozen to deal with a family that is foolishly reluctant. She squints into the moonless night and can imagine the others: dark hunched-over lumps linking the flames together, creating a solemn and single-minded chain.

She had seen it nearly an hour ago. At first, they were a few tiny dots of yellow in the valley, specks that flickered in and out of visibility. If she hadn't been looking for them, she wouldn't have noticed. But she had been looking. Every mother of a child of gifting age would be. It is a night for mothers to stand at windows and pray.

Her eyes ache from the squinting. Still, she can't discern if the specks are moving. The night is so dark that there's no point of reference, no darker tree line or hillcrest to judge distance or movement. She can only see a fire in the village's center and the pinpoints of light that either move away or toward her, she can't be sure.

"Are they coming up the mountain?" Her husband has refused to stand by her, suggesting that watching and fretting is a womanly manner of worry. But he's been checking with her every five minutes or so, as worried as she but unwilling to show it.

"I can't tell if they're moving or if they've stopped. They're too far away, and it's so dark."

The husband is at the stove, and when he's finished, he brings the woman a cup of something hot. "Drink this. You need to relax. You'll give yourself a headache staring into the dark like that."

"Thank you," she says, but doesn't drink. She sets it on the sill, and when it steams the glass she moves it to the floor.

Eventually she's able to determine that they are moving away from the town, toward the mountain. The moon is rising now, and it emits just enough amber light that she can make out the curve of where the mountain dips toward the town. With that edge as a reference, she can see that the dots of light are indeed getting closer.

A half hour later, when the line of torches disappears behind a hill, she still can't take her eyes away. It's the only window in the small cabin, and it faces south toward the town and toward the path that she's taken at least once a day for most of her life. She knows every step of that skinny trail as well as she knows the floorboards in her house. She could run it in the dark if she wanted. So why does that line of greedy men move so slowly? Why can't they get to wherever they're going and be done with it . . . be done with this torture of mothers.

Nearly an hour after the last torch had moved below the edge of the mountain, she can see a glow off to the left as the first comes back into view. Then the second is quickly followed by the third until all six are visible: a line of flickering flames with six dark lumps connecting them.

There are only three houses on the hill: The Thompsons who had given their middle girl the year before, the Ellis family who had a child a few months short of gifting age, and her own family, the Frenches, with one, Lucy, who had just become old enough at thirteen. The mother holds her breath as the procession of light and dark approach the entrance to the first house. It's Ella Thompson's home, a woman with whom she has grown and has loved like a sister. She closes her eyes and says a prayer that is not generous toward her dearest friend. In fact, it offers no remembrances of their sisterly bond. It is the prayer of a desperate mother, a plea to whatever god would allow such a process. It's a selfish prayer, but it's the only one she has. When she opens her eyes, she can see that the prayer has not been answered. The line is still moving, still progressing as one.

"Netty. Come away from the window," her husband says. "Please. Watching won't change what's already done."

She knows he's right. The name has already been drawn. But still, she can't stop herself.

"Where is Lucy May?" She doesn't take her eyes from the dark.

"I sent her upstairs to be with her sister and brother. I told them to pray."

"As if it could do any good." She says it more to herself than to her husband. "Why do we even do this? It's not our tradition. As if a river could curse a town."

"But it's our tradition now. We all agreed to it," the husband says. "And it's our river."

"Still, why do they have to come at night?" she whispers into the glass. "Why do they have to creep up on us like a ravenous serpent?" It's the torches that she hates the most. And now, as they round another corner and come straight up the hill, she can see that there are actually seven of those flames, two at the front, probably to light the path better or to scare away animals. And as they continue their slow progression, those two front torches are like eyes. Two fiery and hungry eyes. She cowers into the curtain.

The line stops in front of the Ellis house, and the mother feels shame at her relief. She relaxes the fists that have been clenched so tightly that her nails have created bloody crescents in her palms. She licks at them unconsciously as she peeks from behind lace, watching with hope as the door to the Ellis home opens. First a crack, then all the way. She can barely make out the shape of Irma Ellis as she steps onto the porch, holding a lamp up to the men, listening, then shaking her head.

Is she pleading? Arguing? Her heart goes out to Irma, a dear woman who has already given two. But she hopes she won't shame herself and her family. After all, giving is an honor. Everyone understands that.

"Do it quickly, Irma, so we can get on with our lives," she whispers aloud, but not so loud that God or the river or the torches can hear. Even she, in her fear, knows that pleading is wrong.

But then, as if a plug has been yanked from inside of her, what little compassion she feels for her neighbor drains out. She watches as the woman turns with the lamp held higher and points a long arm toward the next and only house at the top of the hill. The fiery line turns as one, following the arm's direction. And then it slithers forward.

Alice

ALICE FRENCH WHITAKER
DAUGHTER, SISTER, WIFE
1874–1905

HE KEEPS SAYING IT, OVER AND OVER, LIKE A PRAYER OR A PROMISE. "I didn't kill her," he says, even when no one asks. They assume his guilt now. They stand back and whisper as he walks unsteadily through town. Talking to himself. Speaking of death and innocence. It's as if he's hearing the voices of the dead, and possibly he is. Possibly he's hearing me now, after nearly a decade of ignoring my every word, my every need. I hope he can't stop hearing me.

"You killed me, Edgar." I hiss in his ear and he flinches.

My name is Alice. It's an unremarkable name, but it suited me. I was never an attractive girl, cursed with a nose too long for a face too round. My mother, with her finite capacity to comfort, referred to the protrusion as "aquiline." In reality it was just big, bullying its way into the limited space between my eyes and my mouth from the time I was twelve. It grew with the same relentless aggression as my limbs, resulting in a gangly creature with skin and hair so white some folks in Riverton assumed me to be albino. I resembled a snowy egret, without the grace or beauty.

My father, Dr. Wilfred French, with no sons to treasure, doted on my younger sister Julia. I could never blame him for his appreciation of her. It was as if she had been sculpted by a God hoping to compensate for his earlier artless error. That pride my father felt for Julia transitioned abruptly when his heavily browed eyes fell on me. No academic accomplishment—and I had enjoyed many in our tiny Riverton school—could change that. Despite the recommendations of Principal Newel, Father refused to invest in my higher education. He believed there could only be two options for daughters: either we would be married or we would be a burden. There was little question as to which of those futures Julia would enjoy, if only our father could find someone suitable. I, however, was destined for the latter.

But Father underestimated the desperation that can exist in a lonely man's soul. Sometimes, all a man needs are the warmth of a woman's parts and someone to feed him thrice daily. Even I was well equipped to handle those joyless tasks. Shortly before my twenty-fourth birthday, a spinster by local standards, my father was approached by Edgar.

Edgar Arthur Whitaker, a twenty-nine-year-old farmer from Madison, had tried unsuccessfully for the hand of Julia. He had been scouring the surrounding towns for months seeking a sturdy girl to marry, take home, and put to work. But Edgar put aside those requirements when he laid eyes on the sixteen-year-old beauty. He was quick to appreciate those large blue orbs, her hair the color of autumn oak leaves, and skin that seemed to generate its own soft light. But as lovely as Julia was, a farmer's wife she would never be. It was ridiculous that a man more than a decade older, with nothing to show for those years of labor but a bit of tanned muscle, would think he could abscond with my father's only prize. Even Mother, a woman who was disinclined to openly belittle others, was amused by Edgar's stumbling advances.

It was a year later that Edgar, even more desperate now, turned his attentions to me. When he arrived at our door, I assumed he had returned to craft a better case for Julia's hand. But my sister was giddy with the news that Edgar was vying for mine. She grabbed my arm and guided me out to the front porch, where we could sneak peeks into the sitting room. There my parents and Edgar sat, civilly chatting over cups of tea. I was taken aback, considering how they had reacted to him the first time. I've never blamed Mother for her passive acceptance of Father's decisions. She was a woman whose story had been written for her, and therefore must have assumed mine needed authorship as well. However, I was surprised and even saddened that she considered Edgar an appropriate penman. Whereas I had accepted Father's displeasures with me, I had always thought Mother to be more embracing of my less-visible attributes.

"He has a certain charm," Julia said as we stole peeks through the curtains. Edgar struggled there with a saucer balanced on one knee as he sipped from a cup that looked ridiculous in his massive paw. "This is just like that book you love so much, the one by that woman."

I was surprised that she would reference a novel, since reading was not her pleasure.

"You know, that one about pride. The romantic one."

I laughed. "You've never read *Pride and Prejudice*."

"I haven't, but you've gone on about it so often I don't need to."

I squinted through the curtains, trying to grasp what Julia must be seeing in the disquieting scenario I could not. "I think you need to read more, Julia. In no way does this resemble the beginnings of a romantic novel. From the looks of it, I'm inclined to compare it to a comedy, or most likely one of Poe's horrific tales if it goes on much longer."

Julia rolled her eyes as if it were she who understood the world more fully. "You're too cynical, Alice. This could be your future if you would open to it. Mr. Whitaker is a fine, hardworking man. He has his own farm, and he's not so unpleasant to look at."

"Really? Didn't you all laugh at him the first time?"

She picked at a cluster of invisible lint on her gloves. It was her nervous habit when she was dissatisfied with the conversation. "You obviously misunderstood."

"I think not. You did it openly."

"No, Alice. We were laughing at me, not Edgar. We were laughing at the image of me amongst pigs and chickens. Could you imagine?" She giggled too ambitiously. "You must admit it's an amusing thought considering how I am."

"But you could imagine me there? Surrounded by pigs and chickens and all of whatever that entails?"

"Yes, I could. You're good with animals, always taking in the strays. And you're a far more resilient person than I. Whereas I would be overwhelmed by the challenges, you'll rise to them. You're strong and adaptable and so smart. I'm sure there's a lot to learn, but you'll take to it quickly. And Edgar couldn't ask for a better companion. You might even be happy there. Anyone can tell that you're not now." She turned that lovely face toward me with so much sincerity and humility—whether it was real or feigned—that I loved her more in those seconds than I had ever loved her before. I glanced back at the scene that appeared to be developing into what could be my future. Mother's smile was static as she listened to Edgar's story. Her eyes widened at some distasteful detail.

"But look at him, Julia. He's like an ape at a tea party."

She joined me at the window and burst into giggles before hiding her face in a pillow. "You shouldn't make fun of him while he sits right there. He may be your husband soon."

The reality hit me then. *Husband.* The word felt foreign, like a jagged bone in a bowl of stew. Julia lowered the pillow and took both of my hands in hers. The gloves' fabric was cool against my sweating palms.

"You'll be good for Edgar. He'll take care of you, and you'll help him become a better man." She looked down at our conjoined hands and smiled. It was an amusing assemblage: mine like long white anglers entwining the shorter, thicker clusters of hers. "I will miss you, but this is your best option. There may not be others."

Julia had a point, although I doubted it was hers. She, and my parents by proxy, was probably right. There was little chance of exiting my limited life in Riverton or even improving upon it. I could plainly see the road that lay before me if I stayed there in Father's house. I would grow old with my parents. I would take care of them at the end, and I would do nothing of significance beyond that. I would be Auntie Alice, a sad and pitiable woman. It seemed that a life with Edgar offered, at the very least, a possibility of the uncertain.

"You could make him smile, Alice." She was doggedly enthusiastic, as if her future depended on the settling of mine. I suppose it did, in some way. Julia was approaching the marrying age herself, and possibly it had been planted in her mind that an older, unmarried, and unattractive sister would not make an acceptable impression for suitors and their families. It occurred to me then that she bore a responsibility I had never understood. Her burden was to marry well, while I was allowed a modicum of choice.

"He has a lovely smile, but he doesn't show it nearly enough," Julia said. "You could help him with that." As if by cue, a smile did curl at the edges of Edgar's mouth. But the reason for it was not lovely. Father had just extended an envelope to him, and Edgar's lips parted into a crooked grin as he counted its contents.

There was no courtship. Edgar had little time or patience. The arrangements had been made, and the dowry had been accepted. My departure from my "certain" life was quick and with little pomp. The wedding, if one could call it that, was at home in the parlor, attended only by my parents and my sister. Julia was as lovely as always in a pale green dress with matching accessories. I could not be similarly described in mother's starkly white wedding gown. She had insisted that I wear it, despite the differences in our shapes, and there was no time for alterations. It rose well above my ankles and drooped in places that called attention to my lack of womanly growth. But the whiteness was its most disturbing effect. Julia gasped when she saw me.

"It's so . . . white," she said, as if I hadn't noticed. "You look like a ghost." And she was right. The dress's pallor matched mine perfectly, as if we had been cut from the same sterile cloth.

What a grim couple we made. Edgar, having come directly from the fields, did not dress for the occasion. He was outfitted in a tattered shirt, faded overalls, and boots that seemed to have collected a great deal of organic matter over the years. He did not arrive with a smile nor did he adopt one. As I approached him on what should have been our happy day, I could see his horror. He had clung to an unrealistic hope that on this one day I might be closer to acceptable. When the pastor suggested we kiss, signifying the loving bond into which we were entering, Edgar was still. He was like a child who had not received the gift he had been promised. I felt sad for him, but only briefly. I leaned in and put my lips to his. They were colder and stiffer than I had expected, and they seemed to harden beneath mine. It was to be the only kiss we would ever share. For that I am grateful.

Our marriage, our arrangement if you will, limped along for nearly six years without significant highs or lows. It was a dramatic change from my life before, and in that way it was as I had hoped. It was not, however, a Jane Austen novel as Julia had suggested. I cooked, cleaned, tended to the cows, the pigs, the chickens. The cooking and cleaning came easily, since Mother had given me an education in both. The other tasks were more strenuous. My job was to keep the farm alive, to ensure that the livestock and the chickens and even Edgar did not fail in health. I had never experienced that kind of responsibility—the life-and-death kind—and it was so overwhelming I had no time to bemoan my circumstances. Every day was a challenge; it was a ritual of vigilance.

The care of the livestock was a task that required training, and Edgar was surprisingly patient with me. He taught me well, and I took well to it. There were many times during those six years when I felt close to him. He loved the farm, and sometimes it seemed as though he almost loved me now that I belonged to it. I say "almost" because he never expressed it in any way that I could qualify as affection. There was a tenderness there sometimes, a softer center that would seep through his integument. We would be delivering a calf or tending to an ailing pig and there it would be: a lightness, a gentleness, and that smile that Julia had appreciated. But the moment would be fleeting. As quickly as I noticed it, the softness would be gone. He would pull it back and slam the portal closed as if he were afraid of it opening too far and swinging out of his control. Those glimpses, as fleeting as they were, maintained me. They gave me hope for more, and a reason to stay.

Each of us bore our responsibilities solely, and in that one way it became, in the early years, nearly as predictable as my life before. Edgar immersed himself in his own work. He tended to the fields and dealt with the structural repairs, which were considerable. The house, the barn, the fences were quite old and in need of attention. He spent his time mending structures while I spent most of mine with the animals. We rarely spoke of our days.

Even the weekly coitus was enveloped by the predetermination of time, place, and expectation. Mother had advised me of that unpleasantness, warning me of a man's weight, his odor, and the unnecessary proliferation of hair. I recognize now how close we are to beasts. Edgar would be a marvelous illustration of Darwin's theories. There is no other logical reason for why a man such as Edgar should be blanketed with so much dark fur. It seems that he, and possibly all men, have one foot firmly planted in the genetic mire of another species. It would explain so much.

In Mother's way she was helpful with my introduction to sexual congress. Of course, I was aware of its existence. I was an avid reader, after all. But Mother was quick to point out that it was not the enlightening experience of novels.

"It can be quite odious," she said, although she didn't qualify. "As well as messy and unsanitary," again without details. "You will do best to relax and allow Edgar to do the work. Men like to be in charge."

It was a brief conversation, uncomfortable for both of us.

She offered one last piece of advice that was helpful. It had come to her from her mother, and she swore that it would "get you through the worst of it." She suggested I memorize a poem, something to silently recite during the process. It was a distraction that she herself had employed.

"What poem did you choose?" I asked, excited by this new intimacy.

Mother paused, considering, as if the detail might be too personal. "I chose *Love's Secret* by William Blake. I had always loved his work, and it's a beautiful poem."

"I suppose, but it's quite short, isn't it? Did you repeat it or was there another?"

She flushed. "No. Once was enough. I only hope you are as lucky. And don't worry. At some point he will get bored and seek other distractions. You'll be fine." She patted my knee and gave me such a loving look that we both teared. And that was all.

I was not a fan of Blake or any of those old men. I found my poem in the works of Adelaide Procter.

A Woman's Question.
Before I trust my fate to thee, I recited silently,
as Edgar thrust and moaned,
Or place my hand in thine,
Before I let thy Future give
Color and form to mine,
Before I peril all for thee, question thy soul
Tonight for me.

It was a long poem, but rarely did I get as far as the sixth stanza, my favorite, before the experience was over.

ALICE

Lives there within thy nature hid
the demon-spirit Change,
Shedding a passing glory still
On all things new and strange?
It may not be thy fault alone—but shield my
Heart against thy own.

It became my practice to sing the final stanzas aloud as I washed myself with a good amount of lye soap and hot water. It was a ritual that became as much for my soul as my skin.

Our years moved forward in the way that a workhorse pulls its plow: back and forth, steadily trudging through soil and rock until it either dies or is put down. Except for the weekly coitus, we were like business partners. I did my job and Edgar did his. When we spoke, it was only concerning the farm. He left me alone for the most part. He had his own room, and I occupied the smaller adjoining one. When we were not working, I had my books and Edgar had his pipe and whiskey.

My life with Edgar would have been unbearably lonely if not for Emma. I smile when I think of her. Whereas Edgar could have been likened to the dark, my dear friend Emma was, at least for me, a most brilliant light. She owned the neighboring farm, a smaller one at seventy acres compared to ours at over two hundred. She, with the help of her nephew, was a vegetable farmer, and we shared a fence that was close to the chicken coop.

"You should wear a hat, Missus," she said on that day we met. It had been months since I had moved to Edgar's and nearly that long since I had conversed with anyone. There had been no visits home, and my parents would not come to the farm. Purveyors and buyers came through, but they always dealt with Edgar. When there was reason to go to town, he would insist on doing it alone.

I held a hand up to darken the afternoon glare. Still, I could only see a silhouette against an expansive white sky. "I beg your pardon?" I quickly glanced around to see if Edgar was in sight. He was not.

The woman tossed something to me, and I managed to catch it before it landed in the dirt. It was a soft, wide-brimmed hat with yellow tie strings.

"It was my sister's," she said, as she lowered herself from the horse. "I seen you out here most every day. That hat will be good for rain and sun. A girl as pale as you needs protection." She put a hand across the fence. "Name's Emma. And I guess you must be the missus. Heard Edgar got himself a bride."

"Alice," I said. Her hand was thick and rough, but it held a warmth, like flesh that has worked hard but has also been touched. She nodded and then glanced toward the hat which was nearly forgotten in my other hand. I released her grip, loosened the tie-strings, and settled it in place. It fit nicely.

"Ellen wore it every day till she passed on. Long time ago. Looks good on ya."

That was the beginning of our friendship. It started with a gift, and it continued that way although her companionship was the best that she brought. She stopped by the fence once or twice a week, always with a few pieces of fruit or vegetables. In return I gave her eggs. It was a secret exchange, since Edgar was not a man who either gave or received. If he had known of my friendship with Emma, I'm certain he would have ended it, one way or another. As time passed, Edgar had become a man who did not appreciate the joy of others.

I don't know the seed of Edgar's hatred and mistrust of the world, since I was not privy to his thoughts or his history. But in our sixth year that seed seemed to take root and grow. Although the farm was doing well by then, and Edgar was more financially solvent than he had been, he swelled with even more hate and misery. It was as if he blamed the world for allowing him a small slice of success but not the entire pie. By that year it became obvious that I would not bear children, and Edgar hated me for it. My infertility was, in his eyes, God's curse on him and his future. Whenever I was within reach, a proximity I learned to avoid, he directed his misery at me: sometimes with his hands and sometimes with whatever was available. I tried desperately to alleviate his discomfort, and hopefully to quell mine, but it was a fool's errand. A rabid dog does not respond well to petting.

I wonder if the need to comfort is within a woman's design. Since I had no children, it's possible that I focused those instincts on Edgar. There's no other explanation for why I felt so compelled to make his life more comfortable as he made mine less so. I wonder if it's God's way of helping us move through our woman's work. If I ever meet Him, I will let Him know that it was not a gift helpful to me.

"Perhaps the arthritis would lessen if we had indoor plumbing," I suggested one evening in February as I ladled the hot potato soup into his bowl. He had been complaining loudly all winter about his aches, and he blamed the damp cold of the outhouse for aggravating it. On a recent trip home for Julia's wedding—an event that was considerably more lavish than mine—I had spoken of his complaints. The plumbing was my father's idea, and I mentioned it to Edgar, since he respected Father's opinions above mine.

"He thinks that we can afford it now that the farm is doing well." I said this in the casual tone I had learned from Mother, one she had employed when trying to acquire some new furnishing. I should have known better. I should have respected our boundaries.

He turned his face up to me, as if I had dislodged some mental blockage. His gaze was clear and nearly intelligent in its brightness. It reminded me briefly of those moments of tenderness in our earlier years, when we would work together in the barn and he would smile at some wonder of nature. But I had misread him. His face was like the sky when there is just a touch of sun before the darkness cuts across it. I saw that cloud pass through Edgar, and I was frozen by it.

"We?" He stood slowly, his face filling with a dark rage. "This is *my* farm. Not ours, not your father's. I'll decide how to spend the profits. You ugly, barren, useless woman. How dare you speak of what's good for me."

The explosion was like nothing I had known, in man or beast. It was volcanic in its power, emanating from some deep place within him. His body seemed to expand and radiate. I'm not sure if it was he physically, or the power that swelled from him, that sent the tureen of boiling soup into the air, tumbling and then covering me with burning liquid.

The pain was immediate. I ran outside, threw myself into the snow, and rubbed fistfuls into my face and scalp. My clothes held the heat against my skin, and I pulled at the fabric, tearing it away and pressing the cold into the burning areas of my neck and chest.

Edgar stood in the doorway saying nothing. Clouds blew from his nostrils like the breath of an angry bull. I continued to rub the snow into the burning areas, pleading with him to help. He went inside and I hoped, foolishly, that he would bring burn salve from the kitchen, that maybe he would feel sorry for what was surely an accident. But in a few moments, he was back at the door with something in his hand. He threw a blanket at me.

"You're so damn smart, ain'tcha?" His words were full of gravel and spit. "You and your rich folks. Telling me what to do with what's mine. Well, you ain't that smart, 'cause I was already planning for it. I'll be getting that indoor shithouse. But I'll be damned if you ever use it." Then he slammed and locked the door.

I spent that night in the barn, wrapped in a blanket and mounds of hay. If only Edgar had taken the time to know me, he would have been more cautious with his ire. If he had, he would've understood my creative nature and I might still be alive.

Fortunately, through that dark period there was Emma. She never acknowledged the scars from the burns or the bruising. I did my best to conceal the evidence. We always kept our conversation light: discussing the animals, the weather, her deceased sister, her nephew who had a family of his own. Only once did she make reference to my troubles, and even then, she disguised it as a neighborly gesture, although her meaning was clear.

"If you ever need help, Alice," she said, looking toward the fields where we could hear Edgar cursing a tired horse or possibly a stump that refused to be freed from the earth. "Help with anything at all, just ask. I'll do what needs doing." That was all she said, and I pretended to accept it at face value.

It was so strange to have those two people in my life. One feeding me with joy while the other sucked it out as quickly. As unoffended as Emma was with my appearance, Edgar was quick to show his disgust, as if I were a reminder of his failings. He had been burdened with an infertile woman, and there would be no child who would grow and lighten his load. He'd see me and growl something indecipherable through gritted teeth, not directed at me but more as an aside to some internal cohort, his invisible confidante with whom he now exchanged a constant grunting dialogue of anger and regret, even within the throes of coitus.

Those particular assaults became more brutal in the sixth year. They were administered with the foulest of language if it could be called that at all. It was a degrading and vicious attack on my gender and my lack of adherence to what Edgar thought of as "womanliness." He began taking me in the way that a dog takes a bitch, from behind and with my face shoved deeply into a sweaty pillow. With each thrust, he pressed my head deeper. I struggled for air while he groaned, swore, and eventually released. The time it took for him to achieve that was, thankfully, briefer now. I would barely get through my first three stanzas before he was out of me and into his room. It was as if the violence of the act was all he needed. He would finish quickly but with a torrent of hate, gripping me tightly around the neck and the waist, pounding and pinching at my back and breasts. It was like the assault of an avalanche: fast but destructive.

It was in that festering year, after countless humiliations and assaults, that I saw my future clearly, as I had seen it years before.

Again, I knew there would need to be a change if I were to avoid an even darker path. Life would never be better for me as long as Edgar was in charge of it. I was being swallowed by his darkness, and there would be no end to it until one of us was dead. If I allowed it to go on, I had no doubt that the dead one would be me.

But in that clear vision I could also see a future without Edgar. It was a pleasant one that included the farm, my animals, and maybe even my only friend Emma. In the aftermath of such a lovely dream, I was left with a twinge of sympathy for Edgar. After all, no one would miss a man who neither gave nor received.

It was Emma who acquired the rat poison for me. I was down in the dirt one day, examining a chicken, when she bellowed out her usual, "Mornin'!" Even after our years of friendship, the power of her voice still surprised me. She was a woman of size in all ways.

After our usual back-and-forth about the weather, her aches, and the vegetables she offered along with how to cook them, I brought up the rat.

"Emma, you know so much about farming. Sadly, I'm still stuck in the learning phase after nearly seven years. I'm concerned about a rat we have near the barn. I think it's getting into the feed and making the cows jittery." I asked her if she knew of where I could acquire something to rid us of it.

"Are you sure it's rats? Could be feral cats. They'll spook the shit out of a cow, 'scuse my language."

"Oh, I'm quite sure it's a rat. I've seen him up close."

"Why doesn't Edgar help you with that? I know he goes into town, seen him at the feed store." Emma clearly did not like my husband. Her mouth turned down whenever she said the name. There might have been bad blood between them, one of those disputes that erupts between neighbors. Whatever the cause, I recognized her dislike of Edgar as a measure of her goodness.

"Yes, he could, and I'm sure he would, but the barn and the animals are my job, you see. He has so much to do already, and I—"

"I know, Alice," she said. "No need to explain. How big's the rat?"

"Very large," I said, and I extended my arms in a best estimate.

Emma laughed. "Looks more like a dog, but I get your point. It's a bigun. I'll get the right stuff, dontcha worry."

And the next week she brought me a ten-pound bag of it. "It's good for the biguns. More poison. Might take a while, depending on how fast he eats. And there's probably more than one. You shouldn't skimp on it. You want me to put this out for ya?" She quickly jumped down from her horse and made for the fence. Emma was older, nearly fifty I expect, but youthful in her movements for such a large woman.

"Emma, no," I said and searched the horizon for Edgar. "I think I should do this. I know where the rat lives. And Edgar wouldn't appreciate it."

"You're right. 'Nuf said." She looked toward the fields. "I won't make it worse for ya."

"Thank you, Emma."

I touched her shoulder without thinking, as if the moment required it. I allowed my fingers to linger there, taking in the texture of her shirt and the firmness of her shoulder. It was the only time I had touched her, except for that first handshake, but it was the same warmth I remembered, rushing out of her and into me like water filling an empty vessel.

It was only a work shirt, but it was softer than any of Edgar's. I ran my index finger slowly along the seam, watching as if it were not me engaged in such tenderness. I stopped where it met the overalls and all that abundance that Edgar had considered womanliness. The seconds that I paused there seemed to go on and on, and in that pausing of time I got a sense for real affection, like what I felt for my parents and Julia, but different. I felt like I was moving, running through endless fields, and the air seemed to be rushing past, cool against my heated cheeks.

But I wasn't moving at all. I was perfectly still with my fingers laid softly against Emma's dusty shirt. She didn't move either. We each stood like that, frozen, staring at my fingers paused above in that area between bone and breast. I removed by hand and we each lowered our eyes, to our feet, to the dirt below them, and to the fence that separated us. Old rusty wire and rotting wood. It was a fence that had been built fifty years before, built to separate two properties. I was both angry and grateful that it was still doing its job.

Who knows for how long we might have stood there if our time hadn't been interrupted. I heard the sound of hooves on the road and quickly turned to see the clouds of dust. "It must be a buyer," I said, withdrawing my hand. "Edgar will want coffee for them."

I turned back to Emma and noticed the redness that had climbed into her face. It was so endearing I couldn't help myself. I leaned across the wire and kissed her softly on the cheek and lingered there for several long seconds, allowing that warmth to pour through me again. We separated without another word or a glance between us. She mounted her horse and waved goodbye, and I hurried back toward the barn with the bag of poison, feeling an unfamiliar mixture of embarrassment and thrill.

You would think that poisoning someone would be easy, especially when the intended victim is a glutton. As exceptional a cook as I was, thanks to Mother, I had discovered early on that I could feed Edgar anything as long as there was plenty of it. When he pulled a chair to the table, it was with the intention of filling his face to capacity and sending that half-chewed mass into his ever-expanding belly. It was a wonder to watch, but I had learned not to. I placed the food on the table and quickly left the room. When I started my routine with the poison, I would sneak back to the door and watch. At first, I watched out of fear, wondering if he would taste anything peculiar. Later I watched for the pleasure, relishing that each meal was pulling him further from me and closer to his end.

I was mindful of where I put the poison. I had no intention of killing myself, since I was looking forward to a future, one that would not include Edgar. Therefore, I chose one source: his bread. I was not a bread eater myself, and Edgar could easily devour an entire loaf in a single sitting. I mixed a half dozen handfuls into the flour bins that I reserved for breads. It was a messy task to get them evenly married. Then I used the mixtures as needed, creating all of his favorites: sourdough, rye, soda. He seemed satisfied, although his only method of expressing it was a grunt in a slightly different cadence than those normally used for disgust. I had learned to recognize the limited vocabulary: a grunt which rose in timbre expressed approval. My poisonous breads received many guttural accolades.

But weeks passed, weeks of passionate baking, and I saw no change in Edgar. Even his sexual releases were full of his usual ravenous energy. His routines, rising early and in the fields all day, did not vary in the least. He was a large man, and possibly my doses were too meager. I doubled the handfuls.

It was a month after I had begun the process that my sister came to visit. Julia, a most unlikely comfort, was now a lift for my ailing spirit. It had been more than a year since I had seen her now that she was married and living in Bangor. We melted into one another, and our mutual need was unsettling. We had never embraced with so much purpose.

"Alice, what's wrong?" There was a slight withdrawal as she regarded me. "You look . . . terrible."

"And you are as subtle as ever, my dear sister."

But I knew her assessment to be true. I hadn't noticed the changes until that morning when I was preparing for her visit. I was never one to spend time in front of a mirror, but that morning I had seen the dark circles under my eyes and the blotches of red that traveled out of my collar and skipped in angry patches across my face. I had been fatigued for weeks, and there was pain in my feet that I had never experienced before, but I had assumed it was all the result of my increased work on the farm. And, of course, there was the stress of my unsuccessful attempts with the poison. That had been an emotional drain in itself.

"Are you ill, Alice?" She held me at arm's length. With one gloved finger, she gently touched the splotches and circles. The fabric felt cool against the heat of my skin. I closed my eyes and absorbed it. "Have you been around some poisonous plant? Or maybe an insect?" She glanced around the bleak kitchen as if the creatures might be lurking in the corners or about to descend from the rafters. "It's probably spiders." She shivered at the word and lifted her skirts from the floor.

I began taking the tea, cake, and plates out to the porch. She hurried behind me, empty-handed except for her frilly skirts. Her heels clicked delicately on the floor that had only known the rough soles of work boots and mud galoshes. After I had brought everything out and arranged the table, I settled into the less sturdy rocker and suggested she take the better one.

"Well, Alice? Do you think it's from an insect or something more serious?"

In all fairness to my sister, it is possible that she was actually concerned for my health and not worried about the possibility of a contagion. I shrugged and pointed again toward the other rocker. She tested its solidity and checked around the edges for webs and nests before settling in.

"I honestly don't know," I said. "But I'm certain it will clear up soon. Now, may we please talk about you?" I glanced down and noticed that the rash had started on my arms as well. I unrolled my sleeves to cover them. "How is your life in the city? And how is Benjamin?"

In reality, I didn't care about her husband. He was an arrogant and disrespectful man. However, my head was pounding, and the obvious courtesies were all I could muster.

She removed the pins from her wide-brimmed hat and set it on the empty chair. She did not remove the gloves. I would have been surprised if she had. I hadn't seen my sister's naked hands in years, not since she was twelve or thirteen, not since either Mother or Father had referred to them as "manly" and "stubby." The gloves had appeared shortly after, gradually developing into an obsession of colors and fabrics and, most importantly, disguise. How sad it must have been for Julia, after years of praise and adoration, to finally learn that she did, after all, harbor a flaw.

She let out a dramatic and weary breath, as if the action of settling had taxed her. "Now, about my life. Well, in a word, it's wonderful. It's so unlike the dreariness of Riverton. They're starting a symphony in Bangor. Isn't that wonderful? I just love city life."

"It sounds, as you say, wonderful. And Benjamin? Is he wonderful as well?" Already I was looking forward to her leaving. I had forgotten how unnerving her self-absorbed presence could be.

She took a large bite of cake and chewed it slowly, indicating with an index finger for me to be patient. But how could I be? Her chewing was so loud, like the sound of hooves trudging through gravelly mud, plunging, and sucking. As it went on and on, I felt the first waves of nausea. When she took a long sip of tea to wash it down, it was like the slurping of a barn animal. I swallowed hard at the sour saliva that enveloped my tongue.

"Benjamin is wonderful, of course," she said, finally. It occurred to me that the large bite and prolonged sip had allowed her time to think. Apparently, Julia had something on her mind. Ordinarily, I would have congratulated her, but this time it seemed to be something for which I needed to keep my cynicism in check. She was worried, distracted.

"And now it's my turn to ask, what's wrong, Julia? Your note suggested an urgency."

She giggled, but there was no humor in it. "And you call me direct? Apparently, we can't just chat like sisters?"

"I'm sorry. It must be the heat. I'm suddenly not feeling well, so maybe we should get to the point."

"Well, you're right, it is somewhat urgent. You see, Benjamin has had some recent—how should I put this?—setbacks. They're temporary, of course, but still, they're troubling."

"Setbacks? I wouldn't think a man like Benjamin Taylor would have setbacks." There was a hint of my usual sarcasm. My attitude was being taken hostage by a thumping behind my eyes.

All I wanted was to splash myself with cold water and then collapse into a sleep.

"Everyone has setbacks, Alice. My word, I imagine even Edgar has setbacks."

If only he would, I thought.

"And speaking of Edgar, I understand he's doing well." She glanced around the porch: at the poorly mended screen, the missing tread on the steps, the worn and splintery woodwork that needed attention. "But he's careful with his profits, isn't he?"

A sharp pain stabbed at my insides, and I curled into myself, taking short breaths until it eased.

"My word, Alice, what's wrong with you?" Julia leaned forward and rested a hand on my arm. "You are ill, aren't you?"

I could feel the sweat collecting on my brow. I wiped at it with a napkin. "I suppose I am. What bad timing this is. I had hoped I would have more energy for your visit today, but I'm feeling as though—"

"How long have you been ill?" Her interest was genuine and I welcomed it.

"It comes and goes. I think I'm just very tired after nearly seven years. Farm life can do that, you know." I said this to the woman whose only job had been to marry well. The pain relaxed and I straightened myself to take another sip of tea. My hand trembled.

"Have you seen a doctor?"

I laughed at her naiveté. "The nearest doctor is in Skowhegan, Julia. What would you suggest I do, walk ten miles? I've never learned to handle the horses by myself, and Edgar can't leave the farm just because I'm suffering from a little fatigue. It's a busy time. I can't be sick."

"That's ridiculous. Everyone gets sick. I'll take you to Riverton. Father will look at you. That way we'll have plenty of time to talk." Julia jumped up and grabbed her hat. As she stood there, holding the frilly thing in her gloved hands, I realized how inappropriate she looked standing in the middle of my squalor. She was like an expensive trinket that had been dropped into a privy.

"No, Julia. Please." I reached toward her and saw that the trembling was getting worse. "It's nothing to worry about. Edgar would be angry if we went without his consent. And I don't want to bother him now. He has a lot on his mind."

But it was I who was distracted. It occurred to me in that moment that Edgar may have been poisoning me.

"What do you need, Julia?" My need was for this conversation to be done.

"Whatever Edgar will allow. I think a few hundred should help. It would mean so much, Alice. You'll ask him, won't you?"

I nodded but she talked on. Whatever she said then was lost on me. A vital cord to the outer world was being severed, while I was keenly aware of what was happening to my insides. My stomach churned and twisted like a sack of angry snakes that searched frantically for a way out. Julia's words bounced and echoed and made no sense.

Even now, from my omniscient perch, I am confused by the speed at which things changed then. I have no idea how long Julia spoke to that shell of me while I struggled with the pain that coursed through me. It traveled into my hair, my skin, and my feet that throbbed against the bonds of old leather. Even now, I see it in a blurred sequence of moments that end with my sister standing in front of me, her expensive hat gripped roughly in both hands and tears running down her cheeks in dark wet lines. She is pleading. I can see that now, although I can't, and couldn't at the time, hear her words.

The snakes hissed and growled as they explored the limits of my gut. And then, discovering an opening, they bolted for the exit. My insides convulsed, and a tsunami flew out of me and onto Julia, covering the gloves and the hat and a good portion of her blue dress in a flood of thick yellow with streaks of red.

Death by poisoning is quite unpleasant. I do not recommend it. I was wrong about Edgar. It seems that I was responsible for my own demise, although he is certainly accountable. If it had not been for his cruelties, I would never have touched the deadly powder, or inhaled it. I had breathed in a good amount in my angry process, not to mention the quantities I had absorbed through my skin. I had handled it carelessly. My only defense is that I was blinded by hate, and possibly love.

Julia, even within the depths of her disgust and self-concerns, had tried in her own limited way to save me in the end. I was in no condition to argue with her when she nearly dragged me to her carriage and rushed us to Riverton, scolding me the entire way for not dealing with my poor health sooner. Father was quick to recognize the enormity of my illness and brought me to the hospital in Farmington. By the following day my hair was coming out in clumps, the vomiting increased, and the bottoms of my feet were so sore I couldn't put weight on them. The rash increased and quickly moved in crimson patches across my entire body. I was dead four days later.

The autopsy was done at Father's insistence. He was concerned for Julia, of course. He couldn't allow his prized possession to be disfigured or possibly killed by whatever dreaded disease had taken me. Although he was certainly saddened, I think he was relieved to learn of the poison, to know that I had not brought some farm-bred contagion into his home.

Death brings with it a degree of insight. It's apparent to me now that the size of the rat is more important than I had thought. And the cooking had diminished the potency. I, on the other hand, had absorbed quite a lot. Traces were everywhere: on my skin, in my hair, on my clothes, and in the kitchen.

Emma has been very helpful in the investigation. Her memory, somewhat flawed and possibly fueled by whatever bad blood had flowed between her and her neighbor, was that Edgar had asked her for the rat poison. My innocent peck on her cheek may have flummoxed her into memory loss. More likely is that she understood my intentions with the poison and hoped to assist me now that my efforts had failed. What a sweet and honorable woman. Whatever the reasons for her story, it has been convincing.

Poor Edgar. He would have been better off as a bachelor. Men are so afraid to be alone, and when they are no longer alone they hate us for the intrusion. He's awaiting trial. For the past week or so I have visited him, whispering encouragements that have had quite the opposite effect. He is a less powerful man now. After an entire life of having no control over my future, it has been wonderfully satisfying to have had even a little over his.

The end is a compassionate transition, not the sad and painful one that we are led to believe. We get to stay in the world for just a little while as we watch the remnants of our lives get packed into boxes or burned in un-ceremonial pyres. We get to wander about, checking on our loved ones and their grief. There was more of that than I had expected. I watched as Mother and Father blamed each other for their part in my marriage. For Father, it was more anger than hurt. He prattled on about retribution and shame, while Mother did her best to ignore him. She swallowed her guilt and lamented in private.

Julia has had too much on her mind to grieve in any way that could be assessed as sorrow, although it must have appeared as such to others. She's been crying, she's been praying, she's spent too many days in her room. Friends and neighbors have brought her gifts of solace. But it's clear that her mourning is more for herself than for me. Benjamin has lost nearly everything, due to an affinity for horses and poker and anything else that requires a wager and no skill. Luck, however, has had no affinity for him. I've watched Julia with true empathy as she's considered her future. It seems ironic that the one she may choose will be the one I had been so afraid of for myself. I would love to console her, to let her know that a life with Mother and Father would not be the worst a life could be.

But as my time wears down, I have chosen to return to Edgar. After all, he had been, for a portion of my life, my master. I wanted to leave him with something that would demonstrate my feelings, some memento of our life together.

I am about to pass along a secret to you now. It's a secret that you will learn soon enough—some of you sooner than later. You see, Nature is quite generous at the end, allowing us to let go without guilt or sorrow or worry. She allows us a sense of finality, something more than just the blunt end of life.

And the secret is this:

The most precious gift of death is the one we pass along to the living. It's a lovely ability we're allowed before we dissipate into the firmament. We make this last decision on our own, without judgment or suggestion by any deity or deity's helper. It's our last act, and then it's over. No more wandering, no more spying, and no more whispering.

Every one of us, no matter our station or belief, is allowed to place a single thought into the mind of someone dear: some feeling, real or imagined, that will remain with them until their own deaths. Most souls choose the emotion of a special moment, some sensation that will brighten their loved ones' days until their own end.

My initial gift for Edgar was not so lovely. There were no mutual hopes and dreams, no beautiful days that I wished him to relive, since we had had none of those. No, the experience I originally chose for Edgar was the one that had dehumanized me the most. It was the one that had ripped my head from my heart and had reshaped me into an angry and vengeful woman. It was the one of him and me in the throes of coitus in that sixth year, and I hoped for him to know it as I had. But this time it would be *his* face pressed deeply into a sweat-soaked pillow, barely able to breathe, pleading with me to stop. And it would be *I* who took him in the way that a dog takes a bitch: angrily from behind, again and again, relentlessly. I wanted so much for him to experience my humiliation and pain. It would have been a just bestowal.

But it seems that our hearts soften as the world releases its gentle grip. In my final moments, I have weakened toward Edgar. I have reconsidered that seed that had made him the way he was. I can now see that even he must have been a victim of some injustice along the way. So, I have thought of something that might serve his sickly spirit well.

Instead of that spiteful gift that would have tortured him and given me momentary satisfaction, I am giving Edgar the emotional memory of my friendship with Emma. I am planting in him that sensation of when I touched my dear friend lightly on her shoulder and felt a surge move through me like fresh warm water. And I am willing him the thrill of when I pressed my lips to Emma's cheek, that joyous sensation of when I stood perfectly still, my lips attached to her soft, warm skin, while my heart raced, with no restraints, through fields of fragrant wild flowers.

They are the most treasured moments of my life, and I hope they will give poor Edgar a small understanding of the wonders he has missed.

A Stranger

OCTOBER 12, 1956

I AIN'T MUCH FOR THE BIBLE, BUT EVEN I KNOW THE STORY OF
the apple. It's all about sin and temptation and how a snake talked
Eve into eating one after God told her not to. It's a good story,
but I don't need no fiction. I got my own story of the apple, and
it's a shameful one. It's strange how one little thing can change a
person. I used to eat an apple every day, just like that rhyme tells
ya. But I haven't in nearly thirty years. Now, all I gotta do is see
one and I nearly break down crying, thinking of that poor man,
that day, and how bad a person I am. So I won't touch the things,
'cept for the one I place at his stone every year. Always the same
kind. Always on the twelfth of October. Least I can do.

I can't forget the day, even though I've drunk enough to wash
it away ten times over. All these years and it's still there, wedged
in with the good and the bad, which there's lots more of than I'd
like. It's far clearer than the others. I wonder why that is, why the
one memory you wish you could dig out and burn manages to stay
put longer than any of the ones you'd like to hold tight to the end.
I suppose it's 'cause of the guilt I've harnessed to it. It's there to
remind me that I am not a good woman, not then or now.

October 12, 1956. Gorgeous day. Fall colors against deep
blue. Indian Summer in Maine, that final gift of the kinder season

before the hellish one is heaped upon us. There was a hefty breeze, real warm and summery, coming up off the river, and we mill girls—the four of us—were making a ridiculous show of trying to control our skirts against it. Jane joked that we were like Marilyn Monroes, and we truly thought we were, all giggly as if the wind was being naughty and we were mildly offended by it. Course we weren't, strutting our young legs down Depot Street, clutching our groceries with one hand and barely keeping our undies covered with the other. It was always us four: Jane, plain as her name, with straight dark hair and lips so thin and hard they could split wood; Wilma, who might have been a beauty if only her ma had cared enough to teach her how to style her hair instead of wearing it in a knot so tight it made her eyes slant; and Fattie Lattie, as we used to call her. Always grumpy, couldn't muster a smile to save her life. She was my Johnny's sister. A Thompson, so naturally snooty. Never liked me much. Always looked at me sideways like she didn't trust me fully and was waiting for me to show my true colors. Lattie was smarter than she looked.

We'd just done our shopping at Johnson's after a full day at the mill, so the clean warmth was nice against our bare legs. It swirled up and tickled at the dark and sweaty parts. In those days, the mill whistle blew at 3:30, and the women were let out a half hour before the men so we'd be all cleaned up and ready with dinner and such. It was all about the men and what they'd need after a long day—as if ours weren't longer. So, we were walking fast and talking over each other like we always did on Fridays, laughing about another stupid girl who'd found herself up a stump without a husband. We weren't being mean or nothing, just doing what we do in small towns to pass the time, gloating at our own good fortune at getting hitched before the babies got in us.

We were halfway down Depot Street, nearly to Main, when we heard the horn blast and the screech of brakes. If I live to a hundred, I won't forget the sudden loudness of it. Shot right through the afternoon, it did. You don't hear sounds like that here.

Not in Riverton. Quiet place. Even horns don't get worked 'cept to scare a cow or a deer outa the way. Everybody within a mile must have known something bad had happened.

"Jesus, Mary, and Joseph," one of us yelled. And being the kinda girls we were—the kind to not miss something that might change the pace—we were off and running, hugging our bags tight so we wouldn't lose nothing. Jane was in the lead with her big thighs that came from riding. Wilma and Lattie were next, so close to each other I thought Lattie's swaying hips would send Wilma flying. I lagged behind, cursing the weight of a pork roast I'd bought for Johnny. I was in my early days of wifing then, still trying to please a husband through his belly. Fool's errand.

When I finally got to the corner, I couldn't see much. Must have been twenty mill girls in front of me. I had to stand on tiptoes to peer over shoulders and around heads. But I was pretty skinny back then, compared to most Riverton women, and I was able to squeeze between Natalie from the spool shop and her fleshy daughter, Grace. I pushed my way to the curb, and from that point, so close I could see everything, it was like a scene out of a newspaper. That's how I remember that part: real detailed, and kinda black and white and still. Folks had come out of the restaurant, the post office, and even the Hogpenny, where "lazy, useless men drink away their lives," as Grammie used to say. All eyes on both sides, even the drunken ones, were on the center of the road, a few feet in front of Mr. Johnson's van.

That's where the man was, splayed across the asphalt like something that fell out of the sky, one arm stretched toward a bag of groceries. Traffic, much as we get in Riverton, was stopped in both directions, and everything was quiet as if the volume of the day had been turned way down. Even the wind had quit, like it was holding its breath, like we all were.

Then, in the middle of all that stillness, something moved. It was just an apple, but we all turned to it, 'cause it was the only thing moving. It tumbled out of the man's fallen grocery bag, rolled and rolled real slow, and finally stopped, just like that, inches from the man's face. Strangest thing I'd ever seen. It was like it had purpose or something, like someone was calling it or pulling it with an invisible string.

From where I was standing, no more than a couple feet away, I could see that the man watched it too. His eye, the one that wasn't pressed into the road, followed it as it rolled to him. And when it stopped in front of his face, he looked right at it. Stared *into* it, it seemed. That's when I noticed the kind of apple it was. It was the very same as the ones I'd just bought, the expensive kind I'd planned on baking with brown sugar and a little whiskey. Something special for Johnny.

I'd seen the recipe in *Coronet Magazine*. It was supposedly one of Grace Kelly's, and everybody knows she's got good taste. It called for these expensive varieties that I'd never heard of. Johnson's had them, which surprised me, but I had to ask for them, 'cause they kept them in a special place in the back, probably so folks wouldn't steal them. They'd cost me twenty cents a pound. I remember, 'cause it was a lot to spend on apples in those days. I'd looked them all over, smelled them, felt for bruises. I suppose I was trying to decide if Johnny and me was worth such pricey fruit. The girls were rushing me, telling me to "just buy the damn things." So I finally did—bought four so we'd have em for Sunday, too. Turns out they never made it that far.

It occurred to me, as I stared at the expensive apple just lying there in the dirt of the road, that the man might have bought it for his supper too, maybe even a special supper for somebody. Or maybe it was something to snack on during a long drive to home. I could tell he wasn't from around here. His suit and his shoes were nice, like something not out of a catalog. And there was a hat that must have fallen off when the van hit him, and it was one of those straw ones—can't remember what they're called—and it had a pretty green feather in it, not something a Riverton man would dare to wear.

I felt bad for Mr. Johnson. He'd been sitting in his van this whole time, probably in shock, not knowing what to do, maybe praying even. I could see his lips moving, and then he finally got out, came around to the front, and just stood over the man, pleading with him to get up, asking if he was all right, which he obviously was not. I think Mr. Johnson was crying a little. He looked around at us, his face all red and squished up. We were all being stupid, just standing there, staring like we were watching a play or something. "What should I do? Tell me what to do." He'd always seemed like a weak man, but now he looked damn pathetic. I felt bad for him but I didn't know what to do either. Never seen somebody hit by a car before.

"I'll ring up the sheriff." It was Mrs. Abbott from the hotel. "Better not touch him."

Folks were leaning in, and I could feel Grace's big sweaty boobs on my back, but I couldn't move. I was already closer than I cared to be. And it was because of that closeness I think I saw things nobody else could've, not the way his head was, all twisted to the side. I could clearly see his eye, and it was staring right at the apple. And then—and I swear it—the man grinned. Lying there, belly down and all bent around, he smiled at the apple. It wasn't a big smile, but it was definitely there.

Now, I'm not a thinking person. Never was. In fact, I prefer not to do much of that, 'specially if it's none of my damn business. But that day, that moment, I was thinking a lot. It was 'cause I was so close to him, closer than anybody else. I think that's why I had such a knowing of what was going through his mind. His thoughts—like I was right in there with him—were all about apples. I could see it. He was remembering all the apples he'd ever had, some held to his mouth by somebody he loved, some picked with his ma and pa when he was a kid. He remembered a perfect one he'd given to a teacher once, a young and pretty thing he had a crush on when he was just a boy and hadn't learned yet that apples won't buy love or even better grades. He thought, and

I thought with him, about how the whole world can fit inside an apple, all the sweet and sour of this life. All the bright spots and darkness can be found right there in one juicy bite. I could see it in his eye, the one I could not look away from no matter how much I wanted. I could see it all, his ma and pa and the teacher and somebody he loved enough to share a piece of fruit with. I could even see the inside of the apple, that whole world of sweet and sour life. And it's because of what I saw in his eye that I have so much guilt. I sorta knew him for a minute, saw into his soul. And then I did him wrong. I did him so wrong.

In the next minute, the eye lost focus like it was pulled away from the apple and from all the world. It got dark, the smile went away, and there was no doubt he was gone.

Finally, somebody came. Too late, of course. Mr. Corson, who used his van as an ambulance whenever we needed one, drove up with his horn blasting. His son was with him, and they gently loaded the man in. Then Sheriff Wilson was there telling us to stay back while he directed the van away, down Route 27 toward the hospital in Farmington. After it left, he held traffic back so folks could cross Main Street and be on our way. The whole event, from horn blast to the man's death, couldn't have been more than ten minutes, but it seemed longer. It had made me tired all of a sudden, all that thinking about the man and what I know I saw in his eye. Made my head hurt, too. I couldn't get myself to move yet. I waved the girls on, and I sat down on the curb right near where the man had let out his final breath.

Not sure how long I was there, staring at the spot where he'd been, thinking about what I'd seen in his eye, or what I thought I'd seen. I was too shaky to stand. I felt empty, but full at the same time. Too full of his thoughts to have any of my own. I didn't like the feeling, and I didn't wanna move until I felt steady and back to myself. So I just sat there on the dirty curb, all alone with that poor man's memories flooding my brain. I didn't snap out of it till the second mill whistle blew, the one that tells the men to go home. It'd just be a few minutes before all them, including my Johnny, would be hustling down Depot Street, making a beeline for the Hogpenny, getting their beer and shot of whiskey before heading home to their women.

I stood, feeling a little shaky still, grabbed up my groceries, and slapped the dirt off my rear. The apple was still in the road. It didn't look bruised or nothing, and I thought for a split second to pick it up, being such a pricey thing. I decided against that. It was in the road, after all. But truth be told, I didn't wanna touch it after what I'd seen. It gave me the willies. So I gripped my bags real close to stop the shivers, and I started.

That's when I saw the wallet, just a couple feet from the curb, partly hidden by the brim of the fancy hat. It was a deep red, nearly a match to the apple. I didn't quite know what it was at first—so shiny and big. Nothing like a wallet I'd seen before. More of a billfold, I guess you'd call it. I looked around, but the street was empty. The women were long gone at that point, and I could hear the sounds of men from way up on Depot, talking loud and coming my way. I didn't pause. The apple was one thing, but a wallet was something different. I balanced my groceries in one arm, snatched it up, and dropped it into a bag.

It's nearly a mile from town to what was then our new home. I had lots of time during that walk to consider the man, the apple, and the billfold. When I was far enough away from houses, where there used to be a long stretch of nothing, I stopped, set down the bags, and pulled out the shiny leather wallet. It was still warm from the asphalt, maybe even from the man. His license was in it with his name, his address, and his birth date. It's been so long now I've forgotten all that. It was the money that caught my eye and fouled up my already-rattled brain. There were six twenties, five tens, and a bunch of singles. I remember that well, 'cause it was a lot of money then. Still is, I suppose.

So, I took the bills, folded them and shoved them deep into the pocket of my work skirt. Then I threw the wallet as hard as I could into the woods. I'd be lying if I said it felt good to do that, to get rid of the thing and to feel the bulge of all that money in my pocket. But it did not feel good, not at all. As soon as it left my fingers, I felt guilt and regret, the kind I knew would stick with me for a long time. And it surely has. There hasn't been a day since that I haven't wished I'd done what I knew damn well I shoulda. I ain't no Eve in a garden. I ain't that innocent. Even in my youth I knew what temptation does, how it can make a person lose sight. But in that moment, I didn't care about good and bad, right, or wrong. All I cared about was how hard me and Johnny worked in that smelly mill, and how a few extra dollars might make us feel a little closer to happy.

I started back down the road, but at some point, I musta started crying, 'cause in a few yards I could hardly see through it. I had to put the damn bags down again and swipe the wet outa my eyes. I knew Johnny wouldn't be far behind me, and he'd be wondering why I wasn't in the kitchen already, doing the thing I was supposed to be doing. But when I bent to hoist up the bags again, I could hardly lift 'em. One had gotten real heavy. I knew why, right away. It was the bag with the apples, of course.

I dug through till I found all four. I cradled them in one arm and just looked at them for a minute. Somehow, they'd gotten even more beautiful than when I'd bought them. It musta been the afternoon light, 'cause they seemed to be lit from inside, like those windows in fancy churches. They truly did glow, and for a split second I just wanted to hold them like that forever, to cradle them like they were something alive, something chock full of all sorts of possibilities.

But in the next second I got ahold of myself and did the only thing that made sense. I pulled my throwing arm back and heaved each one of them, with even more strength than I'd given the wallet, into the same woods. Hurt my shoulder a little but I kept throwing. They went high, all bright red and shiny in the afternoon, and then got swallowed by the dark. Each apple went a little deeper, as if my resolve got stronger. I stood there after, thinking about my actions, trying to understand them. But I eventually gave up on the thinking and hustled home.

For years after, every spring before the underbrush got thick, I went back to that stretch of woodland. I spent hours combing through the brush and layers of packed dead leaves hoping to find the billfold. You see, the town had found no identification on that poor man and no one had come to claim him. They even put a drawing of him in *The Franklin*, although *The Boston Globe* probably would have made more sense. Mr. Johnson had his share of guilt, too. Had him buried in Riverside Cemetery with a simple marker. "A Stranger" they called him, which was mostly the truth. I did try to remedy that, but eventually new homes were built in that stretch of woods and I had to give up.

The money came in handy, but it didn't last long. Never does. I bought a few things for the house. Nothing Johnny asked about or even noticed. None of it made me feel any better, but I didn't feel so bad I needed to tell anybody. I guess that's how you know you're a truly bad person, the fact you can live with it.

But I do place an apple on the man's gravestone every October twelfth. That's something, anyway. And it's always the most perfect, the most beautiful, and the most expensive one I can find. Least I can do.

Little Donnie

DONALD HICKEY
THE LORD'S CHILD
1951–1963

WHEN I THINK BACK TO THAT DAY, I CAN'T HELP BUT CONSIDER the "what-ifs." What if it had been raining that morning or if one of the three of us had been sick or stuck to home due to some parental demand. What if we'd gone to a different swimming hole or had a flat tire on the way. It's stupid to consider any of that. It happened, and there's no way to undo it. Even after twenty years, the images are only a little faded. It's like a watercolor now, with each moment bleeding into the next. Until the one moment where everything becomes brutally sharp.

That day, the one that moved us from childhood to the other side of it, had started as our summers always had since we'd been old enough to run without a hand to control us. School had ended for the year, and we were like escapees the way we pedaled our bikes through town, weaving around honking cars and startled shoppers. We laughed and waved back but kept pedaling until we got to the mill road where we dropped our bikes and ran.

Our skinny legs were like windmills, like pistons the way they pounded the field and sent rabbits and rodents and all kinds of bugs flying and jumping to clear the way. It was the freedom that let us run like that, freedom from school mostly but also from time. Hot summer days stretched out as far as we could see, and we raced into them, molting our shirts and our pants and our sneakers, tripping over each other, ignoring the stumps of ryegrass that stabbed at the bottoms of our feet and caught in the clefts of our toes. We were free and still years away from working the fields, or the woods, or the mill with its whistle that told folk when to wake and when to eat. But that day our only job was to cannonball off the ledge into our favorite swimming hole, to be the first to scream up at the sky and claim the rights of "Boss" for the summer.

Because I had grown some over the winter, I was a whole leg-length ahead of Ricky who was two strides ahead of Mavi who was swearing at a pant leg that wouldn't let go. Her long orange curls were stuck to her freckled face, and she kept flicking her head so she could see. She was cursing in that way she always did—loud and with no apology. She cursed the pants and us and even her mother until she finally rolled on the ground and kicked the "stupid-ass, pig-fucking, shit-sucking" pants off.

By the time we got to the river, Mavi was way behind. She was a strong girl, usually the one in front, but she hadn't grown as much as Ricky and me, hadn't developed the lengthy stride that had been gifted to us seemingly overnight. I could still hear her swearing even from up front, mostly swearing at us by then, something about how she'd still be the boss no matter what, and how she'd beat the crap out of us if we thought different. I knew that last part to be the God's honest truth. She was a far better scrapper than us boys, and she never shied away from proving it with fists and even feet, if need be.

I got to the bank first and caught the edge with the toes of my right foot, pushing off and launching high, pulling my legs into a full tuck, throwing my head back and screaming up at the sky, "I'm the Boss!" The air—God, I can feel it still, so warm and clean—poured through my hair and over my skin and I catapulted into it, feeling winter and school and parents peel off me like dead leaves or old skin. It was like that for three perfect seconds, just the way it's supposed to be for me and my two best friends on the first day of our tenth summer. I remember those seconds well, maybe because they were the last good ones of that summer. They felt longer than the bulk of all the seconds that had led up to them, as if the wind and the sun and the shedding of winter held nearly as much time as the winter itself. I can see myself now from the outside, smiling and so full of possibility, a watercolor-memory of a happy day.

But it's the next second that altered that. I looked down. and then I was out of the tuck, pedaling backward, trying to move against the air, trying to reverse my fall and crawl back over all those seconds so I wouldn't connect with the pale-blue fleshy thing that floated right there, right in the middle of our favorite swimming hole, in the exact spot where I was about to be.

At this point, my memories are in pieces, like snapshots separated by blackness.

I'm in the water. The body is next to me, drifting close. I kick at it and it its gives in like soft dough.

Its head tilts and a sheet of dark hair parts exposing one white eye that bulges through blue and veiny skin.

I freeze with fear and sink. My body has forgotten how to work. The air comes out of me in tiny bubbles.

A hand grabs my wrist and yanks until my foot is freed from a tree limb at the bottom.

I'm lying on the large rock at the edge of the river where Ricky has pulled me. I'm spitting out water and sucking in air.

Mavi is above us on the bank, horrified, staring out at the small body with one leg tethered by the branches of a fallen tree.

Then she's gone, running up to the mill for help. And that's all I remember until the next day.

Even after all this time, those snapshots are still there. Mavi remembers more than me, although we rarely speak of it. I suppose we'll keep remembering it until the day we stop remembering everything. For me, the images come back with no reason or warning. I'll be doing some mundane tasks like mowing the field or splitting wood, and suddenly I'll get a flash of it: the whitish eye looking out from under dark wet hair, or the blue arm that kept drifting back and forth with the current, or the stream of bubbles that came out of me while I could do nothing beyond watching them make a dotted trail to the surface. I can see it all, even when I'm trying not to.

It was a few days before we knew the identity of the body. We learned the sad truth when the three of us bought a Coke to share at Babs' Luncheonette. There was a stack of the weekly paper, the *Franklin Journal*, next to the register. Mavi nearly dropped the unopened bottle when we saw it. The headline read:

RETARDED BOY FOUND DEAD IN RIVER

"Oh my God," I said. "That body I kicked was Donnie Hickey."

"And they called him retarded," Mavi said. "That ain't right."

Even ten-year-old kids knew that "retarded" was a bad word to use for Donnie. "Special" was the one we'd been taught. But there it was in bold black ink, the very word that would have gotten my mouth slapped. The three of us went through our pockets and put together the fifteen cents we needed, and with the paper tucked into my shirt, I led the others back to my family's farm and up into the woods to our treehouse. We spread the pages out on the weathered planks and read it together.

"Doesn't that mean murder?" Ricky said when we got to the part that mentioned foul play.

"Can't be," Mavi said. "Who would wanna kill Donnie? He was just a little kid."

Donnie had been two years older than us, but we understood Mavi's meaning. He'd been like a five-year-old, the way he talked in partial words and giggled at pretty much everything. I tried to remember when I'd seen him last. He hadn't been in school the past couple years, not since his folks had pulled him out. The last time was probably the Easter egg hunt at the church. I remembered him being there, because it was unusual for a Hickey to be at one of the church events. They didn't come into town much, usually just stuck to themselves and the others from Happy Valley. But apparently his folks had thought he should experience some things that the valley didn't offer, so they'd brought him in. He was the only one who hadn't found a single egg that day, and it had made him sad, which made some of us feel sad too. My dad had suggested that maybe I'd like to give him one of mine since I'd found so many. He was right to suggest it, and I'd done it, although reluctantly.

"It says they won't know for sure until they do that auto-p-sy thing," I said. "It can't be murder, though. Nobody'd kill Donnie."

We read the whole story again, and by the end it seemed that maybe someone had.

The funeral was at the Baptist church and was as well-attended as any event I'd seen in Riverton. It looked like the whole town had shown up, which struck us kids as odd. The Hickeys were not well-liked in Riverton, but in our naive minds we decided that funerals must help to bury old judgments. Cars were lined up on both sides of the street, and the long black hearse was parked in front.

"I suppose they'll take him to Riverside." Ricky said.

"The poorer part, for sure," I said.

It was a reasonable guess. The lower part of the Riverside Cemetery—the part that often flooded in the spring—was where most of the poorer folk were buried, and the Hickeys were the poorest people I knew. They lived with the Boudreaus in the worst part of Riverton, that stretch of wasteland between the lumber yard and the dump. Folks in town called it Happy Valley. I'd always thought it was a nice name for a part of town that didn't look like it had ever seen a happy day. It'd be a couple more years before I'd learn about the real reasons for the name, about all the drugs and the sex stuff that was rumored to have happened there for generations. But when I was ten, I had no idea about the hateful reasons for why townsfolk would burden such a sad place with the name of Happy.

Ricky's dad, the preacher, was at the church door greeting everyone, looking more done-up than he usually was. I leaned into Ricky and said, "New suit?"

"Yup. Ma and him went down to Waterville yesterday. Sears and Roebuck's. Ma said there'd be newspaper folks here, and she didn't want him wearing that shabby brown one."

His dad frowned down at us as we got closer. "No talking in there, kids. You show respect, ya hear me?"

"Yessir," we said in unison, and we heard it again from behind as Mavi pushed her way up the steps.

"I couldn't find my dress," she whispered, breathing heavy after her bike ride. "Ma hadn't washed it since Janice's wedding. Had to wear these old jeans. Think anyone will mind?"

I didn't think so. It was what most people expected. Mavi's mom wasn't much of a housekeeper. Everyone in town made fun of her for it—behind her back, of course. I thought it was unfair criticism, since cleaning probably wasn't an easy task for the woman. They didn't have indoor plumbing at their place, had to get water in a bucket from a well in the back. There wasn't a bathroom in the house, just a privy down a path into the woods. I'd once walked into the kitchen when Mrs. Goff was washing herself in a metal tub on the floor. She was standing in it, buck naked, moving a sponge over her body and bending down to wring it out in the hot water. I stood there, watching her, barely breathing and too shocked to move forward or back. She looked beautiful to me—all creamy-white with a small patch of dark at her crotch. Her black hair was piled high on her head like a movie star. The steam from the water was rising up over her, and it brought to mind something magical, like a ghost or a goddess. I just stared at her, and my heart was pounding so loud I thought for sure she'd hear. But she didn't. She kept washing herself with so much concentration, like it was the most important task of the day. When she finally looked up and caught me standing there, she grabbed a towel to cover herself, although I'd already seen everything and had nearly memorized it in what was probably no more than a minute. She never said a word about it then or after, nor did I.

"Geez, Mavi, don't your mom do laundry?" Ricky said. "Janice's wedding was over a year ago."

"I know when my damn sister's wedding was, Ricky," Mavi hissed, too loud for church. Reverend Lampert frowned and put a finger to his lips as we pushed past. We squeezed through the adults, looking for empty pews until we found a place near the front.

The service was, in retrospect, typical, although at the time it felt unnecessarily long. The Reverend Lampert made lots of references to Donnie's youth, his "special" qualities, and the loss that would be felt by the community. That last part made no sense to me since it seemed as though Riverton would be perfectly happy to see the whole of Happy Valley disappear. The casket was up front, covered with flowers. It was a closed casket, which was a relief since I'd already seen that body up close and I had no desire to see it again.

At the end, the pallbearers lined up on each side of the box. They were all Hickeys, mostly older brothers of Donnie's. They hoisted it up easily, a little too easily it seemed. It flew up for a second like they didn't expect it to be so light which caused a couple of the flowers to fall off. It occurred to me that maybe the brothers hadn't noticed how small Donnie was. He was a puny kid for twelve, probably fifteen pounds lighter than me at ten, and since the Hickeys were so poor, maybe Donnie hadn't gotten his fair share at the table with all those big brothers and uncles around.

Mrs. Hickey was right behind the casket when it passed. The pews emptied behind the family, and when it was our turn, I scooted out and inched my way through until I was right behind her. I tapped her on the shoulder, and when she looked around, I said, "Real sorry about Donnie, Mrs. Hickey. He was a friend of mine, a really good kid." She didn't say anything at first, just looked down at me like she didn't recognize me. "It's Sammy Taylor, Mrs. Hickey. Henry Taylor's boy. We got that farm over on Maple Street."

Her expression changed then, but not in a good way. Her eyes were bright red without a sign of a tear, and she narrowed them at me. "I know who you are," she said, and she stopped moving. The whole line stopped, and people looked around, but she didn't seem to care. "And you say you was a friend to my Donnie?" Her voice sounded sore, like when a person's been yelling too much. "Maybe you was, but I ain't so sure. Nobody here really cared about Donnie." She said it loud, and people started whispering. "Bunch of hypocrites, coming here like you cared about him, like he was one of yours. Well, he weren't. So why don't you all go home and forget about it. Go home now and forget all about my Donnie. He weren't nothing to you, so you all can stop pretending like he was." She turned back to the casket and gently laid her palm on the dark wood. Her hand was bright red and cracked like she'd been working in the field all day. She wasn't crying. I asked my ma about it later. She said that maybe Mrs. Hickey had done all her crying already.

When we got outside, I asked Ricky and Mavi if they'd heard what she'd said.

"Yeah, but she don't know what she's saying," Ricky said. "My dad says it takes a while to get over losing a kid. It can make a person a little crazy."

"My ma says the same thing," Mavi said. "That losing a kid is like losing a chunk of your heart. I suppose it hurts just as bad even if the kid isn't quite all there."

"Mavi, that's not nice to say, especially not here," I whispered, checking to see if anyone heard.

"I know, I know. I'm just saying that a kid's a kid, no matter what's wrong with him."

And she was right, even though she wasn't saying it properly. The truth was that we'd always seen Donnie as half a kid, unable to do things with the rest of us, having to leave school before he'd made it through the second grade. But even though he seemed like half a kid to us, to his mom he must have been a whole one.

The details of the autopsy weren't made public until nearly three weeks after we found Donnie. I couldn't understand why it had taken so long, but my father suggested that maybe the Staties had plenty of other cases to deal with in the cities, and this one wasn't high enough on their list. Strangulation was said to have been the cause of death.

"That sounds like a bad way to go," Ricky said. We were in the treehouse, reading through the paper I'd grabbed from home. Each of us had taken a turn. Ricky first, then me. Mavi went last because she took so long. She wasn't slow like Donnie, but back then Mavi wasn't taking to learning in the way that Ricky and I were.

"Geez," she said, when she finally finished. "I guess it is murder, huh?"

"Has to be," Ricky said. "You ever try to choke yourself? Can't do it. My brother says it's 'cause your brain won't let ya. And besides, even if Donnie hung himself, he couldn't've thrown his own body into the river. Gotta be murder."

"Poor kid," Mavi said, and it seemed like maybe she was gonna cry, but she didn't. She just got quiet, and we were all quiet for a long while, our heads low like we were praying for Donnie. And maybe we were praying a little at first, but then we were all thinking the same thing that wasn't so much about Donnie. We were thinking that it was now officially a murder. It was the most interesting thing that had ever happened in Riverton since we'd been alive, and as long as we didn't say it out loud, we could be excited to be living within a real murder mystery.

But it wouldn't be a mystery for long, at least not for us.

The town meeting was a couple weeks later. Folks had been talking about having one, but the council was dragging its feet. Apparently, town meetings cost money, so they tend to avoid them until there's a proposal or an emergency. It was finally decided that the murder of a boy qualified. My mother, a woman who is always on the alert for injustice, was not surprised at the reluctance. It was her theory that if the dead boy had been a part of the "real" Riverton, there would have been no hesitation. But since the lives of those in Happy Valley were valued differently, it took some public outrage to make it happen. Although my mother would never have admitted it, I believe that it was she who put the fliers up around town.

They had a large picture of Donnie on them—I think she must have found it among the class pictures of second graders two years earlier—and the caption asked in bold black letters: **WHAT IF HE WERE ONE OF YOURS?** Whether it was my mother or some other honorable person who had posted them, they certainly did the job. Two days later the announcements for the meeting were pasted over them.

The Hickeys and the Boudreaus hadn't been in town since the funeral. Usually, they'd be in once a week for gas or groceries, but they'd stayed away for nearly a month. I'd asked my father about that, about how long it takes to grieve a loss and get on with life. When my mother's sister had died, she'd cried and spent more time in bed than usual, but she'd got right back to business after a few days. She was sadder, but still herself.

"Why don't the Hickeys and Boudreaus act like regular folk?" I'd asked him. Most townsfolk called them Gypsies, another word we kids knew better than to use. It seemed like adults could use whatever words they wanted. They only called them that because they different than townsfolk. But the valley people had lived in Riverton longer than most any of the people who criticized them. "Why don't they come to bean suppers and church and school things with us? Don't they like us?" At that time in my young life, I hadn't learned of the source or the direction of Riverton's hate.

"They're regular folk, Sammy, just a little different than us," he'd say every time I brought up the valley. "They got their wont and we got ours." I didn't understand at first, but he explained. "It's 'cause they got different ways of teaching their kids than us, different ways of living and praying. Just different, not worse." And this time when I'd brought up their absence from town he added, "They probably grieve different than us too. They'll come back to town when they're ready. They just need to be close to their own right now."

Kids weren't allowed at town meetings. My mother told me it was because a lot of Riverton adults didn't know how to talk without being foul. And there were fights often, sometimes with fists. Once with a gun. Of course, those details only made me want to go even more, but there was no persuading.

It was after nine when they got home from the meeting. I could tell right away that it had not been a pleasant get-together. They were talking over each other—not arguing, exactly, just talking like they both had things to say. It was their usual heated disagreements when talking town politics. They didn't even notice me at the kitchen counter eating ice cream out of the bucket. Ma just kept on with her tirade as she reached over, put the cover back on, and tossed it in the freezer before turning her fire back on Dad.

"Henry, you know damn-right-well if that boy was killed in Portland, it would be a whole other story. They wouldn't be patting us on the head, telling us to go home and keep a keen eye on our kids like we were a bunch of idiots. They'd be questioning folks, doing all those policing things they're supposed to. I'm not exactly sure what the process is, and I'm not confident that they do either. I am quite sure their job is not to be preaching to us on how to parent our own damn kids!" Her voice was getting louder, considerably louder than when she was just angry in a usual way.

Dad slumped at the counter across from me. He let out a long breath like he was too tired to keep talking. "Geez, Hazel, it's not like I'm a fan of the Staties. You know that. But they're the State Police. They cover the whole of Maine, not just Portland. And we don't know everything they're doing. We just need to give them a little time, like the sheriff said. It's only been a month."

Ma slammed the kettle onto the stove and turned the knob to high. "It's been *over* a month. And still nothing. You know as well as I do that this is only the beginning. That Statie didn't tell us anything. He just riled us all up, talking down to us like that. There's men in this town who are not going to take that kinda talk. There are men, and you know who they are, that won't wait for the Staties to handle this. Not anymore. They'll be very happy to take on their duties. Franklin Ayers and his buddies are more than ready."

"I'm not so sure about that. He was just mouthing off. They don't call him Crazy Ayers for nothing."

"Well, seems to me you're not paying attention if you don't think there's gonna be trouble. You saw Franklin's gun. And he's more than ready to use it. You surely saw all of them gathering outside after, listening to him spouting theories. And you know at least one of those theories involved the valley. It doesn't even matter that the dead boy was a Hickey, there's people here that are already pointing a finger at that part of town."

"Why would anyone think it was them? It's not like Happy Valley would kill one of their own kids."

"You think Franklin Ayers and his posse have ever had a thought between them? They want action, Henry, and Happy Valley is as good a place to start as any. This town is scared, and that is not going to lead anywhere good. Riverton doesn't give a damn about that poor dead boy. They're just worried about their own kids, and they're ready to weed out a murderer if need be. I surely pray for the valley if the Staties don't get off their lazy butts and take charge."

"Why don't folks like the Hickeys," I said, unable to remain silent.

They both looked at me like I'd suddenly fallen from the sky.

"Sammy! What are you doing up?" My mother turned her fire on me.

I pointed at the kitchen clock. "It's not even 9:30. How come people don't like them? Is it 'cause they're dirty?"

"It's past your bedtime. Get up there. Go on," she said, shooing me out of the kitchen.

"But it's summer. I get to stay up till ten in summer."

"Well, this summer is different, isn't it?" Her voice was shaking—wobbly and high-pitched—as if she couldn't manage it. "And no more staying out after seven. I want you in this house by seven sharp every night till this thing is over." She reached out and pulled me close, hugging me so tight I could hardly breathe. She hugged me like that for a long while, her chest heaving and her whole body trembling. Then she let me go, turned me around, and whacked me on the rear, hard enough to make my eyes water.

"What's that for?" I said, rubbing my butt and backing away in case there was more coming.

"That's for eating ice cream out of the tub. You know better. Now get up to bed before I give you another."

Small-town meetings are intended to stir up action, although the resulting action is not always what the town's looking for. The day after the Riverton meeting, the center of town looked like a military occupation. When the three of us biked through, there were half a dozen Staties questioning pedestrians and stopping cars. Crazy Ayers and his gang were watching, guns at the ready. A couple of times the cops threatened the potential vigilantes with jail if they didn't back off. We watched from a distance as the volatility diminished for a few minutes and then rose up again, causing a replay of cop-versus-idiot.

"I hate this summer already," I said as we pedaled past the chaos and up Main Street, putting some distance between us, Crazy Ayers, and more Staties than I'd ever seen in Riverton. Mavi was in the lead, as usual. She'd decided on her own that since we all hadn't jumped into the river that day, there was no new "Boss" of the summer. And since she'd been the boss the year before, it made sense that she still was. Ricky and I had decided, as usual, not to argue with he decision.

"Yeah," Ricky yelled into the wind. "Maybe we should just go back to the treehouse. Or we could check out that bog out past your farm. My dad says all that land is haunted."

"I'm not going out there," I yelled back. "Folks have died wandering through that place."

"Me neither," Mavi said and she pulled off to the side. We skidded up next to her. "Besides, I got a better idea. Let's go up to Happy Valley, see what's going on." She said it so easily, like it was the most obvious thing to do. I should have seen it for the bad idea it was. But Mavi was Boss, or at least she'd convinced us she was, so Ricky and I kept following her up Main Street toward the one place we both knew we had no business going.

Happy Valley was hot that day, and it wasn't even noon yet. There were no trees along that stretch of West Riverton Road, so there wasn't the shade that cooled most of the streets in town. It was as if God didn't care enough to even give it that. No trees, no grass. Only weeds to break up the gray of dirt and gravel. We slowed down once we got to the houses, checking those run-down shacks on both sides for life. I'd never seen it so quiet. Usually, when we'd be on our way to the dump, someone would be playing loud country music that we'd hear even with the windows rolled up tight against the smell. But that day the place looked deserted.

I'd heard from stories that the Hickeys and the Boudreaus had been there for more than a hundred years, so I'd never understood why folks called them Gypsies. They didn't move around like Gypsies do. I suppose it was because of the way they lived. The houses were dilapidated, held together by scrap wood and pieces of rusty metal. None of them had running water, far as I knew, and that day I got a whiff of the outhouses before I saw them. The smell was like rotting garbage mixed with something else, something sour like bad milk or vinegar. Some of the outhouses didn't even have doors, and I could see into them, see the wooden boxes with the hole that emptied down into the ground. Ricky made a low whistle and put his fingers to his nose. I just held my breath in case anyone was looking. Even at ten I understood how wrong it was to make fun of people's lives, especially since we had no business there.

A dog was licking at the side of one of the toilet boxes. It raised its head as we rode by but it didn't bark, just watched us. The poor thing looked half-starved, like maybe it didn't have the energy to bark. And it was the only living thing around. The whole street was quiet, as if it were abandoned, like a town where no one lived anymore.

"Let's go back," I called up to the others. "There's nothing going on here, and this place is giving me the willies."

"Don't be such a little girl," Mavi yelled back. She seemed to have a plan, which neither of us did. So, we kept following.

But after a while, Ricky yelled up to her. "Mavi, come on. Hold up." We'd passed all the shacks and had entered into the shadier part of West Riverton Road, that long stretch of woods before the dump. She finally pulled to the shoulder, and Ricky asked, "Where you goin'? There's nothing up here except the dump, and I don't wanna go there."

Mavi smiled. "That's what you think, dummies."

"Come on, Mavi," I said. "It's getting really hot. And anyway, this might be where the murderer is, somewhere in these woods. We shouldn't be here. It's too far outa town, and my dad would—"

"My dad would—" Mavi mocked in that high squeak she always used against us. "Go back then, scaredy-cats. I'm gonna find the cemetery."

Damn, if that didn't get us.

"What cemetery?" Ricky said. "What are you talkin' about? There's only one in town."

Mavi's lips curled into a half-smile. "The cemetery where Donnie's buried. I wanna see it."

"He's buried at Riverside. We saw the headstone."

"No, he ain't, Mr. Know-it-all. There's no body under that stone, just the box. You don't know diddly-squat, 'cause he's buried up here somewhere."

"How do you know that?"

"'Cause my mom drinks at the Hogpenny sometimes with Frank Boudreau. You know, the normal Boudreau who works over at the garage. Ma said he was drunk the other night, and he told her that Donnie was buried out here. Happy Valley had their own funeral thing at a special cemetery, one for the Hickeys and the Boudreaus and all those other Happy Valley people. He said this cemetery's really old, older than Riverside Cemetery even, and most of the town don't even know it's here."

Ricky and I looked at each other. He gave me a shrug. I glanced back at the long stretch of road between us and the shacks. I didn't want to ride that by myself, especially not after what had happened to Donnie. It was too dark with all the pines that hung low. I couldn't admit that I was scared, so I nodded and Mavi led on.

Frank Boudreau had told Mrs. Goff that the cemetery was just past the old horse track. The Hickeys had owned all that land since way before Riverton was even a town. The track had been an income for them for a lot of years, but in the 1930s gambling was made illegal in the county. Once there was no gambling, there wasn't much use for a horse track. I'd never seen it myself, but my grandpa had been there when he was a kid. He had some stories about it, but usually he wouldn't get too far into them before my mother would make him stop. She said they weren't stories for kids, but Grandpa had told me plenty. Enough so that I wanted to see it for myself.

We found the track quickly, since the top of the old tower could be seen from the road if you were searching for it. A few turns and a couple of dead ends and we were there. It was rotting and partially fallen but still spoke to the grandness of what it had been: two stories high with a deck at the top. But we lost interest in the structure once we saw the splashes of bright colors rippling through the grass on the far side of the track's oval. They were catching the air and billowing up like cresting waves of reds and oranges. As we walked toward what seemed so out of place and too bizarre to ignore, I noticed the condition of the track. The center was green and overgrown with patches of brush and goldenrod, but the dirt track itself was clean, like it'd been used lately. There were grooves in it: hooves and wheels.

"People don't come out here no more, do they?" I kicked at the dirt that seemed loose and well-trod.

"It's part of Happy Valley, that's all I know," Mavi said, walking fast to catch up with Ricky. "And listen, you guys, Frank made Ma promise she wouldn't tell anybody about this place, so keep your big mouths shut. Ma said it's private property, so the Hickeys got a right to shoot trespassers."

"What?" I stopped in the center of the oval. "We could get shot?" I looked around. A shiver went through me.

"We're not gonna get shot, you big baby."

"Ricky," I called to him, "We should get outa here. I don't like it."

"What the heck *are* those?" Ricky said, not paying any attention to us but looking toward those flashes of color. As we got closer, we could see they were ribbon-like strips of fabric tied to big metal barrels that were mounted on old truck tires. The barrels were cut out on one side, and long poles extended out from there. The bright ribbons of cloth were attached to the backs of the barrels like long banners or streamers, something you'd see in a carnival or a parade.

"What the hell?" Mavi said.

"I know what these are." Ricky circled, looking them over, and then climbed through the cut-out section of one. Two leather straps that looked like reins for a team hung to one side and he picked them up. "I remember these from the church pageant a couple years ago. My dad rode in one. It was that stupid play they did in the field behind Webster Hall. A Romans-versus-Christians thing. It's a chariot, like in those old religious movies."

"What are these things for?" Mavi was playing with a strip of red cloth about twenty feet long and shiny, like the material of prom dresses. She whipped it up and down so it rippled across the grass and onto the dirt track.

"They're supposed to be fire, I think, coming off the back. It looked cool when the horses were running."

Mavi had just jumped into the other barrel when we heard the first scream. It was long and high-pitched, animalistic but undeniably human. Ricky and I reacted to the sound immediately, going headfirst into the bushes. But Mavi panicked and got tangled in the leather straps that dangled off the barrel.

"Oh shit, oh shit, oh shit!" She pulled and squirmed and fiddled with the straps but only got herself more tangled. I was as scared as she was, but I took a couple of breaths and ran out to her.

I fumbled with the straps until I got her loose, and then we crawled back into the bushes next to Ricky. The three of us stayed there for a long while, low to the ground, peeking out through the leaves and trying not to breathe so we could listen. We were huddled so close I could feel the sweat running down Mavi's arm. Gusts of wind kicked at the dirt and made waves of brown dust skitter across the field. The only sounds were the bugs. Mosquitoes dive-bombed our ears while a single dog-day cicada sang high and long, telling us that the day, already a scorcher, would surely get hotter.

Ricky stood up a little and looked around the edges of the field. Mavi stood up next and then me. "There's nobody here," Ricky whispered.

"Where'd that scream come from then?"

As if to answer, a stronger breeze came through the trees powerful enough to move branches and expose a footpath to the right of the oval, about fifty feet away. And on the wind was a second scream, this one longer and scarier.

"There," Mavi said, and I recognized that excited and somewhat dangerous tone. "It came from there. Let's go."

Then the two of them were gone, running low along the tree line. It was either follow or be left behind.

I caught up at the opening to the path and tried to say something, but Mavi shushed me. "Listen." There were moans and voices now getting caught by the wind and bouncing off the trees. We could only hear snippets of yelling and crying. Faint and in and out.

In the next second Mavi was sprinting down the path with us right behind. It was a typical situation for the three of us: Mavi making the decisions and Ricky and I following as if we couldn't think for ourselves. I hated this Mavi then, the one who couldn't be talked out of anything once she got a hankering for it. She was like a dog who wouldn't give up on a raccoon she'd treed. Mavi was my second-best friend, after Ricky, but I still hated how she'd always lead us toward something that would either get me dog-bit or scuffed-up or yelled at by some grown-up who would most likely tell my folks. But what I was hating most at the moment, and what had always bothered me about the three of us, was how Ricky and I never seemed to have a brain without Mavi.

She stopped abruptly and I was crouched so low I ran into Ricky. "There's a clearing up there. We should go through the woods."

"Wait a second." I tugged on Ricky's shirt. "That's gonna make more noise."

"Not if we're quiet, dummy," Mavi said, and she was off.

We crouched lower and tiptoed slowly through the woods, avoiding leaves and sticks, holding branches for each other. Those strange sounds got louder, and I could hear then that it was just one voice. It was a woman, and she was yelling and crying and talking like she was having a heated conversation—but with herself.

Mavi went down on her belly, and Ricky and I did the same, still following her lead as if she knew what she was doing. "It's

Donnie's mom," she whispered when we got a glimpse of her through the trees. Mrs. Hickey was pulling at her hair, banging her head with her fists, reaching up to the sky like she was begging to go there.

The clearing was just what Mavi had said. It was a cemetery, but not like the one in town. It was huge, probably twice the size of Riverside. There weren't any headstones, just piles of rocks—hundreds of them, a few with wooden sticks poking up, but mostly just mounds of what looked like river rocks of all sizes and colors. The piles were close to each other, in groups, some in circles around smaller circles and others in rectangles with a larger mass at the center. There were tiny paths in between, just room enough to walk. The mounds stretched on and on till they curved down to a line of trees and the river beyond.

Mrs. Hickey stretched herself across one of the piles, slapping softly at the rocks and mumbling. We couldn't make out what she was saying. It sounded like another language.

"This is creepy. We should get outa here," I said. Ricky nodded, but Mavi didn't move. Her head was pressed to the ground.

"Wait," she said. "Somebody's comin'."

We could feel it then. Two men passed within a few feet of us, running toward the cemetery and Mrs. Hickey.

"Mama!" one of them yelled when he got into the clearing. "What are you doing?"

"Come home, Mama," the other one said. He was big. I'd never seen him before, but the shorter one I had. His name was Jamie, and he'd come to the church that Easter with Donnie and his mom.

She didn't seem to hear at first, just kept mumbling and patting at the stones. But when Jamie went up to her and put a hand on her shoulder, she bolted upright and slapped him hard across the face.

"Get out," she screamed. "You should be ashamed to be here, both of ya."

"We're sorry, Mama," Jamie said. He rubbed at his cheek. "We loved Donnie." His voice trembled as if he were about to cry.

"We loved him so much, Mama." The big one went to hug her, but when he bent down and put his arms around her, she arched her back and screamed like she'd been scalded.

"Get out, you murderers! You baby killers!" It was so loud and vicious, and it seemed to shake the trees and the ground. I jumped to my feet and started running. I didn't even know I'd done it until I felt Ricky push past me on the right. We were on the path again, running in single file: Ricky up front, me second, and then Mavi right on my heels, close enough that I could hear her breathe. I was running so fast the branches of trees were slicing into my face and arms. I looked back for a second, just as the big guy grabbed Mavi by the shirt and she screamed. Then his other fist latched onto me. He had us both up off our feet as he slowed to a fast walk. We hung from his huge hands like sacks of potatoes. I couldn't even squirm or yell. I was held still by fear and that hand. Then Jamie passed us and tackled Ricky.

"What should we do with 'em?" Jamie said. I could see in Ricky's eyes that he was thinking the same thing, that we were gonna die. I couldn't see Mavi, but I could hear her whimpering.

The big one lowered us enough so our feet touched the ground, but he didn't let go. He and Jamie hauled us along the path—our trembling legs trying to keep up so we wouldn't be dragged—back to where it opened at the track. They tossed us to the ground, just a few feet from where all those streamers caught the air and slithered through the grass like angry snakes.

"Who the fuck are you?" the big guy yelled. Spit flew with every word. "What are you doin' here?"

"They're town kids," Jamie said. He pointed at me. "I seen this one before. I seen him at the funeral."

"You know, we could kill you, and we'd be in our rights," the big one screamed. He was stomping, pacing, and jabbing his massive fist at us. "You ain't supposed to be here. We could kill you for trespassin.'"

"Please don't kill us, mister." Mavi was full-on crying now, and I could see that she'd wet herself. I might have too, but I couldn't feel anything enough to tell. "We didn't hear or see nothin', I swear. And we won't tell nothin' to nobody. Promise. Please don't kill us. Please, please don't kill us." She was blubbering and her last words were sobs. Her face was red and squished.

I wasn't crying. I was too mad at Mavi. It was her fault, every bit of it. I wanted, right then, to beat her up for all the times she'd gotten us in trouble, for all the times I'd taken a belt for something she'd talked me into, for all those times I didn't do something good 'cause she thought she knew better, which always turned out to be the worst thing we could've done. I wanted to beat her up just once before we were both dead, hung by our necks, thrown into the river like someone—probably these two guys—had done to poor Donnie. It occurred to me then that Crazy Ayers was probably right, that the Hickeys had killed one of their own.

"What are you kids doing here?" It was Mrs. Hickey coming out of the path and toward us. Her words and walk were slow, her face white against the dark hair and the long black dress that was torn and dragging behind her. She moved like something dead or close to it. If I'd had any pee left in me, it surely would have taken its leave then. "I asked you a question. Why are you kids here?"

I tried to say something but my jaw wouldn't work. Only Mavi spoke, but it was more of a whine. "Please, please don't kill us, Mrs. Hickey. We'll leave and never come back. I swear."

"Stop crying, girl! I ain't gonna kill ya. I just wanna know why you're here. This ain't a place you should be."

"We're sorry, Mrs. Hickey." It was Ricky. "We were just riding around, exploring, ya know."

But Mrs. Hickey didn't seem to hear him. She looked past him to me. Her face was smudged with wet dirt, and some of it dripped into an eye. She took a corner of her skirt and wiped at it, still looking at me as if she were trying to make a connection.

"You're Henry Taylor's boy."

"Yes, ma'am." I could feel the tears welling up.

"You stopped me in the church that day, the day of Donnie's . . . his town funeral. You claimed you liked my Donnie. You said he was a good kid. Did you mean that? Did you really like my baby?"

"Yes, ma'am."

"You ever make fun of him?" She was standing right over me. She didn't look mad, just real tired and empty.

"No ma'am," I lied. Of course, I had. Everyone had made fun of Donnie Hickey at some point. It wasn't as if I didn't like him, though. I did. And once I knew how it was, I hadn't made fun of him anymore. But I couldn't tell her that.

"You're the one that gave him that egg last spring, at that church thing."

"Yes, ma'am."

"That was nice. I bet your pa made you do it, didn't he?"

"Yes, ma'am."

"Don't matter. It made my baby happy for a little bit. He was a good boy, and he didn't get nearly enough to be happy about. I bet you're wondering what happened to him, ain'tcha? I bet that's why you're here."

I didn't know what to say. I looked at Mavi and Ricky, but both of them were staring up at her with their mouths agape, tears streaming down their dirty cheeks.

"Mama," Jamie said.

"You shut up," she scolded, and she pointed a long, pale finger at him. Her voice was low and hoarse, like it was hurting her to talk. "These kids think there's a murderer in town. It's got their folks afraid to let them out to play, like kids oughta play, like Donnie played. They was friends of Donnie's, at least this one was." She turned the finger to me. "I want them to know the truth. What they do with it, I don't care. So, you tell 'em. You tell 'em what happened to Donnie. You tell 'em right now."

Jamie fell down to his knees and started bawling hard, like I'd never seen a man do. He crumbled like he'd lost all the muscles in his legs. He brought both his hands up to his face and wept into them. Then the big guy went to him and rubbed his back and said words I couldn't hear. He was bawling a little too.

"Mama," he said between sobs. "What if they tell somebody?"

"I don't care if they do." She was talking slow and quiet, but there was a hardness there.

The three of us looked at each other. Some of the fear was gone, replaced by confusion. We huddled close on the ground, quiet as if we were trying not to be there in this private scene we had no part in. Finally, the big guy spoke. But he didn't speak to us. And he didn't seem to be talking to his mother either. He was rubbing Jamie's shoulders and telling the story to some person who wasn't there. Maybe Donnie. Or maybe God.

"We stole them a while back." He nodded at the carts. "They were just sittin' behind the church, nobody payin' attention to them, so we took 'em. Made sense. I mean, we had this track. So Jamie and me rode workhorses down there late one night, hitched 'em up, brought 'em up here." His hand rested on Jamie's shoulder. "Donnie loved the carts. Loved 'em." The mention of Donnie's name made Jamie fold deeper into himself, and he held his stomach like he was going to throw up.

"Donnie did love these carts," Mrs. Hickey said. She had lowered herself onto one of the tires, and she picked up a bright orange streamer and pressed it against her cheek.

"We started havin' races," the big guy went on. "Round the track, one of us in each of the carts, not goin' real fast, 'cause the horses we got are old, too old to be runnin'. But we just went fast enough so those ribbons would catch the air and fly out behind us. Looked real pretty. Looked like fire, I guess. Or rainbows."

"It was something to see, all those colors flying out. Donnie loved them colors. It was magic to him." Mrs. Hickey's lips lifted into a smile for a second, and then it was gone.

"Whole bunch of the families would come up and cheer, drinkin' beers, pretending it was like the old days when they had a real track up here. We were just havin' fun, and it wasn't hurtin' nobody. We only did it once a week, but Donnie would be screamin' for it all the time. 'Let's wace,' he'd say, the way he talked. And then he'd get all excited, gigglin' and jumpin' around. Kids don't get much excitement here, so we'd cave in sometimes and do it just for him." His voice caught when he said that and he paused, swiping an arm across his face. "He'd run and skip behind us. We weren't goin' fast, just trottin' around, and he'd stay right behind so the ribbons would be all around him. He'd laugh and laugh from inside all those shiny colors."

He stopped, blew out his nostrils, and spit out a lump in his throat. "I don't want to tell it, Mama. Don't make me tell it again."

"You go on with it. You need to get it outa ya, and I'm gonna hear it just one more time, a last time. And these kids are gonna hear it too. They're old enough to know that bad things happen. Sometimes they happen when all you're trying to do is make things better. When all you ever wanted was to make your baby just a little happier. And then something happens, and God laughs at your silly plans and puts you right back where you're supposed to be."

So the big guy told us the story, and I wish he hadn't. We were just three scared ten-year-old kids, and it wasn't a story we were ready to hear.

On the night Donnie died, the Boudreaus had tapped into one of the barrels of moonshine they'd been aging for three years. The family had always been good at whiskey. According to the big guy, it was the only thing they were any good at. The recipes were old, brought over by their ancestors from wherever they'd come from, and when they tapped a barrel, it was a big deal. They didn't do it but once a year, and they'd only drink it that night. Then they'd sell most of it to the townies who would line up in their cars in a part of town they'd usually speed through with their windows rolled up tight against the smell. But on those few nights in early June, when Happy Valley would sell the only thing they could sell, the town would roll down their windows to buy it.

It was after midnight on that first day of selling when someone got the bright idea of a buggy race. The big guy said it was Jamie, but Jamie denied that. He blamed one of the Boudreaus. Didn't matter, 'cause the idea went over well with a dozen or so men. They got excited, which got some of the women going too, and then they all made a drunken parade out to the track, followed by a few of the kids who were still awake. Someone, again there was a question as to who that was, decided it would be a good idea to bring along a few jars of the moonshine.

He said it was just another race, but he admitted they'd never done it at night with a couple flashlights aimed at the track. And the moonshine was a new thing too. They'd never had anything more than a few beers. They couldn't say how long they were there, going around and around, racing those tired old workhorses until they could hardly walk. "Go again," someone would yell, and the others would chant it. So they'd go again, slower each time, 'cause the horses and the drivers were too spent for more. Toward the end of it, everyone had left, except the two of them. They were still drinking, passing a jar between them and trying to get the nags to go around one more time.

And then Jamie fell out of his barrel, too drunk to stand. He rolled around in the dirt for a while, first laughing, then swearing at his brother and begging for a fight. That's when he saw something tangled in the ribbons of the big guy's buggy. He stumbled to it, couldn't see what it was at first. It was wrapped so tight by all that cloth he couldn't even make out the shape or size. And of course, he wasn't seeing all that clear. At first, he figured it was a tree stump, or maybe one of those stray dogs that were always following them around. He kicked it a couple of times, and then fell down on his knees next to it. His eyes were barely working, but as he untangled the strips one by one—it seemed to take him forever—he finally saw it was a kid. And then he saw it was Donnie.

Jamie said it was like something you see but you can't believe, so you keep looking back in hopes that it isn't what you know right-well it is. The big guy had jumped down to see what it was for himself, and the two of them just knelt next to Donnie's body, staring at it, thinking it might not be real, just some bad trick of the moonshine.

The boy was filthy from the dust of the track, and parts of his face were scraped clean off, but there could be no doubt that it was he. The big guy grabbed him up, shook him and screamed his name over and over, as if the calling might change somebody's mind up above, as if it were all a big mistake and the screaming could make it right. But Donnie was too far gone by that point. Nobody, not even God, could change that.

It was the big guy's idea to wash him in the river. "We couldn't take him home to Mama like that, all bloody and dirty." he said. They unwrapped him from the ribbons and carried him down to the riverbank, just the other side of the cemetery. They spent a long time down there, washing him over and over, crying all the while and blaming each other. At one point, hours after they'd found him, they started fistfighting, each cursing the other for being so drunk and stupid. During that squabble, they forgot about the body for a few minutes and nearly lost him to the current. That near miss should have made them more mindful, but of course it didn't.

When they figured Donnie was as clean as they'd get him, they brought him up onto the bank and laid him out. They sat beside the boy, apologizing to him for their stupidity and asking each other how they were going to do it, how they could tell their Mama that her baby was dead, and they were the ones who had done it. They stayed there on the bank so long—talking and arguing and crying—that eventually they gave into the moonshine and their weariness. They passed out on the bank with Donnie's damaged body nestled beside them. It must have rained hard at some point in the night because the river rose just a little, just enough. They woke with the noon sun stabbing into their brains, and saw that Donnie was gone.

When they finished the telling, the big guy stood and went to his mom, Jamie right behind him. She was hunched over one of the buggy's tires, tightly clutching that same piece of orange cloth. The boys got down on their knees, put their heads into her lap and cried. She didn't push them away this time. She opened her arms and brought them in. They were like that when we left, all huddled and crying together. But it wasn't that horrible wailing from before. It was softer, like it was coming from a different place. The three of us got up as quietly as we could and made our way to the bikes near the tower. I looked back just once before I left. They were still there, so close, so wrapped around each other that they appeared to be one. Maybe they were praying. I don't know if they do that in Happy Valley. If not, I'm sure it was something close to it.

Our friendship changed after that day. It's taken years to get it back. I think about what Mrs. Hickey had said, about us being old enough to learn about the bad. I think she was wrong. We were far too young to glimpse the horrors of life and death and how different that is for the folks of Happy Valley. The three of us had been given a secret and then told to do with it whatever we wanted. I think what all three of us wanted was to give it back. It's funny how sharing something like that can go either way. It could make us closer, or it could split us apart. We chose the latter. Then both of my best friends left Riverton. Ricky to a religious school in Georgia, Mavi to Bangor with her mom and the new boyfriend. It would be eight years before I'd see Mavi again.

I only saw Jamie and the big guy—I still don't know his name—a few times over the years. They acknowledged me and I did the same. They trusted us with a story that must have nearly killed them to tell. And they surely knew that we had kept it to ourselves. If we'd hadn't, if we'd told someone that Happy Valley had killed one of their own, Franklin Ayers and his drunken vigilantes would have surely done something about it. So whenever I saw those guys in town, I nodded. And they nodded back. It was our secret and our understanding.

Riverton doesn't talk about Donnie anymore. It's possible they've forgotten about him, or maybe they never really thought about him in the first place. It's very possible my mother was right. It could have been that the whole panic in Riverton that summer was just about the kids who were of the real town and not of that section that's always been separate. Riverton will never see Happy Valley as a part of it. I suppose the valley wouldn't want it either. Like my pa used to say, "They got their wont and we got ours."

Mickey

MICHAEL JOHN TAYLOR
GOD'S GARDENER
1910-1963

WORSHIP WASN'T A BIG THING FOR US GROWING UP. MA WAS raised Catholic, so we went to a church thirty miles away, but that was it. Just Sunday. Not much in the way of religious goings-on during the week. My daddy was cautious about it. He had a brother, Uncle Mickey, who'd been bit bad by the religious bug. Daddy always referred to him as "the family fanatic," and it was that fanaticism that eventually killed him.

Uncle Mickey had a big garden at his place in Riverton, and he was real proud of it. He could grow anything from arugula to zucchini. But the larger, hardier squash were his favorites. He called them "God's gift to the poor," 'cause they would grow in abundance, and the picked ones could last all winter without going bad, long as you kept them in a cool place. You couldn't visit Uncle Mickey without leaving with an armful. But the ones he loved the most— the ones he never gave away—were the Blue Hubbard. He called them "divine."

One year, back when I was a kid, Mickey harvested a huge Blue Hubbard that he claimed had the face of Jesus on it. He said you could see it within all the bumps and grooves and splotches of gray-blue. He had our whole family over one night to "gaze upon it," since he figured it was his responsibility to share. He'd put candles all around and encouraged us to pray with him. Daddy made a show of it—I think out of respect for his brother—but Ma refused, and she wouldn't let me. She said it would "expose me to the world's crazy too early for my young mind." Still, I looked at that massive squash long and hard. Couldn't see a face, Jesus's or anyone's, even when Mickey pointed it out. It just looked like bumpy blue squash to me. I was only a kid, and Uncle Mickey wasn't too offended.

He kept that squash under his bed, said he needed it close when he was sleeping and more vulnerable to demons. He'd haul it out—all forty-seven pounds of it—every time he had visitors, which became less and less often due to his inability to discuss anything else. Even Ma and Daddy wouldn't visit much toward the end. They never brought me back after the first couple of times.

Eventually it was just salespeople who'd stop by. They'd want to sell him insurance or a vacuum cleaner, and old Mickey would drag out the Jesus Blue Hubbard, try to get them to pray with him, pointing out the spots and blotches that made up that heavenly face. I suppose a few of them might have gotten down on their knees. When someone's that passionate about something, it's a difficult thing to just walk away. Even a stranger is gonna give the obsession a little time, especially if he thinks there might be a sale in it. Mickey claimed he'd converted a few, had them praying next to him, got them "Jesusized," as he called it. I never heard anyone admit to it, but I suppose they wouldn't. Ma said poor Uncle Mickey was more than a few eggs short of a dozen toward the end. But one thing he was clear about, never wavered on, was his love for that big, ugly squash.

It was sad the way Uncle Mickey went. Apparently, he'd dragged the squash out from under his bed one night to prepare for his nightly prayers, when he had a massive heart attack right there, clutching the thing. That's how my daddy found him, flat on his back with the Jesus Blue Hubbard pressed into his chest. When I think about it now, I suppose it was both a beautiful and a horrible way for Mickey to go, to die under the weight of something he loved so much. Daddy kept that squash for a few months after, I think because it was such a part of his brother. But Ma finally cooked it up, claiming that Jesus and even Uncle Mickey wouldn't want it to go to waste.

It was a good-tasting squash, holy or not.

Maggie

MARGARET HICKEY ALBERTSON
GONE BUT NOT FORGOTTEN
1906–

RIVERTON HAS FINALLY GONE OFF THE DEEP END. TO BE HONEST, it's always teetered too close to the edge of crazy—might have something to do with all that black smoke that's been pouring out of the mill for over a hundred years. Or it might be the water from the river that people keep drinking even though everyone knows raw sewage flows into it from some of the farms upstream. But this crazy is different for Riverton. This time folks have gone full-on nuts. All because of something a drunkard swore he saw on a night he was most likely too blind drunk to see anything at all. But it isn't his story that's the problem here. It's what happened because of it that's made up my mind to do something I've been thinking about since I was a kid. I'm getting out of Riverton. And I'm taking my Mavi with me.

It all began on a Tuesday when I went down to the Hitchpost to get my check. I'm always there first thing Tuesday morning, totally broke come Monday night. I guess you'd call me a pay-check-to-paycheck kinda guy. I'm only twenty-four. Saving's a thing for later.

When I went into the bar that day, Jake—my boss and probably what you'd call my best friend in the world, besides

Mavi, of course—was planted on a stool and staring into space. I'd only seen him like that—so still and pensive—once, the day his pa had died about four years ago. That morning he was drinking Rebel right outa the bottle. It's hard to lose your pa. I know that firsthand.

But it wasn't liquor he was drinking on this Tuesday morning. Nope, it was coffee that was doing the healing, and he was looking like a man who needed a hell of a lot of it. Jake's never been a thinker, not by anyone's standards. I guess you'd call him more of a doer, and usually the doing is not based on anything close to thought. But I could see on that morning that he was a man deep in his own head, so deep he didn't hear me coming in. I walked up, slapped him on the back, and he nearly jumped out of his BVDs, spilling coffee all down his front.

"Jesus, Sammy!" He grabbed a stack of napkins off the bar and dabbed at the wet spot.

"Sorry," I said, although I didn't know what for. I always slap Jake on the back. We're not handshaking people. "What're you doing here so early? Something happen?"

It took him a minute, like he was concerned I might not be the right ear. Jake and I are pretty open with each other, as open as guys get anyway, but he appeared to be struggling with this one. He concentrated on the depths of his cup, stirring and thinking. Finally, he looked me square in the face, got close and said, "I saw something last night, Sammy. I swear I did." His voice was soft, nothing like the boisterous guy I thought I knew. "I just ain't quite sure what it was." Then he did the best he could to describe it.

I should point out that Jake McNally is a decent and honest man. He's like the big brother I never had, close to a dad after I lost my own. Gave me a cleaning job right out of high school when I didn't know what the hell I was doing, where I should be going. I wasn't sure about leaving Riverton with my ma still here, and I'd be damned if I'd work in the mill where my dad took his last breath. Jake helped me wade through that messy time.

With all due respect, and despite everything he's done for me and my ma, Jake McNally is a card-carrying, dyed-in-the-wool, seven-days-a-week drunk. He's one of those guys who doesn't know when to quit, just keeps going until he either passes out or somebody does the right thing and knocks him out. I can't tell you the number of times I've gotten between him and an errant fist that wouldn't listen to reason. My jaw aches with the memory. Still, he is my dearest friend as well as my boss, so when he starts going on and on about something crazy, I tend to listen. Whether he's drunk or on drugs or some mind-bending combination of both, I hear him out. And this is the gist of what he told me.

Jake swears by "everything holy," which is an odd phrase for him, that he was locking up the bar around 2:30 in the morning. That's the usual time since we close at one, then have to kick out the last of the riffraff, clean the bar and the toilets—which always look like somebody exploded in them—and do the money counting, little as it might be. He says he locked the door, turned around to find his car, which sometimes isn't an easy task for Jake, and came face-to-face with Maggie Albertson. She didn't say a word, according to his memory, just started rising off the ground right there on Main Street, ascending (his word not mine) into the heavens. He says she had a glow about her, and when he called her name, she looked down from about twenty feet up and smiled as wide as happy gets.

"Smiled?" I said. "Maggie doesn't smile." And that's a fact. I've known Maggie all my life, and she's never been a smiler. Probably 'cause she's got nothing in her life to smile about, far as I know.

"You're missing the damn point, Sammy." He was in a serious mood, as clear-eyed and cleaned-up as I'd ever seen him. His long black hair was slicked behind his ears, not in his face like when he's been drinking. And his posture was straight-up and square, nearly athletic, not beaten down and slumped like when he's hungover and pissed about life, business, or a fight with his ex-wife. "I'm telling you, Sammy, Maggie was rising right off the ground, floating like a fucking balloon. Last I saw, she was going for the clouds. Headfirst."

I chuckled a little but shut up quick when I saw his eyes squint a warning. "Were you drinking last night?" It was a generous question.

"Course I was drinking, had a little weed too, but I wasn't drunk or nothing. You know I don't get messy when I gotta close." I wasn't entirely sure of that. I'd seen evidence to the contrary. "And I sobered up fast when I saw Maggie. Nearly pissed myself. She was glowing like she had a lightbulb up her ass. Glowing like one of them Chinese lanterns your girl Mavi has on her front porch."

I smiled at that. Any time I hear Mavi's name it's what happens. "Come on, Jake, you were dreaming. You sleep here last night?" I looked to the corner booth where he crashes when he's too drunk to find his car keys. (He often hides them from himself just in case.) If he'd stayed in the bar that night, there'd be some empties there on the floor along with a pillow and a ratty blanket he keeps in the office. But there was none of that. The place was pretty clean, or at least as clean as we get at the Hitchpost.

"Yeah, I stayed here. After I saw that crazy thing, after I stared up at that cloud for nearly an hour, I came back in, made a pot of coffee, and I've been sitting here since. It's no dream, 'cause I ain't even slept yet."

I listened a little more to what seemed to me, at the time, to be a whole lot of bull crap. He went on about the light that came off her and how he might have even heard some music, now that he thought about it. He asked me my opinion, but I had none. When there was a break in the story's loop, I casually glanced at my watch and said I had errands. It wasn't a total lie, but I was more in need of separating myself from the crazy than anything else. I get enough of that when I'm working, stuck behind the bar listening to drunks go on and on about their shitty lives and who's responsible for them. I told him to get some rest, and I'd stop by later. He wasn't listening at that point, just sitting there, staring past the bottles that clutter the back bar, concentrating on that dirty mirror with all the cracks from things being thrown at it. He seemed fixed on some place beyond it, which worried me. I paused and considered for just a second that maybe I should stay, that maybe he needed to talk about what really was making him so squirrely. It was clear that something wasn't right with his head, but I couldn't take the time to dig into it. I had money in my pocket and a lunch date with Mavi.

Still, it bothered me seeing Jake like that. It made me wonder if maybe all his excesses had finally pushed him over the edge. Just because he said he wasn't drunk doesn't mean shit. Drunks never admit to it. I know that firsthand. He's one of a bunch of Riverton folk who've been tainted by too much booze, too many drugs, and too much living with small-town boredom.

Maggie Albertson, the glowing butt of Jake's story, lived midway between the Hitchpost and Longfellow's, where I was meeting my girl for lunch. I figured I'd stop by and check on her. It wasn't like I believed Jake, just thought I'd tell her the tale, see if I'd get a giggle. It wasn't likely, but it was worth a shot. Jake and I were always trying to get Maggie to laugh, not in a mean way. She's a great gal, and we figured she could use one. It was a game we'd play, see which of us could get the best reaction. What we'd usually get was a smirk and an eye roll, maybe a scolding if we were lucky. Then she'd be off doing whatever she'd come to do like she was too caught up in important stuff to be waylaid by a couple of morons.

As I climbed Maggie's porch steps, I was praying her mean-ass husband wouldn't be there. Last thing I wanted that morning was to get into it with him. He's always tuned in to some crazy radio show, something specifically created for his brand of stupid. He listens for hours, gets all riled up, then starts preaching to the first available ear. Why nice ladies like Maggie get mixed up with dickheads like Kenny Albertson, I don't understand. I suppose she wasn't much to look at when she was young, and maybe Kenny showed her attention and a way to get out of Happy Valley, which is not a desirable location in Riverton. Still, I think Maggie would have been better off alone and living in squalor than with Kenny the Bad Penny, as Jake refers to him. "It's just what he is," Jake says. "He shows up, you know the whole day's about to go down the shitter."

I knocked, and before I could change my mind Kenny came lumbering down the hall, his beer belly leading the way by a good foot, his wispy gray hair jutting out like it was electrified. He'd apparently just rolled out of his Big Boy, which is where he lives for the most part. I should have known he'd be there. It's not like he works unless you consider making Maggie work two jobs an actual job in itself. He's on disability for a supposed accident he had twenty years ago. I heard he ran over his own foot, put the car in neutral on an incline and let the car roll over it. Story is he did it three times before he he'd caused enough damage for a claim to the state. But now he was walking strong and fast, like a man with a heart full of need and a quest to unload it.

"Hey there, Mr. Albertson." He likes me to call him that. "Maggie around? I need to talk to her about fixing some bar-stools." Maggie did upholstery for us. I knew Kenny would be okay with me talking to her as long as it involved money.

"No, matter of fact she ain't." He was more worked up than usual. He opened the screen door to let me in, but there was no way I was getting that close. He may be thirty years older, but he could whup my ass if the mood struck him. He'd had lots more experience with that sort of thing. I stayed on the outer side of the threshold and listened to his ranting, waiting for a pause that would allow me an exit.

According to him, Maggie wasn't there when he woke up that morning. I hoped, and apparently Kenny suspected, that she had finally come to her senses and left him for good. "Where the hell would she go?" he yelled and leaned closer. "Her money's still in that hiding place of hers, 'cause I checked it this morning." He considered. "It ain't much, so maybe she's got another I ain't aware of. But she's got no friends she can run to, 'cept you and Jake. You say you ain't seen her though?" He scowled and cocked his head like a dog.

"No sir. That's why I'm here."

"Well, she's got no other friends, so where'd she go?" It was a sad truth. Maggie wasn't popular in Riverton, except with Jake and me. She was a Hickey from Happy Valley, which was one mark against her. The other was that most folks thought she was loony tunes. "Bat shit crazy," they used to say. But as far as I was concerned, the only crazy part of Maggie Alberton was Kenny. "I just want her to come home, so you tell her that. You tell her I won't hurt her no more, that I promise. God, I need her. Can't even find my pain meds, for fuck's sake!" And then his chins—all three—started quivering.

That was my cue. Getting stuck listening to Kenny Albertson is bad enough, but seeing his face get all squished up and weepy is like walking in on your dad in a compromising situation. Not only is it painful on the eyes, but you know he's gonna hold it against you. I backed away and told him I'd keep my radar up for Maggie, and of course I would. It wasn't like her to just disappear without saying something to Jake or me. Wherever she'd got to, I hoped she'd recognize her good decision and not return to her pitiful life with Kenny the Bad Penny.

You may think, at this point, that I shouldn't be so dismissive of Jake's story now that I'd learned Maggie had truly vanished without a word to anyone. But I know enough, even at my age, not to believe every fantastic story that pours off the liquor-stained lips of drunks or out of the skunk-breath lie-holes of stoners. I am a bartender, after all. And I may be only twenty-four, but I didn't just fall off the spud truck. If anyone's been privy to the instability that resides in Riverton, to its downright stupidity sometimes, it's me. I've learned not to believe any of them, not even Jake, much as I love him.

I should have known there'd be plenty of others in Riverton who would not share my skepticism. Folks here are desperate for something to cling to with their skinny thread of hope, longing for that thing that will give their lives the illusion of meaning. I should not have been surprised when I pulled onto Depot Street and was confronted by that desperation and the evidence of how incredibly fast a piece of juicy gossip can circulate in this town. There was a small gathering in front of the post office, spilling onto the street. That may not sound all that strange to most, but in this town folks don't congregate outside like that. They get their gossip—and sometimes even their mail—inside the P.O. Then they're eager to get home or to work or to Johnson's General in order to pass the best of it along. The flag wasn't out yet, and a half-dozen people were banging on the door and windows, trying to see in.

Alva Avery, Riverton's postmistress for about forty years, was always there at seven sharp, six mornings a week even when she was under the weather. It wasn't like her to keep people waiting. Although I'd promised to meet Mavi at noon and it was already 11:45, I pulled over to investigate. I truly wish I hadn't.

"He said she was glowing and heading straight for Heaven." I could hear Ida Wyman before I got out of the truck. Her voice pierced easily through the din of the others. She talks loud due to a hearing problem she refuses to address. I wasn't surprised to see her gossiping, but I was surprised to see folks listening. Generally, she does more talking to herself than to others.

"And she smiled?" It was Phyllis Strong, which surprised me even more. Everyone knows she and Ida have been feuding for years. Something about Beano and an accusation of cheating. But there they were, chatting like girlfriends. Seems gossip has a way of healing old wounds.

"What's going on?" I asked. "Where's Alva?" I tried the door, ignoring the chorus of yells that it was locked.

"She's gone," Phyllis said, excited. "Probably same as Maggie Albertson, bless her heart. Haven't you heard, Sammy? It seems folks are disappearing from Riverton." She patted her hands together in a soft but enthusiastic clap. I hadn't seen Phyllis this excited since her son Gerald had graduated from Riverton High with top honors and a scholarship to Emerson College. She'd thrown a big party to celebrate that occasion, even decorated the house and served cocktails and cake. Everyone was there, except for Gerald. He'd already packed up the Chevy truck his folks had bought him as a graduation present and had made a beeline for Boston, never to be seen in Riverton again.

"Where'd you hear about Maggie, Ida?" If I had leaned a little closer, I could have sniffed out the answer. Ida is one of a half-dozen teetotalers in Riverton who frequent the back door of the Hitchpost in the morning hours, when Jake's there by himself taking inventory and stocking the bar. He refers to their habit as "their morning courage." I suppose some folks need a little something once in a while to make them forget the things they'd hoped for, the things that would have required some real courage.

"I heard it from a reliable witness to the event," Ida said, proud to be so informed. I couldn't help but smirk. As much as I love him, Jake and "reliable witness" should never be used in the same sentence. "And I know just where Maggie's gone," she added.

"Where's that?" I said, like the fool I am.

"The Great Beyond. That poor woman has gone right to Heaven, sure as I'm standing here." Ida pointed to the sky. The others followed her gaze, as if they might get a glimpse of Maggie peeking through the clouds. "And I bet Alva's with her. Phyllis thinks she saw her go last night."

"What?"

"It's true, Sammy." Phyllis raised one hand like a witness. "I'm almost positive I saw her go. I thought it was a dream at first, but it's all coming back now, clear as day. And it's like Ida says. She was lit up and smiling like she'd just won something. I suppose she has, hasn't she?"

"Has anyone checked on Alva? Anyone gone over to her house, see if she's okay?"

They all looked around, confused, as if it were a puzzling concept.

"I'm telling you she's gone, Sammy. And you should ready yourself, too." Ida came close and gripped my arm. She must have had a lot of courage that morning, 'cause I got a face full of it. "You don't wanna be left behind, do you? We're thinking it's gotta be the Rapture. Or at least something close to it. Maybe He's testing it on us, making sure everything's in working order. You know, with it being the first time and all."

I nearly laughed at that one but caught myself. It was clear that these folks were serious and probably unable to see the humor in it. "Not a one of you has checked on Alva, have you?" I looked around but no one looked back. "Course not. You'd rather believe some silly story out of the mouth of a drunk."

"I ain't no drunk!" Ida yelled, spitting a little. "You know I don't drink."

"I'm talking about Jake. That's where you heard it."

"But I didn't hear nothing from Jake," Phyllis said. "What about what I saw?"

"Come on, Phyllis, you were dreaming, said so yourself." It seemed obvious to me that Phyllis was simply one-upping her longtime adversary with a more firsthand account. "What's wrong with you people? This is crazy talk, all this speculation based on a story from a guy who drinks for a living." I checked my watch. "Well, now I'm gonna be late. But I suppose I should check on Alva, since none of you will."

No one moved to offer. They stood there, eyes traversing the sky. Each was surely hoping they'd be next on the list, next to be hauled out of Riverton and straight to the Pearly Gates. I blame that so-called church that sprung up in town a few years ago, started by a guy who'd overdosed, died, and was brought back to life by an overly competent EMT. The guy, Richard something, claimed he'd talked to God while he was dead, was told to start a church in Riverton and get folks ready for the End, as he called it.

So that's what he did. It's not really a church at all, just a bunch of lost and needy folk gathered in Webster Hall, getting all riled up about the Second Coming. It occurred to me that Jake's story was just what the self-proclaimed leader had been praying for.

Even though I'd be late to Mavi, a situation that would surely land me in hot water, I made a quick detour out to Alva's. Sure enough, she wasn't there. Her door was unlocked, of course, and after a few knocks I let myself in. I hadn't been inside the old house since I'd helped her do some odd jobs last spring. It looked the same: neat and nearly sterile, with that sickly pine smell that seemed to emanate from every surface. Her postal jacket was hanging by the door, but I didn't see the purse that she always hung on the hook below. I did a quick search, hoping I wouldn't find Alva on the kitchen floor or, even worse, dead on the toilet. She wasn't either. I left a note on her kitchen table saying I'd been there and folks were concerned, although it appeared I was the only one.

As I'd figured, I was late to Mavi by nearly a half hour. She was in a booth, sketching in her notebook like she always does when she's killing time or trying to calm herself. I slid in across from her, jiggling the table a little which made her pencil go awry. She swore, slammed down the pencil, and gave me a look that was less than welcoming. Mavi's not a person to keep waiting. She's an on-time sort of girl and expects the same of others. When she gets pissed at me, which is often, her green eyes go wide and her orange curls seem to vibrate, spiraling out from that beautifully freckled center. My mother says that Mavi's a little out of balance and probably could use some help in the head department. I can sort of see that, but it doesn't make me love her any less.

I plowed right into my excuse. It wasn't long before she was off the rage train and fully engaged. She was quiet for a long while after I'd finished, and I knew better than disturb her thought process. When she's in a thinking mood, best leave her to it.

"What a bunch of wingnuts," she finally said. "You know what my grandpa used to say?"

I wasn't certain. Her grandfather was a wannabe philosopher, and "wisdom" dripped outa him like snot.

"He always said, 'People believe, in order to avoid believing, the things they don't want to believe.'"

It rang a bell but not a loud one.

"Okay, but what's your point?" I asked.

She shook her head with impatience. "My point, Sammy, is that folks are inclined to believe the things they hope for, things that are extremely unlikely but are so important to them they can't allow themselves to not believe it. They keep believing, even when all the evidence suggests otherwise. I mean, come on, why would any god or universe or whatever-you-wanna-call-it be plucking people out of Riverton? It's not like any of us are all that worthy. Some of us are downright nasty. Nope, the more reasonable explanation is obvious."

"I agree. Too much booze and drugs. Jake's a perfect example."

"Nah, that ain't it either," she said, smiling up at the waitress as she set down a plate mounded with fries that had been drizzled with something bright orange. I was starving, and the steaming mess looked entirely edible. I reached for a fry, and Mavi slapped at my hand. "Get your own, mister."

God, I love that girl. I think I might've loved her my whole life, but I didn't realize it until she and her Ma came back to Riverton. We'd both grown a lot in those eight years she was gone. Once I saw her again, saw her hair and her eyes and that figure that could . . . well . . . I suppose it wouldn't be gentlemanly of me to discuss that. But needless to say, I was smitten. Been smitten ever since.

"If you'd pay more attention to me, Sammy, you'd get what's going on here. It's obvious." Some cheese sauce dripped to her lower lip, and she nabbed it with a flick of her tongue.

"I pay attention, Mavi. I hang on to your every word, my love." I smiled with what I hoped was charm and seduction, coyly rubbing my pinky finger across hers. She was having none of it and slapped me away again.

"Obviously not, my love," she said with more than a smidgen of sarcasm. "It's pretty much exactly like Jake said, eerie light and all. You can read about it in some of those magazines I gave you, if you'd open one of 'em. Shit like that's been happening around the world for thousands of years. As far back as primitive man. Fact is, God ain't taking nobody, much as folks wish He would. What's happening in Riverton is clearly not the Rapture or whatever those zealots are calling it."

"Okay, I'm all ears. Don't keep me in suspense."

She leaned across the table, so low that some of the sauce attached itself to the curls of her hair. "It's aliens, Sammy," she whispered. "I'd bet my left tit. Aliens are snatching folks outa Riverton. And I sure would like to be one of 'em."

I had tried to get her to come home with me, but she wouldn't have it, and I knew better than to press. She was all stirred up with her theories, insisting she "needed to do some research and make some calls." She hadn't shut up about aliens all through lunch— even with her mouth full—and I knew she couldn't wait to get back to her resources, as she called them. They were just a bunch of magazines and books that "proved beyond a shadow of a doubt" that aliens are among us, shoving things up our butts, studying the workings of our minds and our bodies, something I'd been hoping to do with Mavi later. But I ended up going toward home alone after dropping her to her place, not happy about it but fully understanding that Mavi is a girl with her own agenda.

My route brought me past the post office again. If I had been in my right head, I would've gone the long way, avoiding what I should have known was still afoot. And it was, of course. Even more afoot than before. The flag still wasn't flying, and the P.O. remained closed. The group had grown larger, and someone in the middle was holding a big sign that couldn't be missed. **THE END OF DAYS IS NOW**, it read in bold black letters. Ida was the one attached to it. Again, against my better judgment, I pulled over.

The story had grown, as stories do in Riverton. Even as I crossed the street, I caught bits that hadn't been included in the earlier version. In only two hours it had mutated and blossomed into something more colorful, more evolved—a tastier morsel for Riverton's ravenous gossip mill.

"They were so young," Phyllis was saying as I approached the gathering. "And naked. Naked as babies." Tears shone on her face. "Alan looked thirty years younger," she went on. "As handsome as the day we married." She was looking toward the sky, her face nearly ecstatic. Those around her listened with nearly identical expressions.

"Was there light around him, like with Maggie?" someone asked.

Her face shone even brighter. "Oh, such beautiful light. Blue as a summer dawn."

I couldn't keep my mouth shut. "Alan? Your husband?" They all turned on me, excited for a new ear. "He died—what—ten years ago?"

Ida stepped up. "Sammy," she said tenderly but with her usual volume. "The Rapture is not only for the living. The Bible says . . ." She closed her eyes as if the scripture had been printed across her lids. "The trumpet's gonna sound, angels are gonna fly down, and the dead are gonna step right outa their graves, taking us all up there with them."

My Uncle Mickey was a religious man, knew the bible backwards and forwards. He'd quoted a lot of it to me, but that verse of Ida's had not been in his repertoire. I saw then that the leader of the cult church was there now, and it occurred to me it might have been one of his biblical rewrites. He was looking real pleased with himself and how his movement was getting some traction.

"Come on, Phyllis! Naked and blue? The Rapture? I think you've been listening to that quack preacher too much." I nodded toward the man who stared back with more hate than any religious person should possess. His intensity made me snicker, but only briefly. The group slowly moved closer, seeming more like a mob now as they surrounded me.

Phyllis was unamused. "I know what I saw, Sammy. And you should watch that disrespectful tone, mister. You mock me or the Oracle, you mock Him." She flung an arm to the sky. Richard Something called himself the Oracle now, and that's how his handful of followers referred to him.

"Amen, sister." the others said, and it was clear to me as the group parted just enough to let me pass that it was meant as a warning.

Gossip will spread faster than runoff downhill, collecting all sorts of juicy bits along the way until it's as printable and believable as fact. By the following Tuesday, when *The Franklin Journal* came out, there was no escaping it. Jake's vision was now in black and white, which made it about as factual as anything else *The Journal* deems worthy enough for its pages. Everyone had been talking about it, telling new variations, reinventing the one that Jake had started. But now, with the newspaper coverage, it was more than just a rumor. It was becoming real and not something to dismiss.

RIVERTON, MAINE:
THE RAPTURE OR THE INVASION?

There were new claims I hadn't heard. One was about a couple of kids from the trailer park who'd disappeared. Their folks were members of that cult/church run by the Oracle, and it seemed to me their belief system might be tranquilizing what should have been a deeper concern. Kids were missing, but even the county sheriff, Roger Toothacher, was setting his reason aside and considering the Rapture as a real possibility. Maybe because it was bringing so much attention to a town that got very little.

"We ain't dismissing anything at this point," he told the reporter. "The parents think they've gone to the Lord, and I'm not prepared to say otherwise. We got no evidence of foul play. No reason to ignore multiple reports that support that possibility."

My stomach soured.

The story filled half of the first page and nearly all of the third. There were interviews with people I didn't know, and I thought I'd known everyone in town. Turns out there's a whole lot of unbalanced folks living in the cracks of Riverton, and they crawled out long enough to get their names into *The Journal*. There were even stories of pets taken up, beloved dogs and cats that had suddenly disappeared. Some folks claimed they'd actually seen their loved-ones go, all naked and blue—which had become a given—rising into the heavens. One old man said he'd seen his wife go up on a Friday.

"But she came back down on Saturday. Guess God didn't want 'er after all. I suppose there'll initially be some bugs in the process."

It was on the third page where I saw Mavi's face grinning out at me in that way she does when she's been told to smile but doesn't feel like it. The caption read: *Mavis Goff, 24. "They can take me anytime."*

I scanned and found her longer quote further down. "There's been UFO sightings all over the state, but the government ignores them. I'll bet my left [expletive] that the aliens are probing Alva's butt right now. And you know something? They can explore mine too, any time they want. Hell, I'll even spread my cheeks for 'em."

I howled right there in Johnson's General. Couldn't help it. My Mavi has a colorful way.

According to the article, the town was split on whether it was God's doing or something extraterrestrial. I had thought Mavi was the only one who was thinking aliens, but it turned out a whole lot of folks were right there with her. Lots of quotes about "evidence" and "cover-ups."

By mid-week, Mavi had organized a gathering of alien-believers to be held in Simon Gardner's cow pasture on Sunday night. Gardner owned all the land behind Webster Hall where the cult held its meetings, and I think he didn't like The Oracle much, probably jumped at the opportunity to piss him off. There was bad blood there, had to do with the torches the leader used every Saturday night for his "gathering parade," as he called it. He and his few followers would flame up their torches and march around town, calling for the sinners to "repent before it was too late." They'd usually stand outside the Hitchpost for a while since that was where most of Riverton's sinners collected. They'd sing their old, tired songs about demons and the fires that await them, but I don't think they ever got joiners. It was just the usuals walking around, singing, and preaching. When they'd get back to the hall, they'd stick those lit torches in the ground along the walkway leading up to the doors. Mr. Gardner had complained about it in a town meeting, saying it was a fire hazard for his hayfield, but nothing had been done to stop it. So, he had donated the field for Mavi's gathering, even mowed a substantial section of it and built a stage out of hay bales.

When Mavi gets excited about something, she's a rolling ball of fervor. She'd made a bunch of fliers and put them up all over town and in the two towns over. Cute drawings of a flying saucer and a beam of light hauling smiling stick figures up into the sky. Not as artistic as her usual stuff, but it made the point. **SEEK THE TRUTH** was printed across the top, and further down it mentioned a speaker for the Sunday night gathering, some guy who claimed to have been abducted by aliens when he was on a fishing trip in the Allagash. Mavi had contacted him and even sent him gas money. That's my girl: stubbornness and generosity rolled into one gorgeous package. Was I worried that she was getting too wrapped up in a ridiculous and highly unlikely expectation? I was, a little. But I also recognized that Mavi is one of the brightest people I know, and if she believes in aliens and thinks they're beaming folks up out of Riverton, I would not be the one to try to convince her otherwise. I suppose I wasn't so sure she was wrong.

Those fliers weren't up more than an hour before most were torn down. Mavi made more and those were torn down too. She must have done that three or four times before Saturday. Finally, we caught the guy in the act on Saturday night. We were on the way to the Hitchpost—she and I and her dog Precious. She always brought Precious to the bar. Jake liked the mutt for some reason. I thought it was the ugliest dog I'd ever seen. Looked like a cross between a wall-eyed rat and a potbellied pig. Anyway, we rounded a corner and there he was. It was that damn cult leader, the Oracle. Mavi did not refer to him as that. She called him Richard Motherfucker. And when we caught him that night, she said it right to his face.

"Richard Motherfucker, what the hell are you doin'?" Mavi screamed at him. And then, without another word, she handed me the leash to Precious and went right up and punched him hard in the arm.

"What am I doin'?" he said, shaking the crumpled flyer at her while rubbing his shoulder. "I'm making sure you don't corrupt the minds of my followers, that's what." Then he ripped the flyer in half and tossed it to the ground. He shouldn't have done that. From where I was standing, it appeared that Mavi got taller and broader.

"Followers!" She spat the word at him. "You should be ashamed of yourself, getting all those poor folks thinking they're gonna be carried off to Heaven. And giving you money for the honor! If there's truly a God, I hope the aliens take you up and use you for spare parts." Even from a few feet back, I could see her hair getting electrified. She was like a cat readying herself to pounce on some prey she'd cornered.

"Mavis, honey," I said with as much calm as I could muster. "Maybe we should—"

"Stay out of this, Sammy," she called back without turning. "And let me tell you somethin', Mr. Oracle . . ." She leaned close to him. I couldn't hear the rest of what she said, but I saw a lot of back-and-forth before his expression changed from smug to hate. He tossed the crumpled fliers back at her, letting a good number of them hit the ground, and then he stomped away muttering more swear words than any so-called religious leader oughta know.

We smoothed the fliers and taped them back up around town, then went on to the Hitchpost in silence, Mavi in the lead with Precious and me trying to stay clear of any residual wrath. When she'd had a couple shots of bourbon and half a beer, I saw the relaxation move over her, so I asked about the encounter, suggesting that maybe it wasn't right to talk to a man of God like that.

She called to Jake for another shot and a bowl for the dog. She poured some of her beer into it, set it on the floor, and threw back the shot. The dog lapped loudly while Mavi made cooing sounds to her before turning back to me.

"He ain't no man of God, Sammy. That's an insult to the real ones. He's just a con man. Gets people all riled up about sin and burning in Hell. Takes fools' money and feeds 'em bull crap. I mean, come on! The Rapture in Riverton? He's milking this one big time."

"So, what did you say to him?"

"Don't matter. Let's just say I reminded him of a time he'd prefer to forget." She downed the rest of her beer. "I knew him before he came here. Ma thinks he followed us. His real name is Richard Hanson. She dated him for a little while shortly after we'd moved to Bangor, after that other loser dumped her. God, that woman has shitty taste in men. But this one she saw through quick, kicked him to the curb when he did some not-very-nice things. Ma says he's like a booger you can't get off your finger."

"Why didn't you tell me you knew him from before?" Then a horrible thought occurred to me. "He didn't do anything to you, did he?"

"I didn't tell you, 'cause it ain't any of your business. And that time in Bangor is not a period of my life I choose to dwell on. Besides, just because we're dating don't mean you get to know everything about me. Let's leave it at that."

Mavi had never been one to lay all her cards out. She'd told me once that parts of her life were "on a need-to-know basis." I figured she'd eventually tell me the important stuff.

Whatever she'd said to Hanson, it did the trick. Those fliers stayed put, and they managed to attract a lot of attention. So much attention that on that Sunday night, the night of Mavi's big event, there were nearly fifty people lying in the field, a couple dozen others on the edges. The ones in the field didn't seem to care about the cow flops and gopher holes. Mavi tried to get me to join them, but I held my ground and stuck to the sidelines with the other doubters. "Honey, only way you'll get me lying on cow shit is if you're lying on top of me." She just smirked and went back to her people in the circle. She hadn't brought Precious, for which I was grateful. It would've been my job to attend to Her Royal Ugliness if she had.

A massive banner lay off to one side, held flat against the field by rocks. Someone must've spent a lot of time on the thing. They'd sewn a few white sheets together and then painted on it with big black letters. I had to stand atop a few bales to read it.

WELCOME TO RIVERTON
PLEASE TAKE US AWAY

There was a smaller sign off to the side.

WILL SPREAD CHEEKS
FOR
TOUR OF SHIP

There was little doubt as to the author of that one.

The scene was pleasant for a couple hours. Everyone was just lying there in a big circle, staring up at the night that was so full of stars it looked like snow fall. They were holding hands and humming, which was both flaky and cool. Made me feel peaceful just watching. If someone hadn't seen the signs, they might have thought folks were meditating or possibly praying. It occurred to me that most of them weren't really hoping to get abducted at all. They just wanted to be part of something that was different and more interesting than their normal. There was an air of hope and optimism that went way beyond any desire to see a spaceship, much less board one. It felt like everyone was wanting the same thing, something more from their lives in Riverton. And the act of doing the hoping like that, all together in a hand-holding circle, was nearly religious. Made me feel hopeful too, even though I was just a bystander.

The guy from the Allagash started speaking from atop the hay bales. He had a nice voice: loud but deep and soothing, like a dad telling tales from the old days. Folks were quiet, listening to a story that was so detailed and heartfelt even I started to believe. He was very convincing, speaking about his friends and how they'd initially been afraid to tell anyone about what they'd seen and felt. I remembered I'd read something about it but I'd never heard the specifics, and he was sharing plenty. He spoke about how the four of them were on a two-week fishing trip and they kept seeing a bright light on the horizon, bright as the sun, he said. Then one night it shone right down on them, so strong they had to cover their eyes to avoid going blind. Next thing he knew, a chunk of time had passed and he had no idea what had happened.

He'd just gotten into the deep end of it, telling about what he'd remembered under hypnosis, describing scenes from his time on the ship—real disturbing stuff—when the sounds of singing drifted onto the field, soft at first. It seemed to be coming from all around us, and it gave me goosebumps, like maybe angels were coming down from Heaven. It was that kinda night, when things don't make much sense and almost anything is possible. I couldn't make out the words, but it sounded creepy the way it echoed around the field. Then I saw the torches approaching from around the corner of Webster Hall, about a dozen of them, and the whole scene changed from something cool and near-holy to something closer to dangerous.

The people in the circle weren't lying flat anymore. The sudden strangeness had interrupted the magic. Slowly they sat up, one by one, looking dazed like they'd been pulled out of a trance. The guy on the stage stopped talking. He looked over at that double line of torches, mumbled a stream of what seemed like swear words, then waved a goodbye to the audience and bolted for his car. Maybe he'd been through a similar scene before. Maybe he knew the possibilities of what could happen better than we did. But in the first moments when our two groups caught sight of each other—the torchbearers and the stargazers—those of us in the field had no understanding of the gravity of it. We were still caught up in a misguided sense of peace and hope.

The torches got close enough that I could make out the faces of people I'd known my whole life, faces that showed a hateful anger I'd never seen there before. I saw Ida and Phyllis standing side by side, their mend still holding. I saw a few regulars from the Hitchpost that had been absent from their usual stools of late, apparently choosing to go to the other side, just in case. Hanson stepped out in front. He was carrying one of those blazing torches, and he pointed it at the group still sitting in the circle on the ground, too confused to move.

"You folks really think aliens are coming for you? Come on, people, it's a lot of horseshit, and you know it. We're in the middle of the biggest thing to ever happen to Riverton, an opportunity to rise up outa this hellhole and be with Him, and you're out here staring at stars like a bunch of certified morons. You all got your heads up your buttholes, listening to that crazy girl." He reached the bales and jumped up to the top level. He looked pretty big up there, tall and broad, his dark hair greased flat against his head and his shoulders wide like a football player. He could've made a good hero if he hadn't been such a thug. His voice was big too, like a real preacher's. "God is calling us Home, people. You'd be wise to listen to Him instead of an unbalanced female." His words carried across the field as if they were God's own, and I suppose his followers figured they were. I saw in that moment the pull of the man and why he'd been able to convince so many to follow. But I also saw the hate.

Mavi was halfway there before I noticed. She was a fast mover when she had reason. A couple of the church men saw her coming and stepped in front of the preacher. She isn't a big girl, but she's an intimidating figure when she's pissed.

"This is private land, ya know," Mavi yelled, and she planted herself solidly just a few feet in front of them. "Mr. Gardner gave us permission." Gardner came forward and stood next to her. He isn't big either, but he's powerfully built, being a man who throws around bales all day.

Hanson didn't move. He spoke in that thunderous voice that the sinners of Riverton can't escape on Saturday nights, no matter how high they crank their unholy music.

"Thou shalt have no other gods or anything you think is a god," he yelled. "In other words, praying to some damn aliens is not okay with the Lord. You're giving our town a bad name. He's chosen Riverton. And it's my job to get you folks saved before it's too late. You best get those knees to the ground and palms together, people. Come on now, it's repentin' time."

I should have gone to Mavi then, but my brain had stopped giving me signals. It felt like I was on pause, watching something I had no part in. I didn't move, and I'm ashamed of it.

Mavi yelled up at him. "I ain't getting on my knees for you or no man, 'cept maybe my boyfriend." A couple of guys turned to me and smiled; one elbowed me in the ribs. Still, I didn't move. "And I don't need no repentin'. At least not to you. So why don't you go back to your crazy-ass church and let us get back to our own damn business." She spat out those last words, and even from across the field I could see the spittle shine orange in the light of the torches.

"You be careful how you talk to me, girl."

"Oh, I'll talk all right. You want me to tell all these people about the dirty old man you are?"

"You shut up, you whore. You daughter of a whore."

Things sped up then. I believe the pastor made the first move, went to touch her or hit her maybe, and Mavi wouldn't have that.

She moved fast between the guards and punched him hard in the crotch. He crumpled and rolled. Before he even hit the ground, two of his men were on top of her. The torches—forgotten by the fists that now had more important tasks—arced high and landed on the mound of bales and in the dried grass that surrounded them.

My brain finally kicked in and I desperately tried to get to Mavi. But my legs had jellied and it was like running through deep sand. All those people were still sitting in a circle, still confused. I yelled for them to move, and I crashed into a few, stepped on a few more. My progress was slow and frantic, hampered by folks who'd suddenly realized the gravity of the moment. They moved in all directions, bumping into each other, bumping into me.

Before I could get close, the flames started. They sprung up like fountains, causing me to lose direction as I dodged each new blaze. I kept getting turned around by someone crashing into me or by one of those fiery eruptions. I'd stop and spin and search for Mavi, and I could see her still far away, rolling around on smoldering grass. A dozen or so others were in there too, so intent on their fight that they were ignorant of the danger that was rising around them. I could hear the punches landing, the swearing, the threats, but I couldn't get close enough to help anyone.

The folks on the edges, the ones who'd been curious enough to watch but not enough to lie in cow shit, were the ones who had the mental wherewithal to help. Some had blankets they'd brought to sit on, and they threw them over the larger blazes and stomped out the flames. Others just used their feet, jumping up and down on the smaller outbreaks or poured out thermoses of liquid that hissed and smoked. They maneuvered through the half dozen duos that continued their battles, seemingly unaware of anything beyond the faces they punched.

It was chaos. Folks screaming at each other, the sounds of punches hitting the mark, smoke filling the field, and someone hysterically crying from inside of it. It was like that for what seemed like hours, but it wasn't more than fifteen minutes or so.

Fifteen of the most frenzied minutes I've ever experienced. And then it all stopped. That fast.

I'm not a believer—pretty much in anything—but something amazing happened then, and I don't think I'll live long enough to understand why amazing things will happen exactly at the time they're truly needed. But if there had ever been a moment in Riverton's history where something amazing was needed, it was then. Two of the many divisions within our little town were literally at each other's throats. Only something amazing could've stopped it so quickly.

And it *was* amazing, at least it seemed. I didn't notice it at first. I was too intent on getting to Mavi while avoiding flames and punches and darting bodies. It wasn't until one of the stargazers stopped suddenly, right in front of me, and pointed toward the horizon. I nearly knocked him over when I ran into him, but he kept his focus—his mouth was slacked and his eyes were wide and bright blue from the reflection. Someone yelled, "Wow!" and another cried out, "Oh my Lord!"

As fast as that, as if the crazy had been sucked out of the field, it all stopped. Fists paused. The shouting and cursing tapered until there were barely any sounds except for the gasps and the final crackles of flames as they turned to smoke and ash. Everyone, even those in the throes of rage, stopped what they were doing and looked toward the horizon. A field of bright faces were turned in the same direction as if they'd been hypnotized as one.

It was just the moon, but unlike any moon I'd ever seen. It filled about a quarter of the sky like it was about to crash into us. It was so blue it made everything—the field, the bales, even the faces that had been filled with rage a minute earlier—bright with a blueish glow. Every face was turned to it, most with jaws that hung open as if to breathe it in. A few of the religious ones had dropped to their knees, and I could see their lips moving silently. Others were tearing, as if the beauty of it had dislodged a memory of joy or desire.

The color changed slowly, moving from blue through purple, red to orange, and eventually to a bright and normal yellow.

Through all those changes, no one moved or made a sound louder than a gasp or a whisper.

When folks started moving again, it was like we'd all just woken from the worst drunk and couldn't figure out how we'd gotten there. I was like the rest, looking around with a mix of embarrassment and joy. The fighters were brushing the grass and dirt from themselves and each other. Some were shaking hands, some hugged, others just walked away, possibly too full of shame to do more.

I saw Hanson, looking like maybe Mavi had gotten the best of him, signaling his people back toward Webster Hall. Ida and Phyllis were dusting off each other's coats. Phyllis pointed out a smudge on Ida's face, then licked her finger and rubbed it out. Mavi waved to me from across the field. I waved back and we met in the middle. She hugged me hard, like she hadn't in a long while. Not that we were having problems. It just felt like she'd been holding back and now she wasn't.

"I think it's time to get the hell out of Riverton," she whispered close and then kissed my ear. She didn't need to say it twice. I felt it too, so I gave my notice to Jake the next morning.

I had thought that Mavi might change her mind about leaving town, that it was just an impulse brought on by the strangeness of a crazy Riverton night. I couldn't imagine her leaving her mom. But once again, she pleasantly surprised me. "We're only going to Portland, for fuck's sake. It's not like we're moving to East Bumfuck. Jesus, Sammy, grow up." It was a response that both pleased and humbled me. I suppose she'll be doing that for as long as we're together.

I don't know what happened back in the field. It's hard to believe that one remarkable moon could've changed people. I'd like to think that everyone in Riverton suddenly came to their senses, that sharing a moment of wonder had reminded them they're all part of the same town. But I've lived here long enough to know that sense doesn't come easily here. Minds don't change much in Riverton.

I did my final shift at the Hitchpost last night. Mavi didn't come since she was still packing. "Anyway," she said, "those losers are more your people than mine." And that was the truth. As the night went on, I realized how much they all were a part of my life here. As messed-up as most of them are, they've been family. Like it or not.

It was a long night. Too many shots turned into too many tears. I'm not sure if the tears were for me or for themselves. I think it's hard for some to see others make the changes they wish they'd made. Jake cut out early since he's not drinking these days, but he pulled me aside before he left.

"You need me, you call," he said. I was already drunk, but I nodded and hugged back when he pulled me in tight. He turned at the door. I thought of my dad in that moment, and I realized how much Jake was like him now—twenty years younger but the same kind of man inside.

It took me nearly an hour to get the place empty. I had to physically encourage the last one to the door. It was Maggie's husband, Kenny, and I was praying he wouldn't turn nasty on me. He seemed to have mellowed a little, and he allowed me to push his massive bulk all the way across the room and through the door until I was able to lock it. I could hear him on the other side, calling up to Maggie as if she might come down once she heard him pleading. I listened for a minute, almost feeling bad for the old guy, but I had work to do.

There was one task for the night I hated doing the most. In accordance with the cleaning schedule, I was to do a thorough washing of the old oak floor. We do it the last Saturday of every month, but it looked like it hadn't been done for a few. I did one more shot and then got down to the doing. I put the chairs on the tables and rolled up the big rug where folks are supposed to wipe their feet before coming in, although not many do.

The envelope was stuck to the bottom. I peeled it off and wiped it clean of the mold and muck. Some of the ink had smudged, but under a good light and with a little squinting I could make out the two names scrawled there. "Jake and Sammy." I opened it carefully with the fruit knife. The inside wasn't easy to read. Looked like it had been written by a kid in a hurry.

> *Dear Boys,*
>
> *Sorry I didn't clue you in, but I'm leaving. I'm not telling you where to. Don't want Kenny finding me. He's hit me for the last fucking time. You boys been good friends, but it's better you don't know.*
>
> *Alva's in the car waiting for me like the patient girl she is. God I love her. You weren't in the know, but she and I have gotten real close over the years. We've finally decided to go for it.*
>
> *Sammy, don't you stay in Riverton. Get out and see the world while you're young. And take that big-mouth girl with ya. She's a keeper. Jake, you make sure he does. It's too late for you, you old drunk, but you need to help the boy.*
>
> *Love ya both,*
> *Maggie*
> *P.S.*
> *In case you never saw, you guys made me smile. Nice work, 'cause it weren't easy.*

I read it twice, thought it through twice more. Then I folded it in half, shoved it deep in my back pocket, and got to work, the whole time going back and forth about whether I should tell Jake or not. I finally decided on *not*. There was no reason. It didn't explain shit. We still don't know what happened to those kids from the trailer park or any of the other folks who were claimed to be missing. Maybe Maggie and Alva got sucked up, whether by God or a spaceship, right after she'd put the letter under the door. Maybe Jake had seen it happen after all. Or maybe he was just too fucked up to know what he was seeing. There were a whole lot of "maybes," and I was sick of thinking about it, sick of God and aliens and mostly Riverton.

"Fuck it," I said to myself and to any other damn thing that might be listening. "It don't matter no more."

I finished up the cleaning around three, locked the door to the Hitchpost for the last time, left the key under the rock like usual. Mavi and I—and Precious, of course—are off. No plan. Just getting out of Riverton. I heard a quote once about making plans and how stupid it is 'cause God just laughs at them. I believe that laughing part. If He or She or even the aliens needed a laugh, they've surely had a good one. And if any of them need to find us, if they need to suck Mavi or me up into whatever, they'll know where to look.

Hell, we'll even spread our cheeks for them.

Uncle Amos

Amos Taylor French
1933–2003
A Teller of Wild Tales

THERE'S A PLOT OF LAND—ABOUT TWENTY ACRES—JUST OUT-
side of Riverton, a few miles to the east. It's an area folks steer
clear of and have done so for over a hundred years. There's been
stories about that rectangle of forest and bog, tales that go back
nearly to the beginnings of the town. And whether town folk
believe them or not, you'll find that most will heed the warnings.

In 1948, a young lawyer from Boston bought the land, despite
the stories and the discouragements, at a very reasonable price. A
branch of his family had come from Riverton and he'd spent several summers there that had been some of the best of his life. He
saw the purchase as a connection to his childhood, a place to retire
someday on what seemed to be a beautiful and mysterious acreage.

By 1980, shortly after his wife had passed, Amos French sold
his practice in Boston and moved into the cabin he'd built more
than thirty years earlier. He got to know his land well. It was a
small piece compared to his neighbors, but it was diverse. Fields,
woods, river, and, of course, the bog. It was that last area that
fueled the rumors in town, the stories he'd been hearing since
he was a child. But unlike those who skirted that part of town,
Amos was drawn to it, especially to the marshy woodland that
dominated about five acres directly in his land's center.

For the next twenty years, his life there was uneventful, as are the lives of most retirees who stay close to home. Lots of walks in the woods, swims in the river, hikes into the mountains beyond. His only sister and her family visited occasionally, but not so much in recent years. His sister and her husband had grown less fond of Amos, even a little skeptical of his sanity. However, there was one nephew, Jasper, who visited more often than the rest. The two had grown close and the boy had quickly become Amos's favorite.

On a fall afternoon in 2003, Jasper, concerned because he hadn't heard from his Uncle Amos for well over a month, drove up to Riverton from his college in Boston. It wasn't like his uncle to not call or write every couple of weeks. And Jasper's birthday had passed without a word, an occasion that had always brought a card or a trinket. Since the old man wasn't answering his calls, Jasper made the five-hour trip.

He sensed immediately that something was wrong. It was evident in the first moments of his arrival. There was none of Amos's usual warmth. No slamming through the screen door to embrace him. No tender slap on his cheek for having been away too long. The smile was forced, and his posture was tentative, held in a place between welcoming and territorial. He let Jasper in, of course, and the nephew, exhausted from the drive, took a seat at the rickety kitchen table.

They chatted briefly. Amos made no offers of tea or libation—which was odd—and all the while he kept glancing toward the cabinet over the sink, the one Jasper knew well from when he was a teenager sneaking sips of gin. Since it now was nearly five in the afternoon, the boy assumed his uncle was considering his usual: a gin martini with a splash of dry sherry. "One olive, and make it cold, good boy," had been the instructions since Jasper was ten. It seemed unlikely that the old man had abandoned his love of spirits, so Jasper stood and approached the cupboard. "I think it's that hour, Uncle Amos. Shall we have our usual?"

The old man stood too quickly, toppling his chair.

"Not yet," he said loudly, but Jasper had already opened the cabinet door. That's when he caught movement in the darker recesses. At first, he thought it was a mouse or possibly a larger rodent. And then his vision adjusted, and he caught sight of the thing crouched behind a bottle of scotch. One rabbit-like ear softly curled around the bottle's edge, and an eye—bright green and round as the moon—blinked at him with as much wonder as Jasper blinked back. They were mutually astonished, equally petrified. The boy jumped back and yelped, and there was a metal on metal rattle as the thing scurried for coverage behind a larger bottle. Jasper slammed the cupboard door and turned to his uncle for explanation.

"Well, that's just great," Uncle Amos said as he angrily righted his chair. "Now you've scared the little bugger. And he had just started to calm." He shouldered his nephew aside, inspecting the cupboard, and snatched out his bottles of choice. "He'll probably be gone for a while now, so we might as well drink."

While his uncle made the cocktails, muttering his annoyance all the while, Jasper reopened the cupboard just a little and carefully peered inside. The thin chain that had made that rattling sound was visible now. It snaked around dusty bottles of port and sticky liqueurs before disappearing through a hole at the back.

"What . . . is *it*?" he said, uncertain of the correct pronoun.

Amos pinched two olives from a jar, plopped them into the glasses, and handed Jasper one before taking a very large swallow of his own. "I've named him Puck, for obvious reasons, although he is not nearly as amusing as his namesake. And as to 'what,' I'm guessing he's some sort of elf. A wood elf, probably. I've been telling you for years there are unusual creatures here. But you, like everyone else in the family, assumed I was going wacky."

The old man's disappointment was difficult for the boy to hear. His uncle had always expected more from him than the rest. But in this regard, Jasper had let him down as much as the others.

"Crazy Uncle Amos," he went on as he stared into his glass and stirred the remaining liquid with his finger. "I know what you all think."

"I never—"

Amos gulped the last of the martini and smiled. "But now you'll believe me, won't you?" He gathered their glasses and brought them to the counter for a refill, ignoring that Jasper had barely touched his.

The boy went back to the cupboard for another look and carefully moved around bottles. The chain was now tight to the wall, and a trail of detritus led to the hole: crumbs of moist wood, moss, and what appeared to be bug carcasses.

"Don't bother looking. He'll be in his quarters for a while. I should cook dinner, since I suppose you'll be staying." It was less an invitation than a piqued assumption.

Uncle Amos was being true to his reputation as a distrustful and unreasonably private man. Jasper's mother had labeled him with more descriptive adjectives. "Cantankerous," "An old fuddy-duddy," "Too arrogant to be reasoned with," and "Precariously unbalanced" were just a few. His mother was forever seeking more scorching labels for her brother.

"Now that you've seen the truth, I expect you to keep this between us. Understood?" Jasper nodded, unconvincingly. "I'm serious, Jasper. If you tell your mother, I'll disown you. Am I being clear?" The raised eyebrows were static until the boy nodded and crossed his heart. He knew the threat to be meritless. Even as his uncle's closest and dearest relative, Jasper stood to inherit nothing more than a modest cabin on a few acres of boggy landscape. And the old man could never be angry with him for more than a day. "I'm glad you've seen for yourself, but who knows what my sister Harriet and her rapacious husband would do with the information." The old man had little love for his sister lately. His feelings were based on good reasons which included a recent and unsuccessful attempt at having him moved to a home.

The details came out in snippets, spread out over the course of a spaghetti dinner accompanied by two bottles of juicy Cabernet. Each of Jasper's questions were followed by a long silence, followed by a strained and calculated answer. At first the particulars leaked out in dribbles, but by the second bottle, they flowed easily, as if he'd been needing to tell them all along.

"Where did you find him?" The nephew kept the questions short. The uncle's responses were likewise.

"In the bog. Where else?"

Of course. The boy should have known. Uncle Amos had always referred to the bog as "the magical center" of the land. To Jasper, it had been an area to avoid, a place where a person could get lost and possibly drowned in the holes that were said to lead down more than a hundred feet into an underground lake. Amos had claimed to have seen things there, had even mounted expeditions around the edges with his nephews and nieces when they were still within the age of belief. But his narratives were always held in question—by Jasper's parents and eventually by Jasper himself, to the boy's shame.

"And you were able to catch him?"

"It was easier than you would think."

"I can't imagine that such a thing would just come to you."

"He *didn't* come to me. Don't be daft, Jasper."

"But why did he—how did you—?"

"He was unconscious, of course. How else could you catch a wood elf?" He took a long pull from the wine bottle. By the second one, he had given up on the glass. "He'd fallen. Out of a tree, I suppose. And I thought he was dead."

"So you—"

"So I gathered him up. He'd been a living thing, even if he was dead. And besides, he was my first piece of evidence that I was not an old fool seeing things in the shadows. He was proof of all those years of stories, reason for the hikes around the bog with you children. I figured I'd finally be able to show someone—you, most likely—that my stories were not just that. I'd show you that I wasn't going senile and becoming too old to be here alone. And then maybe you would stand by me in my battle to stay. So, yes, I gathered him up and I brought him here."

"But he's not dead." Jasper glanced toward the cabinet, both hoping and not hoping to see those green moons peeking out from the door's crack.

"No, he is very much alive." There was disappointment in the words. He followed his nephew's eyes to the cabinet. "And he's not pleased with me, not one bit. Therefore, the chain."

As if in comment, the chain dragged across wood followed by a pounding on the cabinet door.

"He'll be wanting his beer." Amos got up from the table with an effort that spoke to a month of sleepless nights. "Never should've gotten him started on the stuff." He grabbed a bottle from the fridge and popped the top. "He'll only drink Guinness now. Anything else he spits at me."

"How much does he drink?"

"Two of these a night, and for such a tiny thing. Can you imagine?"

Jasper could not. Then he wondered what would happen once the beer was processed? An hour later he heard the answer. At first, he thought the faucet had been left on, it was that loud and substantial.

"He has a soup bowl in there. It'll overflow if I forget to empty it before bed. I've done that before." He shook his head with disgust. "All that liquid in one little body."

After dinner, they retreated to the worn leather armchairs in front of the fireplace. They spoke of family, especially his disgust with Jasper's oldest sister and how disappointed Amos was with her defection to what he referred to as "the dark side," his moniker for the Republican Party. They discussed Jasper's classes, his future plans, and his search for meaningful relationships. It was the usual dialogue between loving uncle and favorite nephew. For an hour they hardly mentioned the little beast who had gone quiet, even though it was the only thing either of them could think about. Then they heard the chain rushing across the cabinet floor again. There was a metallic snap followed by a thump, as if the creature were making a dash against his restraints.

"I don't mean to question your judgment, Uncle Amos, but chains seem a little excessive. I mean, he's just a little guy."

Amos smiled. "Little guy, indeed." He reached for an old decorative box that he kept under his easy chair. "Like most people, you probably think wood elves are sweet little creatures."

Jasper, like most people, had never given them a second thought.

"Well, they're not. At least they're not always." He packed a purplish bud into a carved bone pipe. "I've learned something from this experience. Possibly too late, I'm afraid. You see, if we leave the magical alone, it'll mind its own business. But if it's tampered with—well, you just don't want to do that." He lit the pipe and sucked in deeply. "I tampered. And *this* is what I get." He jabbed a thumb toward the kitchen.

"I'm confused. Why not just let him go? Why chain him in there?"

Amos extended the pipe, but the boy waved it away. It seemed important that one of them should remain alert, considering the circumstances.

"Let me tell you something about wood elves, Jasper. You see, I've done quite a lot of reading on the subject now that I'm involved with one. Most, especially those of the Northeast, are vindictive little creatures. They don't take well to interference. The proper thing to do would have been for me to leave him there to die, maybe take a picture. But I didn't do that, did I? Instead, I brought him here. And after I had, I found that he was still breathing. I nursed him back to health with broth and beer. It's what he likes, a little too well it seems. I was trying to make him happy, so please don't judge me."

The boy wasn't judging exactly, but it did occur to him that a small being with a large temper might be best kept sober.

"Anyway, it took several weeks to get him on his feet. I even made a little hovel for him in the wall behind the liquor cabinet, through that hole. Cute place with a bed and a chair. It took me a while to do it, too. Had to cut through the outside wall, then board it up again. Pain in the ass, but I felt obligated. I had saved his life, and now I was responsible for it. And like I said, releasing him without some sort of agreement didn't seem smart. I was in the hopes that we could communicate at some point. So, I did all that for him because I thought I should.

"But was the little bugger thankful? Did he even give me a thin-lipped smile of appreciation? No, sir, he did not. The ungrateful rodent bit me!" He pushed back a sleeve and pointed to a small, circular wound on his forearm no larger than a dime. Jasper leaned closer to see the circle of tiny dots that appeared bright red with infection. "It hurt like hell, it did. So I flung him across the room. Natural reaction to getting bit like that. He banged his little head against the wall and was knocked out cold. I felt bad for just a minute. Then I got the chain. That was three weeks ago."

"But what will you do with him?" Jasper asked as he loosened his belt that had tightened from the dinner. He sunk deeper into the old leather. "You won't keep him locked up like that forever, will you?"

The question hung in the air for several long minutes, hovering amid the sweet aromas of burning wood, wafts of smoke, and Amos's garlic-rich pasta sauce. The old man stared into the fire as people do when a dilemma weighs heavily, as if a best solution might present itself from between log and flame. "I need to get him back to the bog," he said. "And I'd like to do it without losing a finger in the process. Maybe you would help with that now that you're here?"

Jasper nodded, against his better judgment. He would not say no to his uncle.

It was a problem that seemed to have no easy solution. Each possibility presented another problem that neither of them could resolve. A box or a bag? He'd tear it to shreds with those teeth and claws. A drug? The wrong amount could kill him, or, even worse, intensify his aggression. More beer? Intoxication seemed like a bad idea. Drag him into the woods by the chain? It sounded both dangerous and cruel. They went back and forth like that until the logs became embers, the embers became ash, and what was left became nothing more than a pile of cold gray. Still, they stared into it and discussed the problem until Uncle Amos rose with effort and grunted a "good night." He slowly climbed the stairs to his room and indicated the one off the living room for Jasper.

There would be very little sleep that night. Jasper would question whether what he saw only briefly could really be as his uncle assumed. It could just as well have been an unusual animal, some cross between a rabbit and . . . and what? A frog? A Gila monster? Those eyes were not of an ordinary animal. They were unworldly the way they glowed, like balls of bright green algae. As Jasper drifted toward sleep, he decided his imagination and his uncle's stories had surely affected his vision.

But then, barely moments after he had closed his eyes and relaxed his grip on the day, all hell erupted.

There were screams—or something like screams—at first. They pierced through the quiet and the blackness, unlike any human screams Jasper had ever heard. They were a series of trilling screeches so loud and alarming that he bolted out of bed and immediately crashed into the corner of the bureau. He hardly felt the pain. That sound seemed to fill his head, the room, and the entire cabin. There was an urgency to it—barely broken by breath—as the scream grew into one long and warbling cry.

In the next few seconds, a similar sound started from outside, but louder and more piercing. It was an angry cry, like a hate-fueled call to battle. Without turning on a light, Jasper went to the window and pulled back the curtain just a little. There was only a sliver of a moon, but even in that minimal light he could see the shine of their eyes. Round and bright green, at least twenty pair. They captured the moonlight and made a brighter light of their own. He must have gasped loudly, because all the eyes turned as one and blinked. He ducked behind the curtain.

"Uncle Amos!" he yelled as he threw open the bedroom door and nearly collided with his uncle who was bounding down the stairs, heading for the kitchen.

"Stay in your room," the old man commanded, not pausing for a second. He slammed the kitchen door behind him.

What happened in the next minutes, Jasper could only imagine from what he could hear through the door. It was a fracas, a clamor of wood splitting, glass shattering, and screaming from both his uncle and from what must have been that little creature. And the warbling cry from outside continued and escalated until it was nearly deafening, so loud Jasper couldn't hear his own screams. Then a series of cabin-shaking thumps, like the effects of something heavy hitting the wall, made it impossible for him to stay put for a moment longer.

He opened the kitchen door halfway and went still. The entire scene did the same. The screen and interior doors were in splinters, hanging from their hinges. All the bottles and glassware were broken and strewn across the kitchen. His uncle was supine, about a foot off the floor, held aloft by a dozen or more of those little creatures.

"Stop!" Jasper yelled, and the elves spun toward him, their eyes even wider and rounder than before. They paused, looking at him, blinking as one. Then they hissed. They bared their tiny, needlelike teeth for just a moment and released a surge of vitriolic warning, like a gush of hot steam. It lasted for only seconds and in the next they went quiet. They spun back toward the broken doors and proceeded to carry the old man aloft, like a casket, across the threshold, off the porch, and out into the nearly black night.

Through all of that, Uncle Amos did not move. He looked to be unconscious, since he made no sounds and no attempts to escape. They marched with him above their heads, mumbling something in unison. One of them—the one from the cupboard still with a glint of metal on his ankle—sat on Amos's chest, arms folded, looking straight ahead, chanting with the others. Jasper, with no idea of what he could do to help, quietly maneuvered through the kitchen's debris and bent low to the ground as he followed, how could he not? Clinging to the safety of the cabin while his uncle was being taken by these creatures to who-knows-where was not an option.

The woods parted for them. The boy watched as the procession marched straight from the cabin, down the slight hill, and into a thicket of branchy cedars and densely woven brush. The forest opened like that sea in the bible. It parted as a curtain would. Even the roots seemed to pull up and step back, allowing a wide path where there had been none. It welcomed them as they marched into it, and then the gap slowly closed behind them. Jasper, without thinking, crouched and ran as fast as he could, sliding through that diminishing crevice. The branch of an old cedar scraped across his back, and he pressed his fist into his mouth so as not to cry out from the sharp pain of it. But even if he had, the little devils would not have heard it. Their mumbling chant had grown louder and more purposeful as they marched. It was as if they were energized by their proximity to the deeper woods and to the bog.

Jasper followed the procession for about fifteen minutes when he saw the light just ahead. It pulsed slightly, as if it were breathing. The ground beneath his bare feet began to tremble, like a living thing that should not be walked upon. He treaded carefully, avoiding the dark patches of water, testing each step before transferring his weight to the next. It had been said that cows, dogs, and even trespassers who had wandered in too deeply had been taken by the bog's depths. Jasper stayed low and crawled from thick root to solid rock in order to avoid the watery spaces. It was easier now, since the greenish light seemed to be generating from each patch of black water. It was the same light he'd seen in those elfin eyes.

When the procession stopped, he did the same, and he hid on a mound behind a sprawling cluster of cedars. From that point, slightly higher than where the elves lowered his uncle, Jasper could see a gathering of more creatures, some like the elves but others unlike anything close to man. They crept from behind trees, crawled from between roots, and slithered out of rock piles. They surrounded Amos and stared at him. A few kicked at his arms and legs, but Amos didn't move. It occurred to Jasper that his uncle might be dead, but then one of the creatures—not an elf, something smaller with a lot of fur—blew a handful of dust into the old man's face, and he bolted awake.

As slow and as ceremonious as the procession had been, the next minutes were anything but. Amos slumped at the edge of a wide hole with his feet dangling into the pool, his back pressed against the trunk of a sprawling elm. He barely moved. Only his head turned from side to side, taking in the strange gathering of creatures in that greenish glow that made everything seem underwater. He looked confused, not quite awake, unaware of place and reason. The elves continued their chant, but it had quieted to a barely audible hum. It was a sound nearly as soothing as a gentle whisper. Jasper could feel his eyelids getting heavy against his will.

But then another sound brought him back to full alert. It was like a wave crashing hard against rock, so loud it shook him and the roots and stones that supported him. Everything moved and growled. He covered his ears against it, but his eyes remained on his uncle. He watched with a paralyzing horror as a massive hand, a watery limb of gray and green, thrust out from the black water and clutched onto the old man. It closed around him, completely enveloping his thin body, and in one swift yank it pulled him down into the dark pool and out of sight. As quickly as that, the sound and the glow were gone, as were the creatures and any evidence of Amos.

A braver boy might have foolishly run to that spot and tried to save his uncle, but Jasper was neither brave nor foolish. He cowered and remained hidden behind the cluster of cedars until daylight. He didn't sleep. He stared numbly at that spot of black water, barely blinking until sunrise. When there was enough light, he left his hiding spot and stumbled out of the bog and up the hill. His movement was not initiated by thought. It was as if his feet and legs and arms knew better than the thinking parts. He crawled and pulled himself along by tree roots and rocks, slashing his arms and feet on the thorny underbrush, until he made a path back to the cabin. By the time he got there his limbs were sliced and bloody, but he didn't notice. He squeezed past the splintered doors, across the kitchen floor still strewn with broken glass and leaves, and went directly to his room. There he removed his torn and muddied pajamas—barely seeing himself or his surroundings—and slid beneath the heavy down comforter. He slept, without movement or dreams, for nearly twelve hours.

Jasper could have slept longer. It was a comfortable bed and the day was so quiet, not even the usual quarrels between families of crows that started early on a normal day. But that morning was not normal. The woods had gone silent, as if it were tiptoeing through the day. The first sound he heard was a ringing. It went on and on until he woke enough to realize it was a phone.

He reluctantly opened his eyes and stared up at a ceiling that was not familiar at first. It wasn't his dorm room and it wasn't the ceiling of his bedroom at home. Glancing around at the old furnishings he soon realized he was in his uncle's cabin. Uncle Amos. Yes, that was his uncle. And this is his home. *But why isn't he answering the phone?*

He flung back the covers, and the top sheet stuck to him in places, causing a stinging pain on his legs and feet as it ripped away. *Why am I bleeding?* Still naked, he ran to answer the kitchen phone, but when he pushed open the kitchen door, he couldn't understand what he was seeing. The room was in shambles, not at all the way his uncle kept it. *Why is the phone still ringing?* He carefully stepped between pieces of glass and splintered wood to reach it.

"Hello?"

"Jasper? Is that you?" It was his mother.

He hesitated. He looked around at the room again, trying to remember how he had gotten there and, more importantly, what had happened.

"Jasper? Are you all right? I've been calling all morning. Where is your uncle? Why aren't you saying anything? Is something wrong?"

So many questions. And he couldn't summon a single answer.

"Please, honey, talk to me. What's going on?"

He hesitated again, this time longer, searching the room for answers, seeing the door, the upended table, the broken glassware, and the chain that hung without purpose from the liquor cabinet. Finally, he was able to say softly, "I . . . I don't know."

Without realizing, he started to weep. The phone slid from his fist and dropped to the floor. In the next second, he followed it.

Baby

1924

From the journal of Sarah Winslow Linquist:

February 17, 1924

My world has lost its color. All I can see in every direction is an obscene and disquieting whiteness. The snow pounds, swirls, and gathers in corners. It piles onto itself, over and over, until nothing else is recognizable. Everything has lost its shape. White sky becomes white trees become white earth. The world has become one thing: a wild and angry white beast.

Please help me, Lord. I am so very afraid of the white and what it might be doing to my mind.

I NEVER THOUGHT I'D GO BACK TO RIVERTON. TOO MANY MEMO-ries, some of them not so good. I'd lost my dad there. Lost a best friend, too. Nearly lost my brain working at the Hitchpost with Jake. But I also found something in Riverton. It's where I fell in love with Mavi, and because of that I've always held a love for the town, although I've rarely acknowledged it.

When Mavi and I finally left, I'd sworn I'd never step foot there again. After my mother moved to live with my sister, there was no reason to. Even Mavi agreed, joking that she'd taken the best of Riverton with her. "Not you, dummy," she'd say, punching me in the arm as she was fond of doing. "I mean my little girl Precious." It's one of those ongoing jokes between us, but I do believe Mavi loved that ugly dog more than me, may she rest in peace. Precious, not Mavi. The latter lives on, feisty as ever.

Anyway, it had been nearly ten years, time that I set all that angst aside. So I went back, reluctantly, but I went back nonetheless. It was my editor's idea. I'd been working for the *Press Herald* since 1980. Six years later, Portland was celebrating its 200th anniversary and they needed a piece about some of the old families that had helped rebuild the city after the fire of 1866. It was just another human-interest piece to add to an already overdone feature. Most of the readers were sick of the anniversary before we'd even gotten to it. But the paper kept beating that tired drum. In one of the staff meetings, the name Winslow came up as a storyline.

"Sam, you're related to the Winslows, aren't you?" Schlectman was the editor then. Good man, but not one who accepted a *No.* "I seem to recall you bragging about that." He smiled. We'd become close recently so I understood the man's good nature.

"I wasn't bragging, Tom. And it's not even a close relationship. My mother was a Winslow, but all the money was long gone by the time she was born."

"Well, thank God this story isn't about you. I need ink about old family money, something that will bring the reader back to the good old days, or whatever they were. If it's decent, you'll have the full feature."

And that's how I got the assignment. I was to research the Winslows and write a piece about the family that still had its name on buildings and streets around the peninsula. My mother would have been a great place to start, but she'd died a couple years earlier, and she had never been one to talk about that part of the family. She seemed to be embarrassed by their wealth, their position, and their loss of all of it. She'd been more comfortable with her small-town life and the family that she'd created with my dad.

It was in the Portland library, on a loop of microfilm, that I first caught a glimpse of Sarah Winslow. The family resemblance hit me immediately, but she was far more beautiful than the muddied genetic line that came after her. She had the same dark hair as my sisters, but hers was long and wavy, pinned away from her face with ribbons and fancy combs. Even her dark, wide eyes were familiar. But her face, the shape and texture of it, seemed to have been created by a more skillful artisan, one who appreciated the softer and smoother line. In each of the pictures she stood out among the small-city socialites that surrounded her. Perhaps it was the strength in her posture, unusual for a seventeen-year-old girl. Or it could have been the way she aimed her dark gaze directly into the camera's eye: deliberate and amused.

There was little information in any of the clippings about her, just those few photos. Most of the stories concerned her father and the family business, their social activities. The tags only listed her as a guest along with a half dozen others, some of whose last names I recognized from my tours through Portland history. One picture from 1920 showed a large outdoor party at their estate in Riverton. The place was a stone-and-log structure, large enough to be considered a lodge, with a lawn that rolled down to a mist-covered lake. Sarah was pictured bent over a croquet mallet. Her long curls were held back by a scarf, and her head was turned up to the camera, one thin eyebrow raised as if to say, "Watch this."

Then I found her obituary from 1924. There she was referred to as Sarah Winslow Linquist with no mention of a husband and no clue as to how she had died, only that she "had passed away at her home in Riverton." She was twenty-four. I scrolled back to find a wedding announcement but there was none. The picture that accompanied the brief obit was a studio portrait. She was smiling slightly, and in that negligible lift at the corners of her mouth I saw what appeared to be a challenge: either for the camera or for life.

The family vanished from the society pages after 1930. The Great Depression had done a number on the shipping industry, and the father had committed suicide shortly after the collapse of Wall Street. The last piece I found was a five-line entry in the gossip column. It stated, in not very sympathetic language, that "Mrs. Harold Winslow, once the Queen of Deering Highlands, has plummeted from her lofty perch. No longer the matriarch of Winslow Manner and the hostess for countless social extravaganzas, Mrs. Winslow has abandoned our fair city, accompanied by her two surviving daughters. She has returned to Akron, Ohio, the land-locked port of her less-advantaged youth."

"So, no Winslows left in Portland?" Schlectman scanned my pages. He hadn't asked me to sit, but he never did. His spare chairs were always occupied by books and magazines. I stood on the other side of the wide desk piled high with copy. Two cigarettes burned in an ashtray nearly filled with the filters of a long day. A cirrus cloud of smoke clung to the drop ceiling, making the stuffy room feel smaller and more claustrophobic.

"Nope. That whole Winslow line died out, at least in Portland. And my grandmother died when my mother was young." I was sweating hard and I kept swiping at it with the sleeve of my shirt. It was mid-October, but only according to the calendar. The whole state was baking like it was a week in July. The windows of the building had been closed and covered with plastic for the winter, a routine that was apparently dictated by the date rather than the thermostat. Fans were the only attempts at relief. Schlectman had three of them going, but all they managed was to circulate the gray cloud that seemed to be growing larger and more threatening.

"I could follow the story to Ohio," I said. "But that's going to move away from the Portland connection. Or I could just find another family." I was hoping for the latter. There was something about that picture of Sarah Winslow that spoke to me of bad endings. I would have been hard-pressed to explain it to Schlectman, so I simply added, "Nobody's gone into the Neil Dow family for the anniversary. I could dive into them."

"Been done. Couple years back. Anyway, I'm sick of that self-righteous prick." He scanned my notes again, underlining some, slashing others. It was several sweaty minutes before he spoke again. "The Winslows, they were here for—what—over two hundred years and then they get wiped out by the crash? That's a hell of a lot more interesting than the Dows." He examined the photos. "Who's this girl? Pretty little thing."

"That's Sarah Winslow. She died at twenty-four. Her obit's on the next page."

He flipped to it. "Hm. Not much ink for a debutante. How'd she die?"

"I couldn't find any more than what you've got there. She died in Riverton, but that's all I know."

"She buried at the Evergreen? The Winslows have that big monument. You been there?"

"Well, that's another thing. They have a whole section with markers going back to the late 1600s, but Sarah isn't there. Harold Winslow, the dad, is the last one—1930."

"Okay, this might be interesting. I'd want pictures of the houses, include some of these old pics too. Give me stuff about how the Depression affected Portland, how it changed the status of the family. Go to—" He checked a page. "Go to Riverton and get pictures of their summerhouse if there's anything left of it. And maybe there's someone there who knew this girl, Sarah. It's only been sixty years; someone might still be around. See if you can find out why there's no mention of a husband or how she died. Might have been a scandal. People love that shit, especially when it dirties the rich." He started to hand me the notes, then pulled back. "This could be good, Sam. You won't let your family connection or your past get in your way, will you?"

"Nope. Not a problem."

"Good. But if it does, you let me know. Agreed?"

"Absolutely, Tom." It never occurred to me that any family issue could get in the way of my job. My parents were long gone, and my sisters and Mavi were no longer connected to Riverton. But I had no idea then how deeply a family connection can run.

Two days later, I crested the hill that winds down into Riverton. There it was, just as I remembered, and I needed to pull off to the side to absorb it, to ready myself. It was overwhelming to see it again. The view was as stunning as it had always been. Three white spires poking out of the center of the valley, like candles stuck into the middle of a sprawling, autumn cake. The river, as blue as the October morning sky, twisted out from between mountains, bisecting the town and snaking a path through farms and woods until it disappeared around a hill of greenish gold. The last time I'd seen the place was in my rearview, on the day Mavi and I left Riverton. I hadn't kept in touch with anyone, not even Jake. There was no logical reason for why I'd cut everyone out. Maybe it was guilt. I'd left, and they hadn't. My escape from Riverton had felt like the gift of a brand-new life. I'd won the lottery, and then I'd kicked my friends to the curb.

I sat in my car for nearly a half hour, allowing the past to flash at me like clips from old movies. Ma and Dad drinking tea in the farm kitchen. Ricky and Mavi running through tall ryegrass ahead of me. Happy Valley and the many sorrows that lived there. I thought of Donnie Hickey and Jamie and the big guy, whose name I never learned. And I thought about the event that had decided my destiny, the night a crazy preacher had nearly burned the town down.

I stayed there until I'd seen enough, until I'd convinced myself of the need to move forward with the task that had brought me home. When I was sure of my readiness, when I'd talked myself out of turning back and telling Schlectman to give me another story, I pulled onto the winding road that would lead me, against my better senses, down into the valley and back to my hometown.

It was well before noon, but I knew my first stop had to be the Hitchpost. I couldn't land without seeing Jake, the man who had been a big part of my life in Riverton. I went to the bar's back door, knowing it would be open and that Jake would probably be taking inventory or doing the money from the night before. He sat on a stool, back to me, hunched over the bar. My first emotion at seeing him there was concern. Was he drinking again? Or back on the drugs that he'd sworn off the night he'd seen Maggie Albertson rise up into the clouds? But when he spun around, my concern dissolved. His eyes were clear. His graying hair, his clothes, his whole demeanor were clean and kempt. He was a man who had seen—or thought he'd seen—something life-changing and had made the best of it.

"Sammy!" Even his movements spoke to a rebirth. "Where the fuck you been, you little shit?" He jumped up and pulled me into a hug that forced the wind out of me—along with a good portion of my trepidations about coming home. When he finally let me go—and it was he who decided when it was time—he poured me a cup of strong coffee. Then we got down to the business of catching up.

"I've kept track of you," he said, and his implication was obvious. I had drifted away, but he hadn't let me go. "You're pretty good at this writing crap. And I've noticed you go by Samuel now." He rolled his eyes. "A little uppity, don't you think?"

"Only in print. Still Sammy to my friends."

We talked about Mavi and her art career, my family—what was left of it—and his new "true love," who he promised I would meet before I left again. Eventually we got around to my reasons for being there.

"I should've known it'd be about work. You wouldn't just drop back into Riverton without good reason. Not your idea, was it?"

I smiled. No need to answer.

"I'm afraid the Winslows were a little before my time, so I won't be much help to ya. I knew the name, of course. Lots of money. I didn't know you were related."

"It was my mother's side. She didn't get any of it, obviously."

"I think they had a huge place up on Pinnacle Pond. Just a pile of rubble now. Burned down back in the '20s or '30s maybe. You should check it out."

"Who in town would know the history of that?"

"I'd start with the library. Talk to Thelma Woodard. She's got the town's history in her back pocket. She'll remember you, town star that you are. That old girl remembers everything." He punched me in the shoulder when I stood to leave. "Don't be such a fucking stranger, Sammy. You got roots worth keeping."

As I made my way from the Hitchpost to the library, I considered the possibility of staying for a couple of days. Whether it was seeing Jake or seeing the town again, I didn't know. It suddenly felt like the right thing to do.

Not much had changed. The Victorians along Depot Street were just as charming and well-maintained. Johnson's General still had ads from the fifties taped to the windows. I passed the post office and wondered who had taken Alva's place. A block later I came to the library—a small white structure with columns, full-length arched windows, and massive double doors. The building had always struck me as strange, as if a statelier library from a big city had been shrunk to fit the town. The door was as heavy and loud as I remembered. Thelma Woodard, sitting behind the highly polished desk, squinted and then smiled as I came through.

"I was wondering if we'd ever see your handsome face again." She stood and came around to give me a hug. I hadn't been in the library since high school, but Jake had been right about her memory. She pulled out a chair near her desk and patted the seat. "Here. You sit down and tell me everything, Sammy. How's the big city treating you? How's that crazy wife of yours?"

It took a half hour to get around to business. Then I showed her the pictures of Sarah and laid out the few articles I'd brought. She looked over everything, rose from her chair with a little difficulty, and went through a door marked "Private." In a few minutes she was back with two thin leather volumes.

"These can't leave the library, but there's not much here anyway. I found Sarah Winslow, but nothing about a Linquist." She bookmarked three pages in one, two pages in the other, and nodded toward a long table. "Set yourself up over there. Take your time. I'll make copies of anything you want." She headed back to her desk, turned, and added softly, "There's not a day goes by that I don't think of your mother. She was one of a kind, that one." I agreed.

There wasn't a lot of information on Sarah. There was a mention of her death, but it offered no details. Harold, her father, was referenced a few times in two of the chapters. There were pictures that I hadn't seen before, including a full-page shot of the estate on Pinnacle Pond. Another was of Sarah and a girl at a party near a bandstand. The caption read:

"Two Riverton beauties enjoying a Saturday night dance behind The Herbert Hotel.
Sarah Winslow and Charlotte Holmes, 1917."

I brought the books back to the desk after I'd taken notes. "Thanks, Miss Woodard. Not much, but it's a little something." I opened the book to the last picture. "Do you know this girl? I suppose she'd be in her eighties now. Charlotte Holmes?"

"Sure do. That would be Charlotte Thompson."

"Judge Thompson's wife? I remember them. Friends of my folks, I think."

"That would make sense. I know your mom was active in the same clubs. Some folks think Charlotte's a bit uppity, but I like her. She makes nice donations to the library every year. The Thompsons are pretty well-off now, so I suppose that's why people talk bad about them. It's just jealousy, ya know."

"You never heard of a Linquist living here?"

"Nope. No Linquists in Riverton, far as I know. But there used to be a whole bunch of Swedes or Norwegians that lived up toward the mountains. Daddy called them 'woodspeople' because they didn't come into town much. He said they were all crazy."

"They moved away?"

"I suppose. Or died. Daddy used to tell a story about them, that they'd all got drunk one winter off moonshine and killed each other. Not sure if that's true. He had a lot of stories. And I don't even know if their name was Linquist, just called them 'woodspeople.'"

"What about Pinnacle Pond? The Winslows owned a large house there."

She chuckled. "Large house? More like a mansion. It burned down a long time ago, but I've been told there's still the foundations of the main house and a few smaller ones. A complex, I guess you'd call it. When I was a teenager, some of the kids—the wild ones—would go up there to party." She swiveled in her chair, pulled a single-page map from a file cabinet, and highlighted a road and an area near the pond. "If you go up there, be careful. Those foundations aren't safe. Couple of the kids got hurt pretty bad."

I thanked her and started for the door when she called me back. "Wait, Sammy. It occurs to me that you should talk to Jim Trenholm. You may not know him, keeps to himself mostly. He owns all that land up toward where the woodspeople used to live, up into the mountains. If anyone remembers a Linquist, he would." She scribbled directions, gave me a final hug, and I was off.

July 4, 1916

A perfect night in Riverton. Every summer I love it more. Charlotte and I went to the dance in town. The music was as professional as any I've heard in Portland or Boston. An eight-piece band with two singers, a man and a woman. Quite the extravagance for the town, I would think. Every-

*one came out, except Mother and Father. They had guests at
the house and a party of their own, as usual.*

*I met a very sweet man at the dance. I think I was for-
ward, but I couldn't help myself. I was quite drawn to him.
Handsome, but intelligent as well, and able to talk on so
many subjects. We spoke French most of the night, which irked
Charlotte. I hope to see him again, but apparently he seldom
comes to town. I will certainly keep my eyes open for him. I
believe he could be a dear friend and a welcome change from
the boys in Portland.*

I found Mr. Trenholm at his farmhouse a few miles outside of
town, on the top of a big hill that looked down on Riverton. I
could hear the sounds of splitting wood when I got out of the
car, and I followed it to the back. The man gave me a nod when I
approached but he didn't stop working.

"Mr. Trenholm?" I said and extended my hand.

"Ayuh. That'd be me." he said between swings, ignoring
my gesture. He was a big man, over six feet and broad through
the shoulders. Curly white hair billowed from his collar, and it
matched the thick crown that showed no signs of thinning. I
approached him cautiously, keeping an eye on the ax. He didn't
stop swinging it until I said my name. The ax paused at the top of
the arc, and then he brought it down hard into the tree stump he
was using as a block.

"Your Henry Taylor's boy, aren'tcha?"

"I am, sir. Did you know him?"

"That I did. Worked with him at the mill for a time. Damn
shame how he died. Nobody oughta die at work." He pulled a rag
from his back pocket and wiped it roughly over his forehead, neck,
and into the deep crevices around his mouth. It left his face red
and raw. "What can I do you for?"

"I'm doing a story for the *Press Herald*. It's a piece about some of the old families in Portland. The name Sarah Winslow Linquist came up in connection to Riverton. Did you know her?"

"I did. Knew her husband George too."

"So that would be George Linquist?" I pulled out my notebook and started writing. "You knew them well?"

"I suppose. Much as any man knows another." His speech was slow and wary, and he kept looking back at his woodpile as if to apologize to it for taking a break. "They lived a few miles down there." He jabbed his thumb toward an expanse of rolling forest that ran along the river and then up into the mountains. "Never met none of the Winslows, 'cept for Sarah. Oh, and her father just once. Didn't take to him much. But I knew the Linquists. They owned that whole valley and the mountain at one time." He swept his arm across everything in view, thousands of acres of green. "That clearing at the top is where George was born, his father too. George lived on that piece of land till he died. He was the last of 'em."

"How long ago did he die?"

He leaned on his ax and studied me. "You don't know shit about them, do ya?"

"No, sir. That's why I'm here."

"Well, George and Sarah both died down near the river, in a sweet little cabin way back in those woods. Musta been around '23 or '24."

"It was 1924, according to her obituary. But there's no mention of George."

He snickered. "Not surprised. Sarah's father woulda kept that outa the papers, I'm sure."

"Mr. Trenholm . . ."

"Call me Jim."

"Jim, I hope you don't think this is too forward, but would it be possible for me to go down there, to see the cabin? Miss Woodard at the library said you own all this land now."

"Thelma? That old woman talks a lot, don't she? Didn't think you was supposed to do that in a library." He spat a wad of something brown into the grass. "But yeah, that's right. I bought it from the town after they died. The Linquists had been deeded the valley and the whole mountain when the town went official. The land went back to the town after George died. No heirs."

"So, what do you think? Could I go down there?"

"You really wanna see the cabin? Not much left. Why would you wanna see where someone died, anyway? How's that gonna help you write a story about Sarah?"

"I'm not sure it will, but I won't know until I go there."

"Hell, you'd never find the place yourself. Road's not even a road no more. Probably get lost and then I'd have to go out and find ya. Ain't got time for that." He stared at the stack of wood, then back at me, and blew out a long-frustrated exhale. "Ah, for chrissake, friggin' day is half gone anyway. I'll tell you what, son, you come back here in an hour and I'll take you there myself. It's a lot of miles through the woods, along the river. We'll take the tractor far as we can. Then you'll have to get a little dirty if you want to see her."

"Her?"

"The cabin. You'll feel her when you get down there. Can't have a thing like that happen without leaving a little something behind."

"A thing like what?"

He didn't answer. He looked me over and made a sucking sound through his teeth and spit out another stream of brown. "Go over town and buy a pair of boots at Johnson's. You won't get too far with those fancy slippers." He nodded toward my tasseled loafers, and I was embarrassed at how delicate and inappropriate they looked.

"Thanks, Jim. I appreciate it."

He grunted and got back to his woodpile.

An hour later Jim was waiting in the driveway. He looked at the boots and nodded approval. Then we were off: he sitting in the tractor and I hanging onto the back hoping I wouldn't fly off every time he hit a gopher hole or made a quick turn to avoid one. We rode like that for a half hour, and when the path got too narrow, we went on foot. He didn't speak for most of the way, but it seemed as though the proximity of the place loosened him a little, or at least softened him.

"This ain't easy for me. I'm one of the ones who found 'em, ya know." He walked slowly so I could keep up.

"I didn't know that. Sorry, Jim."

Even with the new footwear I was stumbling and slipping. The path was muddy, overgrown, and blocked in spots by blowdowns. The day was heating up and a fog rose from the moist ground—an eerie effect in a place that didn't need one. I kept hearing twigs snapping in the woods, but I couldn't see far enough to tell what had done it. Jim just kept moving at the same pace, glancing over his shoulder occasionally to make sure I was still there.

"I really appreciate your bringing me down here."

"Well, nobody else woulda. Most folks don't know about this place. And if they do, they sure as hell don't want to come here. Kids used to years ago but no more. Can't say I blame 'em. There's a weird feeling in these woods, gives me the creeps. Truth be told, it makes me a little sad too." He jumped across a stream of mostly dry rock with just a trickle of cold mountain water making its journey to the Carrabassett. "I haven't been here for, geez, it's gotta be forty years or more. For a while I'd come back a few times every summer, picking wildflowers on the way, setting 'em at the door of the cabin. Sarah loved wildflowers, 'specially those brown-centered ones. I used to see her picking 'em up on the ridge while I was cutting the fields. She'd wave a big hello and I'd wave a big one back at her. I guess I had a crush on her. Hell, course I did. She was a beauty, and I was just hitting my teens." He smiled with the more pleasant memory. "We're almost there. You gonna make it?" He looked back and chuckled at my lack of stamina.

"Yup," I said between heavy breaths. Jim was in his late seventies then, but I couldn't see evidence of it. I did my best to keep up with the man who was more than twice my age.

A mile or so later we crossed another stream, this one larger and with the remnants of what once served as a bridge. "Careful here," he said. "Watch where I'm steppin'. You won't go through as long as you stay on the crossbeams."

On the other side, the land opened. The sun shone fully now that the canopy of massive pines and oaks was behind us. Dozens of moss-covered stumps dotted the area, evidence of when the clearing had been cut decades before.

"That path we just come down? Used to be a logging road back in the day. It was George's road. He and his pa used it, probably his grandpa before them." I looked back at the path that was barely visible now. It looked more like a deer run than anything made for human travel. "They were all loggers. Whole family of woodspeople, cut mostly Punkin' Pine and Hack for the mill. Only ten miles from town, but woodspeople didn't go in much. No reason to. They killed or grew or made most everything. Even booze, unfortunately. And it wasn't that good stuff that comes outa Happy Valley. Their moonshine could rot out your whole insides, brains and all. Not sure how they drank it, but they did." We rounded a cluster of old birches and stopped. "There she is, what's left of her."

It took me a minute to see it. Finally, I made out the peak of a roof, just a few feet off the ground now that the walls had partially caved. It was barely visible through the brush that had grown around it, but I could make out the conventional angles of the steep pitch and the corners. The whole cabin couldn't have been more than ten by twenty. As we got near, I got a sense of what Jim had spoken of before: the feeling of something there, something alive. It was a closeness, a heaviness. It could have been the thickness of the woods and the moisture evaporating from it. Or it could have been my imagination fueled by Jim's unease.

"I was barely into my long pants that day we found 'em. Still a kid, but thinking I'm a man already. Well, that day went a long way to crossing me over, I'll tell you that. I think I aged a decade."

"Can you tell me about it?" I pulled out my camera and took a picture. It was the only one I got.

"Don't do that," he said, and he put a hand over the lens.

"Why not?"

"'Cause folks died here. It ain't respectful."

"Sorry," I said and put the camera away. "Is it okay if I take notes?" I reached for the notebook but paused.

"That's fine. You can take your notes, not that I'm gonna say anything worth noting. I'll tell ya some of the story, but I ain't getting into details. You'll have to go elsewhere for those. You wanna sit? You look like you could use it." He nodded toward a couple of stumps. I settled onto the closest one. The moss was thick and warm from the sun and it felt good after the hike. Jim remained standing.

"George grew up in a bigger cabin up the mountain. It's probably gone to the land by now. That's what nature does: takes back what's hers. The old folks passed on a couple years before this all happened. George, just like his pa and his grandpa, had lived his whole life here. I don't think he'd ever left the woods until he was a teenager. That's how they were. They cut timber and hauled it into town by team twice, three times a year, but George never went in until he was nearly grown. His two older brothers had always done it with their dad. But then, after a few years, they'd got a taste of life off the mountain and they didn't wanna come back. They took off one fall with the money from their last haul. Musta been a huge disappointment for Grace, their mother. They were bad ones, they were. Not George, though. I think he stuck around just 'cause his brothers hadn't. He was like that, real good boy."

I kept scribbling, glancing up occasionally at his face. It remained calm and expressionless as he stared into the woods, as if the memories were all there, waiting for him.

"The town worked two mills then, and old man Linquist did the bargaining once the older boys were gone. He was pretty good at getting the best dollar. The mill bosses hated to see him coming. He'd get the two of them fighting with each other over the haul, one outbidding the other, and the loser would storm off swearing. Linquist loved it, I imagine. He was a mean old sonofabitch."

"George didn't go to town with him?"

"Not for quite a while. I suppose the old man was afraid of losing him too. But eventually Linquist was too old to do it himself and had to start teaching the kid the ropes. By the time George was eighteen, he started taking over the hauling and the selling. Better than the old man, people used to say, 'cause he was a charmer. Honest too, clean through. Old man Linquist was far from charming. What's the opposite of that? You're the writer."

"Irritating maybe?"

He laughed. "Ayuh, that would describe old man Linquist all right. Irritating as hell. But George was different. Everybody liked George. He didn't get those mill families fighting like his pa did. His way was to joke around, get 'em all laughing until one finally gave in to the other. And then, when the deal was done, he'd take them all out for a few drinks at the Hogpenny. That was his way. Yessiree, George was a lot of fun to be round. Damn good man." He looked over at the rooftop again and shook his head. "I don't know what happened that winter of '24. Nobody does. Nobody that's alive anyway. It's just a lot of speclatin'. But we can figure that at some point during that long stretch of winter George musta changed. 'Cause he did something bad then. Real bad indeed."

"Wait, Jim. I'm confused. What did George do?"

Jim looked at me and shook his head. "You really don't know shit, do ya? Well, that don't surprise me much. I suppose old man Winslow paid a lot of money to keep that out of the papers. And he paid the Staties a chunk too. There were rumors for a while, but nobody was talking, so the stories lost their fuel. I wasn't about to say anything. I was just a kid and my dad had made it clear that I was to keep my mouth shut. I think Winslow mighta got to him, too."

"Keep your mouth shut about what?"

He looked at me hard, as if he were deciding. Finally, he said, "Nope!" He gritted his teeth and shook his head. "Goddamn it, kid. I told you I wasn't gonna get into no details, and I ain't doing it. I've been tryin' like hell to forget this story, and now you got it going through my brain again."

"Come on, Jim. You can't just give me half a story and leave me hanging. What happened?"

"The hell I can't. This is my land, ain't it? Told ya I'd bring ya down, and I done it. You want some juice for your paper, you'll have to get it somewhere else."

"Sorry, Jim. I know this is rough on you and I apologize. But I'm not asking just for the paper. I'm personally invested in this story. My mother was a Winslow, remember?" I knew when I said it that I wasn't being completely honest. There was a story there and I wanted it for myself, sure. But mostly I wanted to write it. For Schlectman and the approval that would go with it.

"Well, that's just too bad, ain't it? I'm no gossiper, and this is not good stuff to talk about, no matter what your reasons. Talking about evil gives life to it. Maybe I'm just a little superstitious, but I'm too old to change." He was silent for a long time, staring off toward the clearing that sloped down past what was left of the cabin, toward the river. "Sorry, kid, but that's enough. I'm in need of gettin' outa here. Talking about this makes me feel a little sick in the ticker. If you want more details, and I'm sure your paper will, you might wanna talk to my friend Arthur Thompson. He's not as superstitious as me, maybe 'cause he ain't got this place in his backyard. He's the one who was with me that day, and he probably remembers more about it than me. He's a few years older but still sharp as a tack."

We started walking back, him in the lead again but walking slower as if he'd tired. Farther along he stopped and turned back to me. "I will tell ya one more thing, since I know you'll be talking to townsfolk about this. I want you to know that none of them know shit, 'cept for Arthur. They're just making up stories. Some of them are gonna claim there was a rope—a noose—hanging from the beam, twenty, thirty years after it all happened, pieces of skin and hair still on it. I've heard that rumor more times than I can tell ya, but I never bothered to put them straight, 'cause I ain't no gossiper. The fact is Arthur and I got George down from that rafter, and we couldn't get that piece of rope off him. It musta been on his neck for months, digging into his throat. We had to leave it there, like it was part of his skin, and then we hauled all the bodies out on a pung behind a couple of Dad's hosses."

"All the bodies?"

"Ayuh, all three. George and Sarah and the little one. She couldn't have been more than a coupla months. Damnedest thing the way their bodies were when we found 'em. George was hanging from the beam, just a few feet from his only family, but Sarah was still sitting in a chair in the kitchen. One of her arms was wrapped tight around that little bundle like she was rocking her to sleep. We hauled Sarah and the baby out just the way they was, still huggin'. Couldn't bring ourselves to separate 'em."

July 22, 1921

 George took me for the long hike up the mountain to meet his mother and then to see the cabin he'd built near the river. Grace is a wonderful woman, so smart and true to her name. His father is quite the opposite, but George had warned me of his manner. Can't imagine why Grace married him, but I suppose he has his good side.

 I love the cabin. It could certainly use a woman's influence, and I promised him that I could be that if he was so inclined. It was forward of me, and I'm sure he understood my meaning.

 I am in love. And very happy.

By midday I had already decided to stay at least one night. I stopped by Winter's Inn to get a room, and while I was there, I called Mavi to let her know. She sounded a little envious that I was in Riverton, even though she'd never admit to it. I knew that she would have loved to have joined me if she could have, but an upcoming exhibit had been keeping her anchored to her studio. There were questions about her old house, the school, and Happy Valley, to all of which I had no answers. Despite her annoyance with my lack of information, she asked me to give her best to Jake and to put some flowers on her mom's grave. I agreed to both.

The Riverside Cemetery is just below Winter's Inn, which sets on a hill overlooking the river. It's separated from the cemetery by a plot of field that appears to have never been mowed. It's filled with tall, fluttering ryegrass and all varieties and colors of wild-flowers. I walked through it and filled my arms with as many as I could hold. Daisies, devil's paintbrush, clover, and those yellow ones that Jim had picked so often for Sarah. I found my family's markers first—my parents and a bunch of Tilsons, Taylors, and Frenches. I read through a dozen of them, noting the dates that went back a hundred years and trying to remember the stories I'd been told about the people who lay beneath them. I placed small bunches at each.

Then I came to one I'd never noticed when I was a kid wandering through the old stones. It read *Sarah Winslow Linquist, 1900–1924*. In Portland, I'd spent an hour looking for it in Evergreen Cemetery, but here it was. It was a nice marker, obviously something that had cost old man Winslow some money. There was none for George, just an empty spot where he might or might not have been buried. I thought it was possible, considering the circumstances, that he hadn't been buried with her. But it was odd that there was a plot there with nothing on it. I laid most of the yellow flowers between the two. I took a picture of her stone and turned to leave. But then a small piece of flagstone caught my eye. It was partially toppled and nearly covered by weeds and moss. I righted it the best I could and brushed away the moss to read the one line. *Baby, 1924* was etched into the dark gray rock. The sight of it—upended and barely readable—brought a sadness into my throat. Mavi and I had decided against having kids, but I could still imagine the tragedy and the loss that comes from a baby's death.

The discovery of her grave flummoxed me enough that I nearly forgot Mavi's mother, Maxine. She was farther down, in the poorer part, but I found her eventually. I knelt beside her simple stone and thanked her for Mavi, leaving the rest of my flowers with her.

Judge Arthur Thompson's house was easy to find. It was the largest in Riverton: a sprawling white Victorian surrounded by nearly an acre of well-maintained lawn and gardens. It held a full wraparound porch and a widow's walk that must have offered an impressive view of the river and the mountains. When I pulled up, he was sitting on the porch and he waved me in. Jim had told me that the man was in his eighties, but I wouldn't have known it. He stood tall and trim like a runner, no curl to his posture at all. He extended a hand to me, and there I felt his age—the bony knuckles and gnarled fingers of arthritis. I loosened my grip a little.

"Jim told me you were coming. Hadn't talked to him in a while, so that's one good thing you've done." He swallowed the last of a beer and said he was about to have another. He offered me one. I refused, but he insisted and handed me a frosty bottle. "You wanna talk with me on a warm fall afternoon, you're gonna be drinking."

"Thank you, sir. I'm sorry, should I call you Judge Thompson?"

"You call me Arthur. I retired fifteen years ago, and the only ones who call me 'Judge' are the ones I put in jail. Never put you in jail, did I?" He smiled.

"No sir. Arthur, I mean." I took a long haul of the beer. It was good: bitter and very cold.

"Now, what's this about? Jim said you wanted to talk about Sarah Linquist. Hope you're not stirring up trouble. That whole mess was a long time ago. Everyone's dead, and the dead should rest."

I gave him the same details I'd given Jim. I told him about the series, the Winslows, and my connections to them and the town."

"So you're Hazel Taylor's boy. Nice lady. I knew her more than your father, since she was so involved in town politics. You've got some of that Winslow blood in ya, huh? Lucky man."

"I don't know about that. All the money disappeared in the crash."

"There's more to blood than money, son. Still, it's a damn shame what happened to that family. Riches to rags for the wife and the two girls, I heard. But I suppose you know all that. You know about their place up on Pinnacle?"

"I've seen pictures. It must have been something."

He laughed. "It was something, all right. Burned down in the late '20s, I think. Some people said it was the old man who did it. Pissed as hell that his daughter had left a will and asked to be buried in Riverton."

"She left a will? That's unusual for a young woman. Especially back then, I would think."

"I suppose it was, but Sarah was an unusual girl. Very smart, that one. My uncle did the will for her, that's how I knew about it. She'd said at the time that she wanted George to have a say in things. I think she was mostly worried about the baby—she was pregnant by then—and she once mentioned that she was afraid her father would try to take the baby away from George if anything happened to her. She didn't seem to trust her father completely."

"Why was that?"

"Not sure. Probably some history to it, but Sarah never mentioned that relationship, at least not to me. He was a powerful man, and power can make bullies of folks. Some people in town think that of me, but we do what we have to do, don't we?"

"I suppose."

"Her old man was a real manipulator. That's probably why you couldn't find much information about her death. He would have put a cork in that. Lots of money, lots of power. How'd it go with Jim? He talk much?"

"A little, but he was reluctant. He took me down to what's left of the cabin."

The crevices in the old man's brow deepened. He shook his head and let out a long breath. "That couldn't have been easy for him. He was just a kid that day. Nobody, especially a kid, should see what we saw. He was never the same after. He bought that whole mountain about fifty years ago. I think it was for Sarah, a way of keeping her spirit safe or some nonsense like that." He sipped his beer. "But that's not the story you're here for, is it? You want information about Sarah and George. So, what do you want to know?"

"I guess the beginning would be good. Can you tell me how a rich girl like Sarah ended up marrying a woodsman?"

"My wife Charlotte can probably tell you more about that than me. They were close as sisters. I expect her back from Farmington any minute. She's a talker, generally, but I don't know how she'll feel about this subject. That'll be up to her."

"Then maybe you can tell me more about George. Mr. Trenholm said he was quite the guy."

Arthur smiled with the better memory. "Yup, George knew how to turn it on, that's for damn sure. Where he got it, I have no idea. His father wasn't what you'd call charismatic. I don't think he was a bad guy, just didn't like people much. George probably got his congeniality from his mother, but I never met her. He was home-schooled. His mother never came into town, far as I know.

People used to say she was foreign, from France, I think. Some distant relative of the Boudreaus in Happy Valley. Of course, that was just rumor. Riverton does love its gossip. But George did speak French fluently, which was odd for a woodsman. Most of them didn't speak at all. And he spoke real French, not that Canadian crap. Maybe that's where the rumor came from about his mother. And stories had circulated that she wasn't all there, mad as a hatter they used to say. After the discovery in the cabin, they said that George probably got that from his mother too. Maybe that's why it all happened."

"Jim suggested that, but he wouldn't go into details. Do you think George killed Sarah and the baby?"

"Course he did," he said with more certainty than I'd expected. "What else could've happened? It was a simple case of a man going off the deep end. 'Cabin fever' they called it, but I figure it was that damn moonshine those crazy woodspeople made. Horrible stuff. Fries the brain, you know. George had probably drunk too much and went a little nuts. Then killed himself when he sobered up. I've heard more than my share of sad stories, but that one is right up there with the worst."

"Had you ever seen him violent before? You knew him pretty well, didn't you?"

"Pretty well, considering he was a woodsman. No, I never saw signs of it, but he only came into town a few times a year, more than his father had but still not often. In the winter we wouldn't see him at all. We get a lot of snow up here in the mountains, and it seems as though we got a lot more back in the day. Once the snows came, the woodspeople stayed put, hunkered down until spring. They had those stills, of course, and I think that probably helped them through it. So, George did the same thing his father and his grandfather had done: just hunkered down. It was usually about a month after the ice broke in the river that we'd see him. We knew it was spring for real when George came into town, sporting a big grin and leading those four workhorses and a pung of logs.

"That's why we worried that year: no George. And no Sarah either, which worried us even more. It was mid-June before Jim and I could get down there to check on them. Sarah's father had offered to pay someone to go earlier, but it was impossible before June. Ground was too soft. It'd been the worst and longest winter on record, 1924. Still is, I imagine. Just kept snowing. There were actual hurricanes of it, which is a rarity, but that year there were a bunch of them. Storm after storm, blowing and covering the whole town. The drifts were fifty feet high in some places. Buried us until May. Even the train had stopped running."

"Didn't anyone try to get down there on snowshoes or something?"

He laughed at my ignorance. "It's nearly ten miles from town down to that cabin, a lot of it uphill until you get close to the river. You ever try to snowshoe through ten miles of woods and hills with twelve feet of fresh snow under you? Men die doing that."

"Twelve feet?"

"That's what came down on us. If it'd been possible, someone would have tried. And when the snow finally did melt, it was too dangerous by foot or horseback. The ground was like mush. Mud season, you know. It was bad that year 'cause of the lengthy winter. My dad wouldn't let me try, at least not with his horses, and the mud went so deep I would have gotten stuck there till summer if I tried by foot. Spring mud is like quicksand. Sucks you right down. But come mid-June even my dad was worried. The whole town was, but nobody else had the nerve to go. I think they were all scared of what they'd find. So eventually Jim and I volunteered. I was in my mid-twenties, home from Portland where I'd just started my first job with a law firm, still young enough to think I could do anything. And Jim was just sixteen, I think. He was far too young. But the youngins are always taking the risks for the rest of us, aren't they?"

He paused and reached into the cooler for another beer. I was still nursing mine.

"We were cautious. We went on horseback, after fitting them with cowbells so George could hear us coming. You don't want to surprise a woodsman, even a nice one like George. They had those stills and they guarded that swill like it was liquid gold. You don't want to get too close to a woodsman's still. The town hoodlums had learned that the hard way. Even though George was the only woodsman down there at that point, we knew to respect his ways.

"It was tough going. Lots of underground springs. Lots of sinkholes where a horse could snap a leg. My dad woulda killed me if that happened. He was not what you'd call an understanding man. In fact, he would have made me shoot the poor horse and bury it myself. Probably without a shovel."

I had stopped writing, and I clicked my pen impatiently. The judge noticed.

"But you don't want to hear about my dad, do ya? You want the good stuff. Well, Mr. Journalist, there's no good stuff in this story. It's all bad. And we knew it was bad by the time we got to the second bridge. You probably crossed that bridge today with Jim, didn't you?"

"I did. But there's not much left of it now."

"It wasn't much of a bridge that day, either. The melt had washed out most of it. That's when we first knew something was wrong. George would've had that repaired already. And the other thing was that there was no smell of burning wood, no sounds of cutting, which you'd always hear in the spring. It felt as though the whole woods was holding its breath, waiting. So we just paused there at that bridge for a few minutes, listening for any signs of life. I think we both were scared and wanted to go back home, but neither one of us would be the one to say it. We tied the horses there and went on foot.

"Jim noticed the smell first. It was strong once we got to the clearing. There was a barn to one side of the cabin. He ran in right away, but he was back out in seconds, coughing and retching, both his hands covering his mouth and nose. All the livestock were dead. All but one had their throats cut. One cow had been left alive but it had frozen to death. Jim's a softy, and I think he was crying, but he said it was from the smell."

Arthur stopped talking when he saw his wife pull into the driveway. "That's it, son. I don't want Charlotte hearing this stuff, never told her all of it. You can ask her if she wants to talk about Sarah, but I can't guarantee it. We're a little old to be dredging up the things we've been trying to forget."

"Can I ask you one more question? I'm not sure anyone else will know."

Jake glanced out the door at his wife who was opening the trunk to collect her packages. "Make it quick. She shouldn't be carrying those bags."

"Was there an autopsy? Did they know how she died?"

"Throats cut," he said in a low voice as he headed for the door. "Her and the baby. Just like the livestock."

June 14, 1922

   Last night was our first night in the cabin as husband and wife. We are truly blessed. It is so quiet here. Birds, more than I can identify, are calling to each other day and night. It's what I would imagine a jungle to sound like, but it's not threatening. I feel safe here. George says there are dangers and I should be mindful. I'm sure he knows well, but I feel very safe and at peace. I feel at home.

Charlotte Thompson was easy to recognize from that picture I had seen in the library. Her white hair was pulled back in a tight bun, and her pale blue eyes were made even brighter by a blue and white dress that showed a trim figure. Her posture curved slightly, but she moved without evidence of pain. I stood to greet her and she extended her hand. It felt small and fragile within mine, but she surprised me with a strong grip. Mrs. Thompson was a woman who seemed to have learned the importance of that simple gesture, possibly from the years of being a judge's wife. She and Arthur spent a few minutes in the kitchen, putting away groceries, talking. When she came back to the porch, she held a glass of wine for herself and another beer for me.

"Well, Mr. Taylor," she said as she settled into the porch swing next to her husband. "Last time I saw you, you were working at that questionable bar and seeing that wild and overly opinionated girl. You have come along since those days, haven't you? What was that girl's name? Something strange if I remember correctly."

"Mavi," I said.

"Yes, that's right. Mavi. My, but she was a girl on the fast track to trouble, wasn't she? I wonder what happened to her."

"She married me," I said and smiled broadly.

The woman nearly spit out her wine. "I certainly do know how to step in it, don't I? My apologies." Her neck and cheeks had gone crimson.

"No apologies necessary. That was a long time ago. I'll let Mavi know that you were asking for her." I couldn't wait to hear Mavi's reaction. I had no doubt that it would include some very descriptive language.

"Now that I've embarrassed myself sufficiently, maybe we should get down to the reasons for your visit to Riverton. I heard you were a journalist now, and Arthur tells me you're digging up some unpleasant town history."

"I suppose I am. But honestly, it wasn't my idea. Since my mother was a Winslow, it fell in my lap. I'm sorry to be asking, but would you be willing to answer a few questions?"

She glanced at her husband who raised his eyebrows and said, "It's up to you, dear. I can ask this boy to leave and we can get on with the rest of our day." Arthur patted her hand, and she squeezed it back.

"No, we could chat a little." She took a sip of wine. "What would you like to know?"

"It would be helpful if you could tell me about Sarah Winslow. Even though we're related at a distance, I don't know anything. Arthur suggested you were close."

"That's right. I was her closest friend, in Riverton at least. She wasn't from here, as you know. Like a lot of the wealthy families back then, they summered. They'd all come up on the train with their help and all their friends. It was a different town then from what you see now. Lots of little shops and restaurants, activities all summer. That changed when the train stopped coming this far north in the '30s. The Depression put an end to all that."

"It's still a nice town. I'm glad to finally come back."

"It's good to come home, Sammy. I remind my grandchildren of that every time they bless me with a call." She glanced at her husband, who only shrugged. "Now, why don't you tell me what you want to know, so I won't blather on and on and travel too far down memory lane. It can get to be a long and tedious journey."

"I'd like to hear about Sarah and George, if that's okay." I glanced to Arthur for a sign, but he gave me none. Instead, he kept his focus on his wife, monitoring her emotions. "Whatever you can tell me would be helpful. How about when they met? Do you remember that?"

She smiled. "I certainly do. I was there when they met, at one of Riverton's summer dances. There used to be a bandstand in that park behind the hotel. And at least once a month until late fall there'd be a concert there followed by a dance. I think George stayed at the hotel sometimes." She looked to Arthur for confirmation.

"That's right," Arthur said. "He used to stay at the hotel for a couple of days after the mill deal was done, two or three times in the summer."

"Sarah and I always went to those dances. Most of the towns-folk did. One night—in July, I think—Sarah and I were sitting on a bench near the bandstand, and we could see a handsome young man watching the festivities from up on the third floor. He was hanging out the window, looking down on all the colored lights and pretty dresses, big smile on his face. We could tell he wanted to come down, but I guess he was a too shy to do it. So, Sarah waved up to him. I slapped her hand down but she did it again, and then she yelled to him to come down. I was mortified, but Sarah didn't care. She was such a flirt, so outgoing. I loved that about her. I didn't have much experience with boys then, but she'd traveled the world, lived in Portland. City girls knew considerably more than us country girls did. They taught us a lot, believe you me. Not in a trashy way, of course. Sarah was all lady. But she knew how to get a boy's attention, and, most importantly, what to do and what not to do once you got it."

"I've seen pictures of her. I imagine she had no trouble getting George's attention."

"No trouble at all. When you get an invitation from a beautiful girl like Sarah, you do not ignore it. You won't get another. George was down in a flash. And my, what a tall and handsome young man he was up close. I would compare him to that actor in *Gone with The Wind*. What was his name?"

"Clark Gable?"

"Yes, that's the one. He looked just like a young Clark Gable. But that was long before there was a Clark Gable. George was the original. Most beautiful man I'd ever seen." She turned to Arthur again. "That was before I noticed you, dear."

"So that was it? They started dating?"

"Of course not," Charlotte said. "We were only sixteen, and we weren't allowed to date. That was a good way for a girl to get a bad reputation. But George started coming into town more often, usually when there was a dance or something, and they always spent time together, mostly just talking. Sometimes in French, which I didn't speak. I asked Sarah what on earth she had to talk to a woodsman about, and she said they talked about literature and art. I laughed, thinking she was kidding, but she was serious.

Apparently, George knew a little about everything, at least according to Sarah."

"How old was George then?"

"Three years older than Sarah, which would have put him at nineteen."

"So, how long before they got married?"

"Quite a while. Three or four summers, I think. And every year Sarah couldn't get up here fast enough. All she could talk about in our winter correspondence was George and the upcoming season. Had I seen him? Would there be dances this summer? And then when she got here in June, she was a nervous wreck waiting for him to come into town."

"What about her family? Her father?"

"The family didn't know anything. She told me once that her father would probably sell the compound in Riverton and drag her south if he got wind of it. She kept it very hush-hush, until George asked her to marry him in 1921, I think. Yes, it had to have been that year, because Arthur and I had just started dating a few months earlier." She slid an arm through her husband's.

"Was the wedding here in town?"

She laughed. "There wasn't a wedding at all. George and Sarah eloped barely a week after he asked her. They grabbed us and we all went down to Farmington to the justice of the peace. They didn't tell anyone, except Arthur and me. We were their witnesses."

"Then I'm assuming the Winslows were not privy to the marriage?"

"You are correct, sir. Sarah was quite the sneak. That year her parents were in Europe with the younger girls all summer. She was nearly twenty-one and insisted she stay in Riverton. Her Aunt May had agreed to be with her at the compound, but that woman was always three sheets to the wind. She didn't know if she was on foot or horseback half the time. So Sarah took advantage of the situation and moved right into George's place after they got married. I don't think her aunt even knew she was gone."

"She moved into the woods? Why not the estate?"

"You're so young, Sammy. Back in our day men did not live in the homes of their wives' parents. They provided for their wives. And George was very much a typical man in that respect. Sarah moved into his little cabin in the woods. I never got to see the place myself, but she told me all about it. It sounded horrible, but Sarah had a pioneering spirit, that's for sure. I couldn't understand it, a sophisticated city girl like her loving the simple life and apparently being quite good at it. I only saw her a few times that summer, only when George came in with his logs. Each time we got together she would go on and on about her tasks, how much she was learning from George's mother—she was still alive that first summer—and how much she loved being the wife of a woodsman."

"And still her parents didn't know? She didn't write to them?"

"No. She wanted to tell them in person. So, they waited until the family returned from Europe and came up for foliage season. It must have been early October, and Sarah and George didn't waste any time. They went right up to the estate and confronted them. As you can imagine it did not go well, initially. According to Sarah, the first word out of her father's mouth was 'disgrace' followed closely by 'annulment.' And he had harsh words for the aunt as well, but I imagine she was in her usual condition and couldn't have cared less.

"You've probably heard that George was quite likeable. Able to charm the fleas right off a dog, as my mother used to say. Apparently, the two men came to an agreement, after a time. I don't know all the details, but it seems that Mr. Winslow worried mostly for Sarah's well-being, beyond the disgrace and scandal, of course. He eventually agreed to let the marriage stand as long as George promised to put her on a train before each winter so she could spend it with them in Portland. He had no intention of allowing his daughter to live through a single one of our harsh mountain winters, especially in an isolated cabin. In return, he agreed to put Sarah on a train back to Riverton as soon as the snows had cleared. It was a good plan. Unfortunately, as you know, it didn't go well that third year."

"But nobody knows what happened, do they?"

"No," she said, with certainty. "And we never will, will we?" She exchanged a questioning glance with her husband, and he nodded agreement. It was a moment that made me wonder if I were missing something. "It seems pretty clear," she added, "that George went mad with that moonshine they made down there. I had never known him to be a drinker, but it seems I was wrong."

I considered my next question for a moment, concerned that I might be treading on delicate ground. I moved ahead. "Did you know that Sarah was pregnant?"

Charlotte took another sip of wine. She paused long enough that I thought our conversation might be over. Finally, she said, "I knew. And Arthur knew right after she told George. But her family didn't, not until—" She swirled her wine and stared into the depths of it. Her chin quivered slightly and then two thin rivulets made their way down her cheeks, pushing through the rouge and the powder, collecting in the hollows at each side of her lips. She pressed at the tears with a tissue she retrieved from the cuff of her dress. "That was the worst part of it. That poor child. The Winslows couldn't put anything on the piece of flagstone except 'Baby 1924.' Isn't that just the saddest thing? It's been so long and still it hurts."

Arthur put an arm around her and brought her close. "I think that's enough," he said.

"No," Charlotte said and she straightened. "I've come this far and we're almost done." She looked at me and smiled. "You had better get this all down, Sammy, because I'll never speak of it again." She pointed at my pad, and I readied.

"Sarah came up early that third year, it was the first week in May, I think. The snow had melted, and she was not about to wait a minute longer, just had to be with George. There was no way to let him know she was in town, so Sarah convinced me to take her out there. I could never say no to her, especially with her pining for George the way she was. It was driving me crazy. So I took two of Daddy's horses and we went into the mountains toward the cabin. It's quite a long way and the ground was still soft, especially near the river. We got all the way to the first bridge when the horses started to sink into the mud. Really sink, well up onto their legs. I was nervous that one of them would stumble and break something, so I insisted we stop. But before I could talk it over with Sarah, she was off her horse and running. She didn't say a word, just jumped off and started on foot. I yelled after her, 'What about your bag?' It was still tied to the horse. She turned back on the other side of the bridge and waved, told me to just drop it right there. 'I'll come back for it,' she yelled and kept running." Charlotte giggled. "She was like a kid running to the Christmas tree. Seeing him was all that mattered. God, she was so in love. In love and not able to see anything beyond it." She stopped laughing and began to tear up again.

"I didn't see her again until mid-June, when George brought in his first load of logs. That's when she told me she thought she was pregnant. Oh, my lord, she was so excited. She hadn't told George yet. She was going to wait to be sure. Next time I saw her it was obvious, so she couldn't wait much longer. I was happy for her but a little concerned as well. I couldn't help worrying about her and the baby way out in those woods, but Sarah didn't seem concerned in the least.

"I saw her three more times when George came in with a load. She always had an appointment with Dr. Dunlap. I swear, every visit she was more beautiful. I told her she was probably having a boy, since they say that boys give their mothers beauty and the girls take it away." She paused for a moment and her expression darkened. "But I guess I was wrong. It turns out she had a girl after all."

That was all that Charlotte could say as the tears began in earnest. She extended a trembling hand to me and hurried inside, most likely to think about Sarah and the child and the sorrow I had rekindled. It was generous of Arthur not to be openly angry with me. I had stirred up a lot of unpleasant memories. Instead, he wished me well before going back into the house to comfort his wife.

October 25, 1923
   The weather has changed too quickly for me to leave yet. It's been snowing all day and shows no signs of lifting. George is hopeful that it will warm in the next couple of days so that I can make the train for Portland. He's afraid for me, afraid for the baby. But I would be very happy to stay this time, to have my first child in this enchanted place. It's so beautiful with the dusting of white in the trees and the cabin. But George is full of concern, and my appreciation of the beauty is doing nothing to soothe him. I've always wanted to stay through the winter here, but he and my father would not hear of it. Now it may be out of our hands. I welcome the challenge of proving myself to be a true woodsman's wife and a capable mother.

I called Jake that night and asked if he and his new love could get together for a late dinner. "My treat," I said to which Jake replied, "Say no more. We'll see you at seven."

It was good to see Jake so happy. Audrey seemed to be at least partially responsible for the smile that rarely left his face. She was a good fit for the man: fun and, most importantly, sober. Our conversation was easy. Audrey was a natural entertainer, and she told great stories about her work as an ER nurse. Eventually we got around to my work and why I was back in Riverton.

"I know that cabin. My brothers brought me down there when I was a kid. Scared the hell out of me. I can't believe Dad brought you. I didn't think he'd ever go there again."

"Wait a second," I said. "You're Jim Trenholm's daughter?"

She laughed. "Far as I know. I grew up on that farm. Ten of us kids. Three girls, seven boys. My poor mother, may she rest."

"Beautiful spot."

"That it is. Wonderful place for a kid. Lots of room to get lost if you needed it. But that part of the land was off-limits for us. Dad said there were ghosts down there. I think he was trying to scare us out of going, but it made my brothers wanna go even more. They only went once or twice. Spooked the hell out of them too. Even the air feels weird around the cabin."

"I felt that, too," I said. "Did your dad ever talk about that day to you?"

"Jesus, Sammy," Jake said. "Take a break from work, would ya?"

"Sorry." And then I leaned closer to Audrey. "Well, did he?"

She laughed, but then got serious. Her dark eyebrows pulled together, and I could see the resemblance to her father. "He did, but only once. Not a word about it until a couple years ago. I had heard stories from other folks but never Dad. And when he did tell me about that day, it was hard for him. It was after Ma had died. He got real sick, and I think he was thinking of dying himself. I was taking care of him through most of it, when I could. He told me a lot of stories I'd never heard. I got to know him pretty well in those weeks."

"How did he happen to tell you about George and Sarah?"

"I think I asked. Not about the day, but about the cabin and how fucking creepy it is down there. I'd only gone that once, but it stuck with me. I'm sure it'll stick with you, too."

"I have no doubt." I shivered involuntarily, and Jake noticed.

"This story you're working on is getting to you, isn't it?" he said. "That place really spooked you?"

"It has," I said. "And there's something not right about the story, but I can't figure it out."

"You're right, Sammy. Dad thought the same thing, and I think that's why he told me about it. He said he thought Judge Thompson knew something."

"Why did he think that?"

"It had to do with that day when they got down there. He'd gone into the barn himself, and when he came out, Arthur was already in the cabin. It took Dad a few minutes to get himself together enough to go on. The scene in the barn had made him sick. When he was done throwing up, he went in. He told me Arthur was bent over near where Sarah and the baby were. At first he thought Arthur was crying, and my dad said he couldn't blame him, the scene being so horrible and sad. But then he realized Arthur was looking at something on the floor, and when he heard Dad step into the room, he shoved whatever it was into his pocket. Then he kicked a knife across the floor. It landed just under where George was hanging."

"Why would he do that?"

"Dad asked him that after. Even a kid knows you're not supposed to touch a crime scene. And that's exactly what it was, for sure. But Arthur was just out of law school and when he told Dad to mind his own business, that's what Dad did. He looked up to Arthur. Still does."

"Did your dad see what Arthur put in his pocket?"

"He couldn't see it."

"So you have no idea what that might be?"

"No idea at all. And Dad never mentioned it again. I think when he realized he wasn't dying, he felt a little bad about telling me. A while later when I asked him about that day, he shut me right down. Told me it must've been the painkillers."

"Okay," Jake said. "That's enough. This is giving me the creeps too."

And with that the subject was changed. The rest of our night was lighter, easy talk with one of my oldest friends and my newest. It was a good night.

But my sleep was not so good. I lay awake for hours thinking about the couple and the baby and what really happened in that cabin. When I finally fell into sleep it was not a restful one. It was full of troubling dreams, every one of them of snow, whipping torrents of the stuff, coming down in sheets and swirls. And through all that blinding white, so far off within a colorless landscape that I could barely make it out, was a cabin with two tiny windows. In my dream I moved closer, trudging through drifts that gripped at each heavy step. I leaned into the wind and it pelted me with hard icy crystals. As I neared the cabin, I could see the windows clearly. No one moved inside. There was no glow from a fire, not even the trembling evidence of a candle. But amid the starkness of white, one color shone clear. Bright red splashed and dripped down panes of frosted glass.

Schlectman wasn't thrilled with my piece, but he was satisfied enough to make it the feature in the weekly anniversary section. It was mostly about the life of rich folks, fancy parties, and getaway lodges that fell into ruin after the crash. I'd left out a lot, and I think he knew it, although he only confronted me once. "Nothing about the girl's death?"

"Nothing interesting enough to include. Died in childbirth. The baby died too. Happened a lot then."

"I suppose," he said, but he held my eyes a little longer than was comfortable. "Was it good to be home?"

"It wasn't horrible. I'm thinking of going back more often."

And that part was true enough. On my way out of town, I had picked up a real estate pamphlet and I'd been scrolling through it since, looking at land prices, imagining the possibility of a small place near the river that I'd loved so much in my youth. It had occurred to me, as I glanced at the town disappearing in my rearview this time, that it might be okay to be a part of it again, to let the bad stuff go, to be closer to my oldest friend and my roots. I might finally be old enough to love the town again, to see all the good that I'd packed away beneath the bad.

It was during one of my many trips back to Riverton that I learned about Judge Thompson's death and Charlotte's a month later. I hadn't seen them for nearly a year, not since the last time I'd stopped by for a quick hello and a beer. At that time, they seemed to have aged considerably, and it occurred to me that it might be our last time together. Charlotte gave me a long hug when I left, as if she might be thinking the same.

I had finally bought that cabin near the river that I'd wanted. It set on a few acres that had belonged to Jim Trenholm. His daughter Audrey, married to Jake now, sold it to me. Fifteen years after we'd left, Mavi and I were finally able to see Riverton in a better light. Mavi still had reservations, but I convinced her she'd appreciate it in doses. I've been spending more time there than she will. She's pointed out on more than one occasion that the town hasn't changed. But I point out to her that we have, and maybe we've grown enough to accept it and live with it, despite its history and ours.

I was up there alone one weekend, building what would become a deck off one side of the cabin, when an SUV, too wide for the final stretch of driveway, beeped its horn aggressively until I started toward it. A woman with large dark hair stuck her head out the driver's window and yelled, "You Samuel Taylor?"

"Yes, I am. Can I help you?" I approached the car slowly. The woman looked angry.

"I've had a hell of a time finding you, mister. I was about to give up and throw this damn thing away." She held out a small, brown-wrapped package toward me and I accepted it. "I'm Lilly Winter, Charlotte Thompson's granddaughter. She left this for ya."

"What is it?"

She shrugged. "Hell if I know. It's got your name on it, so there ya go. My job's done." She shifted into reverse and backed out the serpentine driveway at a clip that would have taken down a dozen trees if she hadn't been so skilled at it. I watched in wonder and then headed back to the cabin with the mysterious package.

To be opened ONLY by Samuel Taylor, son of Hazel Winslow Taylor of Riverton was printed in large black script across the front. It was taped and tied with twine so excessively that it took me several minutes to open. Once I had, I found a tattered, soft brown leather book with the word "Diary" embossed in gold. An envelope poked from the middle.

Dear Sam,

I'm glad this has found you. You are the only living person who has the right to possess it. Please forgive us for not giving it to you sooner. I was aware of its existence, but I had never seen it until Arthur passed. It was in our safe deposit box all these years. Arthur found it that day in 1924, but refused to share it with anyone. He told me that he had never read it, but I find that difficult to believe.

The content is disturbing, but it explains so much. I hope you will use it with respect and kindness. She was your great-aunt, after all.

Sincerely and warmly,

Charlotte Thompson

Inside the front cover was the name written in the elegant hand of the time. Sarah Winslow. Linquist was added below it. I found myself shaking when I turned the first page, and I needed to stop. The importance of the journal overwhelmed me. I put it down, poured myself a glass of wine, and brought the wine and the book to the rocker on the porch.

The early pages were mostly about parties, crushes, the typical private musings of a young woman. But then I found the first entry concerning George, and it was nearly all about George after that. Their first meeting. Their long talks about literature and art. Her missing him and the letters he sent her. The day he proposed, and the entry that quickly followed about their wedding. There were pages and pages of the plans, the dreams, and the longings of a woman on the precipice of life.

But then I came to January 1924, and the optimism of the earlier pages was gone.

January 17, 1924

I believe there is evil here. Whether it is in the snow or in the trees or in my mind, I don't know. George can't feel it, but maybe he's not as sensitive to it as I. Even the baby knows. It thrashes in my belly sometimes when the storms are at their worst and the wind is like the howling of a hungry monster. The snow pounds at the cabin as if demanding to be let in. I sometimes need to cover my ears and scream to keep it out of my head. George is concerned, as am I.

The baby. What will happen to the baby?

January 25, 1924

It comes down like cresting waves, breaking over us with a heavy, relentless weight. It has blanketed everything: the doors, the windows, the chimney. George is more out than in, fighting the losing battle with nature, trying to save the animals, the cabin, and of course me. He keeps the fires going but he is only one person. I am of no help to him. And soon I will be engaged with my own woman's work. What will happen then?

February 5, 1924

Charlotte Grace Linquist was born on February 2, 1924. Charlotte, after my dearest friend. Grace, after George's mother.

And now we have a child. We have brought a baby into this cold and desolate world. I thought that having Charlotte would give me joy and make me feel more of a wife and a

*woman. But it seems to have had the opposite effect. I carried
her beneath my heart for nine months, worried for her safety,
only wanting the best for her. But now I feel nothing. I suddenly don't want any of it: the cabin, George, or Charlotte. I
want to escape. I want to run and keep running. It's all I can
think about. George will be out in the storm taking care of his
endless tasks, and he will come rushing into the cabin. He'll go
to Charlotte, pick her up, cradle her, calm her. And I will be
sitting in my chair, rocking, not even hearing the cries of my
own baby. How can that be? Am I losing my sense?*

I had to pause from reading that night. I knew where this story
was going and ending, and I didn't want to. I took a shot of bourbon and went to bed, but not to sleep. I lay awake for several hours
considering the cabin, the snow, and the possibilities of a winter
with too much of both.

February 20, 1924
 *We are down to frozen potatoes and a few jars of pickled
beets. There is milk for Charlotte still, thanks to the cows. She
refuses to take mine and I have lost interest in trying. It seems
that I am failing in every way as a wife and a mother.*
 *The snow keeps coming. The sound of it is like a train
sometimes, or like an army of wild beasts. The wind blows the
white into violent drifts that rise well over the roof. George
spends hours trying to keep the doors and windows free of
it, but the storms mock his efforts. They fill everything in as
quickly as he removes it. All the while it makes that sound:
a constant angry wail that envelopes the cabin and pushes
its way into my brain. Sometimes George shakes me, holds*

me tight, consoling me with promises of spring. I'm not even aware in those moments that I have been screaming.

There was only one entry left, and I could tell from the script that it would be a difficult one. The writing was large and shaky. Some words were hard to decipher, but the meaning was clear. Sarah was at the end of her rope and her life. I considered not reading it fully, but I didn't have the fortitude or restraint.

March 8, 1924
There will be no spring.

George is in the barn doing the deed that must be tearing at his soul. He's doing it so that the animals will not suffer further. There's no more food for them. It's either the blade or an agonizing death.

But what about us? Are Charlotte and I not as worthy of his compassion? The snow will win. It's become more than just white and wind. It is alive now and it won't rest until it has devoured us. It's seeping between the cracks in the walls, down the chimney, under the door. It's become an army of vengeful demons, trampling everything with a thousand bloody hooves.

I will not let it trample my child. I've given my baby nothing until now. No milk, no safety, not even love. After ignoring her needs for all her life, I can finally give her something. A quick and painless end.

And that was it, the real end to a story that I had chased for nearly four years. It was the most tragic ending I could imagine, but it made so much more sense than the one everyone had been told.

And from what I had learned of George, he wouldn't have wanted it any other way than to have people believe the worst of him rather than of Sarah. Finally, I understood the truth, that Sarah Winslow Linquist was a gentle soul whose mind was devoured by a hostile Maine winter. The end. I could do nothing to change the end.

Still, I could honor the truth by honoring the dead. There will be a marker for George and a name on another piece of granite where a nameless one had been. It will be nestled between "George Francis Linquist" and "Sarah Winslow Linquist." And I'll go one step further. Under each of their names I'll have a line added, an important one that has been missing. "Loving Husband and Father" and "Loving Wife and Mother." I think Sarah would approve.

CHARLOTTE GRACE LINQUIST
1924
DAUGHTER
"EVERY ANGEL DESERVES A NAME."

*W*innie

Winslow Thompson Winter
1985–1995
"Too Young, Too Soon"

There's a wall through Riverton now.

It seemed to have gone up overnight. But the line of it, the straight and formidable power of the thing, made it feel as if it had been there all along. The postholes had been dug weeks before the town meeting, but no one had noticed, or at least they didn't talk about it. And then one day the road that had been running through Happy Valley for over a hundred years—the one that had always taken Riverton folks and their trash away from the town center and to the dump—was there; the next day it wasn't. The old potholed gravel route now ended abruptly at a 12-foot wall of two-inch-thick, roughhewed pine.

The need for it relied solely on rumor and speculation. Stories had been told about Happy Valley for more years than anyone could remember. The people who lived in that part of town were called Gypsies at best, criminals at worst. "Gypsies" only because Riverton folk, not known for their open minds or their kindness to strangers, thought it to be the best moniker for people with such odd ways. The valley folk had their own ceremonies, their own celebrations, even their own graveyard. They only came to town when they needed something they couldn't make or kill, preferring to stick to their own people in their own village, a little over three miles from the center of town. The criminal label stemmed from the fact that there were always one or two of them in jail. Usually for making moonshine—a tradition for them, passed down for generations dating back to whatever country they'd originated. The only people who bought and drank the stuff were townsfolk. Even Happy Valley knew better, only tasting the quality and power of it on the one night the barrels were tapped.

"They're a bunch of drunks and druggies," someone yelled at the town meeting. "Criminals that got no place around decent folk." Others agreed, and then the old rumors started up again, enriched by the years.

The meeting had been called in July, a few months after a ten-year-old boy, the second one in twelve years, went missing. All the searching by the state police and a few dozen volunteers had turned up nothing. As with most cases of missing kids, dogs, horses, and even wives, accusations were aimed squarely at the folks of Happy Valley. The last time, when that kid from the trailer park disappeared, the town had found a more religious or terrestrial explanation. But the valley wasn't so lucky with this one. The Staties spent weeks there, questioning the Hickeys and the Boudreaus. The search left a mess of the place, made it even less livable than before. One of the cops—a young and ambitious town-boy—took it upon himself to tear down a few of the out-houses, checking in those smelly holes for the body or at least some incriminating bit of clothing. Nothing was found, same as before, but a lack of evidence didn't mean much to the good folks of Riverton.

The boy who'd gone missing this time was a larger concern than a missing horse or a trailer-park kid. This boy was a Winter, the great-grandchild of Judge Thompson and the spawn of two important families. Maybe in a larger town those names and the money that went with them wouldn't have meant much, but in

Riverton, a town of fewer than two thousand souls, the Thompsons and the Winters were near royalty.

So when Lilly Thompson Winter—Big Lil to most everyone—stood and cleared her throat, the room went quiet. Even in a small-town meeting there are moments of respect, especially when the mother of a missing child is a Thompson.

"You all know me, and probably more than a few of you don't like me much. I'm a Thompson, and to some that means 'Queen Bitch.'" A couple of the people snickered, but they hushed up quick. Big Lil wasn't someone you'd make fun of, even in her unkempt and possibly drunken condition. Her long curls were flat against her head, as if she'd just gotten out of bed. Her clothes, stained and wrinkled, seemed to have doubled as sleepwear for too long. They clung unflatteringly to the body responsible for her nickname. There'd be talk about her condition later, but not now. Not while she stood close enough to hear.

"I'll be the first to agree with you for the most part. I've never done much for this town, never asked for nothing either." She paused and swayed a little, put a hand to her forehead and squeezed as if she were pushing her thoughts together. "The thing is, I'm asking for help now. I may be a Thompson, but I'm still a Riverton girl, and I'm worried about what's happening here. You all know my son Winnie went missing a few months back. And you know there's not much hope of finding him now." She paused again, long enough for murmurs of consolation. "The Staties have stopped looking, and I can't blame 'em. But the thing is, I have three more youngins, and I know most of you have kids and grandkids of your own that you cherish just as much as I do them. We all can see the problem; it's no secret. There's been a damn cancer in this town for too long, longer than any of us been alive. It's time we did what we've been talking about for years. It's time we built that wall. And now we have a plan to do it." She nodded toward the back of the room and sat down with a heavy thump that made the chair creak.

Judge Arthur Thompson, Big Lil's grandfather, walked up from the back, slowly and in silence. The room was silent too as he stepped up onto the stage and dragged a large, mounted map of Riverton on an easel from behind the stage curtain. He placed it front and center, then pulled an expandable pointer from his pocket. Still not saying a word, he ran the tip over the map where a wide red line had been drawn. The whole room leaned forward, following the line as it moved through fields, over hills, across major roads, ending at the river at its widest section.

"Any questions?" He turned to the room.

At first, no one said anything. They all leaned closer, squinting at the map, trying to understand the extent of it. Someone, a woman toward the front, let out a low whistle and muttered, "How the hell we gonna do that?" It was barely audible like she might have been thinking out loud, but most of the room grasped her sentiment.

"Don't you worry about that, missy," the judge said. "Got it all worked out. No cost to the town, either. I'm paying for the lumber, the tools, and the hardware. Already had the postholes dug by Jack Healey and his construction crew. Nice work, Jack." He put his hands together for the large man who stood, smiled wide, and took a bow. A few folks joined in the clapping, but most sat confused, uncertain as to what was being applauded. "All you folks need to do is the labor. If everyone pitches in, shouldn't take any time at all."

Someone yelled, "But you got that line running right across the road to the dump. What are we supposed to do with our trash?"

"You think I haven't thought of that? You underestimate me, Willis. I still have clout where it counts. I'm having the transfer station moved over to that boggy land on Maple Street. All twenty acres is owned by the town now due to back taxes. Plenty of space for landfill."

"You're moving a little fast with this, aren't you?" Edna Post called up to the judge. "We don't even know those folks in Happy Valley had anything to do with the missing boy."

The judge stood tall. "Don't be naive, Edna. Who else would've hurt little Winnie? They've always hated me for locking so many of them up. I'm thinking they took him to get back at me. But they hate all of you, too. Mostly 'cause you got what they don't: decent lives and decent jobs. You know as well as I do that there's evil up there, bad goings-on that need to be dealt with, beyond a missing boy, God bless his little heart. Think about that damn moonshine they make and sell to good Christian folk in town, get them all crazy and riled up and doing things they wouldn't think of doing otherwise. It's the devil's work, and you know it. And let's not forget the drugs." A few voiced their angry agreement. "You think that methamphetamine the Staties found on those Riverton boys was made in town? Hell no. We all know where it's coming from." He extended his pointer again and slapped it on the map so hard it nearly toppled. "Right there! That's where all the bad in this town is generated." The pointer rested on the north side of the red line. "I don't care what you call them. Gypsies. Incesters. Criminals. Whatever you call 'em, they sure as hell ain't God-fearing folk. There's evil in Happy Valley, and we need to wall it off, suffocate it till it's dead."

And that was that. The judge didn't need to say more. Amid yelling, spitting, and a whole lot of fist-pumping, the wall won approval. A committee was elected to oversee its construction. Nearly every capable hand in the town was granted a role. Those few that objected, like poor Edna Post, were ridiculed severely until they either relented or receded into the sanity of their homes.

The folks of Happy Valley, that area soon to be isolated, were not a part of the decision or even aware of the process. They continued as they always had. They farmed the few fertile sections within their one hundred and fifty acres. The Hickeys did the majority of the hard labor, while the Boudreaus turned the potatoes and corn into a sellable spirit. It wasn't until July, when two barrels of aged whiskey were ready for sale, that they discovered the wall. Eddie Boudreau, the one responsible for sales, noticed there hadn't been any traffic through Happy Valley in over a month. They all knew that the transfer station had been moved. It had been a relief for those with homes on the road. They'd lived for a hundred years with the holier-than-thou attitude from behind rolled-up car windows, and now they could live easily without it.

But summer had always been their season to sell liquor. Townsfolk, the ones who'd never otherwise be driving through the valley without a load of trash, would be lining up on late-summer nights, waving their green and hoping to score a couple of jars. There hadn't been any of that, not a single soul blaring their horn and flashing their lights. So Eddie had driven toward town to see what was going on, figuring maybe a sickness had taken hold of the place. But the explanation became clear when he rounded a blind corner and nearly crashed into a twelve-foot wall that cut across the road and stretched far in both directions.

"Strangest thing I ever seen," he told some of the others when he got back. They wanted to see it for themselves, so a half-dozen hopped into the back of the valley's one working truck, and they headed down West Riverton Road to where it now ended. They piled out and just stood there for a while, looking up at the twelve feet of thick pine. Some walked along it, examining the construction, listening close as if there might be a word from the other side.

"No climbing over that thing," someone said, kicking at the base if it. But Helen Hickey, a girl who'd always been a climber and proud of it, tried anyway. She took a running start and nearly got halfway up before gravity got the best of her. She fell hard on her back, knocking the wind out of her. Instead of trying again, she stayed there for a few minutes, flat against the gravel, looking up at the structure and cursing its being.

From where they stood, it was hard to tell the extent of it. They split into two groups and hiked in both directions until they got to the ends. It was nearly two hours before they met back at the truck. They had discovered it went all the way to the river to the west, and even farther, to what seemed like the town line in the east.

"Why in hell would anyone build a wall right across the road?" someone asked.

"Sure, as hell ain't for our protection," someone responded, and the group agreed. They shook their heads, climbed up into the truck, and headed back to report to the others.

By October, things had gotten bad in Happy Valley, which is hard to imagine for a place that had always been bad off. They'd run out of gas. Therefore, they had no tractor and no truck. The vegetables in gardens that were too far to harvest on foot rotted in the field. When one of the Boudreau kids got the flu, Mary Boudreau, the child's mother, tried to get him to the doctor in town. She carried the six-year-old on her back all the way to the wall and then along to where it ended at the river. There'd been downpours all week, and the river had risen nearly three feet. Ordinarily, she could have waded in and then gotten to the other side. But the water was several feet up onto the wall by then, and with the weight of her son and the slickness of the rocks, she'd lost her footing. Fishermen discovered their bodies several days later, pressed up against the dam in the center of town.

The folks of Happy Valley knew nothing of the fate of Mary and her child. They had their own problems, and the possibility that Mary had managed to solve hers was inspiration but not impetus. There were meetings, some with just the elders and some with all the families. It was decided that the structure, regardless of the reasons for its erection, would need to come down or at least be scaled. A group trekked out there the next morning. They carried a makeshift ladder, a crowbar, some rope, and a couple of handsaws. There wasn't a plan, just a need.

But when they got there, while they were looking up at the wall and trying to figure out how to conquer the thing, they heard activity from the other side, a few yards to the left of the road. It was loud, just talking at first, but then there came a buzzing, a gnawing vibration against the wood. It got louder, and when the first break in the wall occurred, the Happy Valley folks nearly fell back, it was that powerful. The blade of a chainsaw ripped through one plank and then another, spraying splinters of pine across the dry gravel.

It wasn't much more than a crawl door, but for those looking on, it was much larger. A booted foot kicked the square in, and then a head popped through the opening—a head of mostly beard and long, stringy hair.

"Hey there." A smile parted the dark fur. "You folks got whiskey?" His smile widened but no one smiled back.

Eddie recognized the man. He'd been a regular since he was no more than a kid. Bobby something, he remembered. "What the hell is goin' on?" Eddie yelled, clearly not happy with the wall, the man, or the part of town that had made them both.

The man crawled through the hole, dusted himself off, and looked up at the confused expressions. "Whatcha mean? I just put a hole in this stupid wall, that's what's going on." The confused looks didn't change. "You guys don't know shit about this, do ya?"

"We know there's a damn wall keeping us outa town," someone yelled, and then someone else added, "But we don't know why. So how about you tell us the why before you get any closer." Two of them took an aggressive step forward.

The man, whose name was indeed Bobby, got into a fighting stance, a natural reaction. He was smaller and leaner than the valley men, but he looked capable enough. Three more valley men stepped up, and Helen Hickey was quick to join them.

"Now, you just hold on one second," Bobby said, backing up a little. "First of all, we didn't put this thing here. We didn't do nothing to build it, and me and my friends are getting a lot of shit for that. Can't even get served at Babs's no more."

Another head, equally as furry, poked through the hole. "You okay, Bobby?"

Bobby raised a palm. "Wait there a sec." Then he turned back to the group. "I get it. You're pissed. But we just cut a hole in this thing, so don't shoot the messengers. Can they come through?"

Eddie turned to the others. Reluctantly, they agreed. Two more men came through the hole, each one asking about whiskey.

The walk back to Happy Valley gave folks time to absorb the information and the accusations. They heard about the fate of Mary and her child, and that led to some screaming and crying. The accusations concerning the Winter boy confused most of them, but got others even more angry. "They already searched our homes, for fuck's sake. Made a mess of everything. Why us?"

Bobby shrugged. "Who else we gonna blame? Don't matter now anyhow. Workmen setting up the transfer station found his bike two days ago, at the edge of that bog everyone knows to stay away from. Not a bright kid, obviously. Probably wandered in there and sunk right to the bottom."

"Poor kid," one of the women said.

Another agreed, bowing her head slightly and whispering a small prayer for the rich boy.

By late fall, the door in the wall had become larger, and then large enough for a car to get through, since some thirsty townsfolk didn't like the long walk that offered no shade or view. Happy Valley made use of the opening too, but less so. Shortly after that first breach by Bobby and his thirsty friends, Eddie made the three-mile trek into town and bought gas at the one station that would sell to him. A few townsfolk gave him hostile looks, but others were more pleasant. One woman—Eddie thought her name was Edna—gave him a light peck on the cheek and told him, "It's good to see you here. Hope your family's okay."

There was no move to tear the wall down, even after the need for it had been disputed. Judge Thompson quashed any talk of that, reminding folks of the years of evil that had certainly been spawned there. It had been his idea, after all, and there weren't many Riverton folks who thought it would be intelligent to challenge the well-respected judge. "It's best to remind people of what's what and where's where," he was quoted in *The Franklin Journal.* "We got our little place, and they got theirs. Just the way it is. No disrespect. No offense to anyone." Some were quite offended, but most kept it to themselves.

As for the valley, they're just fine with "their place." Now that the dump has been moved, they don't deal with the traffic and attitude. They're a little closer to deserving the name they'd been ironically saddled with for generations. It's a happier place, now separated.

It appears that the wall will stay. Youngins from both sides have already begun using it for messages of love and hate and unfriendly suggestion. Harsh Maine weather is having its way with the untreated pine, turning it into more of an eyesore than a barrier. Remnants of the ugliness will be there for years, reminding us all of who in our small town belongs where.

ℒD Wuz Here

1948-1988

He was a nice man. And I don't say that much, 'cause I hate most people. He used to come up every fall, like clockwork for about twenty years. Always stayed in the same cabin, number twenty-eight. Said it was his lucky number. Don't seem like it was though, huh?

—Natty Simpson, Owner of
the Sunset Motor Lodge, Interview with
Sheriff Wilfred Tufts, Franklin County Police.
October 20, 2015.

There ain't much to bury. Just a skull and a few bones. Parts fell off in the move. We're combing Route 16 for more. They found what's left of him wrapped in bits of rug and plastic when they were putting the cabin up on blocks at a place up Maple Street owned by a Benjamin Taylor. Know him? Don't

seem like many do. Christ, the body musta been dragging that whole way from Skowhegan.
—SHERIFF WILFRED TUFTS, FRANKLIN COUNTY
POLICE, IN A CONVERSATION WITH BUD WILLIS,
THE HOGPENNY LOUNGE, RIVERTON. OCTOBER 20, 2015.

No, Martha, I'm keeping the cabin. Just because they found a body under it is no reason to abandon it. I don't know why you care. You'll never come up here, anyway. By the way, I'm paying for the burial and I don't want an argument. I'm just doing the right thing. It was a . . . a human being, after all. I'll call you next week when things are settled here.
—BENJAMIN TILSON TAYLOR, OWNER OF CABIN
NUMBER TWENTY-EIGHT,
IN A TELEPHONE CONVERSATION WITH HIS WIFE,
MARTHA.
OCTOBER 20, 2015

CABIN NUMBER TWENTY-EIGHT, SUNSET MOTOR LODGE, SKOWHEGAN. OCTOBER 1970

"This is perfect." The young man squeezes past the heavy woman, trying not to rub against her. It's difficult not to, considering her size and the way she's planted herself just inside the door. She doesn't move, and she doesn't seem to mind his proximity. "It's perfect," he says again, more to himself this time. He tosses his bag on the bed and does a slow turn, taking in the rustic charm of it: the knotty pine of the walls, the beamed ceiling, even the furniture that walks the line between old charm and Goodwill.

"Well, glad you like it," the woman says, although her tone doesn't convey it. "Now how long did you want it for?"

"A couple of weeks, maybe longer."

"Can't be longer than two. We close for the season on the thirtieth, head down to the Carolinas. No insulation in here, and it gets damn cold come November." She points to a thermostat on the wall. "At night you'll be needing that. Turn it up to sixty-eight, no higher. It's gas, like the stove. Both the pilots will need lighting. Instructions on the wall over there, next to the heater. And there in the kitchen." She doesn't move, just points, like a stewardess or a traffic cop. "Do I need to run you through it?" She cocks her head and stands with her sizable weight shifted to one hip, a hand fisted on top of it. Her girth doesn't get in the way of her style. She's a pretty woman, with generous features that coordinate with the rest of her. Her dark hair is clipped to one side, so that the ends slither and point toward the cleavage that rises nearly to her neck. A pink floral scarf creates a waist just under her breasts.

"No. I can probably figure it out. My name's JD, by the way."

"Natty." She pumps his hand just once and holds it for an uncomfortable few second. "So, two weeks up front. That'll be—" She squints toward the ceiling as she mouths the math. "One ten total. That includes sheets and towels twice a week. That work for ya?"

"Yes, ma'am." He reclaims his hand and pulls the cash from his wallet. She counts it bill by bill, snapping each and holding it to the light.

"There's an extra ten here. You want change?"

"No. Just privacy."

"You won't have no problem with that. This year's been slow. Place is only quarter full, and the cabins are so far from each other you'll think you're alone. You expecting company?"

"I, uh—"

"I don't really care. I only ask 'cause if you need another bed, there's one in the closet there."

"A friend's coming up. Will that cost extra?"

"Nope. Cabin's for two. But if you have more it'll cost ya." She turns into the doorway and then back. "By the way, JD, my daughter Dorrie brings by the linens and towels Mondays and Thursdays. She's only sixteen and a bit of a wild child, if you know what I mean. I'm not gonna have to worry about her stopping by here, am I?"

"I'm sorry?"

"You will be sorry if you touch her. My husband don't like it when guys look at her, even though it's her own damn fault. Brain of a child and the body of a woman. No offense, but I don't know you for shit. You look like a clean-cut and upstanding young fella, but I've been fooled before. I won't have to come banging on this door, will I?"

"No, ma'am, you don't have to worry about a thing. In fact, how about I leave the sheets and towels on the porch those days and she doesn't even have to come in. Will that work?"

"Yes sir!" For the first time she shows a hint of a grin; it's a crooked one, nearly a sneer, but it's a grin nonetheless. "You do that. Shove everything in a pillowcase and leave it on the porch. I'll tell her to throw the clean stuff on a chair out there. And don't tip her. I like knowing what money she's got. Girl's got habits already."

He follows her out. She moves like someone who is alien to the process, swaying her weight from side to side in the effort of lifting each leg. She isn't old, probably in her early forties, but she moves like a person who has lived with her heft for decades. Her legs are like two pylons that are sunk deep in mud. She pitches back and forth, releasing each foot from the earth and then planting it. One foot, then the other. The old wooden treads of the porch moan from the load, complaining as if they've endured it for too long and are sick of the task.

After she's sped off in her golf cart—"My chariot," as she calls it—JD checks the time. He has about three hours: enough for a shower, a trip into town for food and liquor, and then a call home to let his mother know that he has made it to where he isn't. That last task worries him. She isn't well, and he's her only connection to life. He will need to keep the call short. The longer he talks with her, the more likely she'll catch him in the lie. He isn't good at lying, never has been. But he figures that it's time to get better, considering he might finally have something worth lying about.

The unpacking is quick. He leaves half of the space open in each of the drawers. In the closet he uses only five of the ten hangers, doubling up on some so as to be fair. The toiletries go into the bathroom cabinet and he keeps his to the left. He looks around the main room for what's missing. "Flowers," he says and makes a mental note to get some in town. Then he remembers another decorative touch that he'd nearly forgotten. He finds it in his backpack and jams the pin part into the top of the headboard. **NO MALARKY VOTE McCARTHY** is printed in bright red on the white campaign button. "That'll break the tension."

And there will be tension, of that JD has no doubt. It's one of two things of which he's certain. The second is that he will need to grovel. That's a given, after what happened in Chicago.

Chicago, 1968

JD has flown in from Boston, Tilly from New York. The press leading up to the convention has warned of possible hold-ups, of demonstrations, of the inevitable road closures. But no one has predicted the extent of it. It takes them each about five hours to get from the airport to the Conrad Hilton. The bus drivers' strike has made it nearly impossible to get a cab. And all traffic is rerouted around the central chaos.

They don't even unpack once they got there, haven't even closed the door completely before they're on each other, feeding nearly a lifetime of famine. It's been almost three months since the New Jersey primary, and they hadn't been alone long enough then to follow through after that one fumbled kiss in the cab.

They were in separate hotels there with miles of obstacles between them. This time they've planned ahead.

JD moves just enough to close the door. He's reluctant to lose contact with the lips and the tongue that he'd been obsessing over since May. That last time had been unsatisfying, like a nibble of a meal that's swept away too quickly. But they're here now, not going anywhere, so he breaks long enough to slide the DO NOT DISTURB sign onto the outside door handle before kicking the door shut.

The passion is clumsy: too many buttons, zippers, ties, all those things that bind and get in the way of progress. The shoes are kicked off and one knocks over a table lamp, but the crash and the sudden change in light goes unnoticed. One pushes the other onto the bed and there's a feverish thrashing. Arms and legs tangle. What is left of modesty is yanked off and discarded.

"Owww!" JD winces and rolls to one side, feeling for whatever is stabbing into the soft flesh of his lower back. "What the hell?" He holds up the round white campaign button and they both burst out laughing. "Why do I feel guilty all of a sudden?"

"'Cause you are guilty," Tilly says. "Guilty of backing the wrong guy."

"Please. I am *not* backing the wrong guy. Humphrey's gonna keep us in that stupid war for another eight years. Think about the number of lives—"JD starts to get up but Tilly pushes him back.

"We are not going to talk about war . . . or Humphrey . . ." Tilly moves down JD's neck, placing kisses along the way. "Or McCarthy . . . or guilt . . . or anything else." He takes the pin from JD and sticks it high into the fabric of the headboard. "We're going to have some fun. We deserve it."

It's their first time together, and there's been more failed attempts than most people could have handled. Each opportunity, the one at the New Hampshire primary and then the two at New Jersey's, were frustrating in their almost-ness. But the men had been smart even in their urgency, recognizing the fallout that would come from being discovered. So they had waited, as mentally and physically torturous as that had been. Chicago is to be their reward for patience and common sense.

It's a typical first time: fast and sweaty. It's as if they both just want to get it over with, get that first one out of their bodies and minds so they can have the real ones, the ones that will matter and be full of what they've been looking forward to, each of them. They want to get that urgency out of the way so they can linger in something that's slow and deliberate. So that's what they're striving for that first night, all night, and by the next day they're nearly there.

"Are you awake?" JD raises himself on an elbow and runs a finger down Tilly's long athletic spine, following the tan ridge of muscle that leads to the shadowy cleft. He pauses there to stroke the patch of blond fuzz.

"Sorta."

"I suppose we should get up?" JD checks his wrist before he remembers that they had both thrown off their watches at some point during the night. They have also unplugged the clock and the phone.

"Why would we do that?" Tilly's voice is muffled by a mound of pillow.

"So we can do our jobs, maybe?" He flicks playfully at the fuzz.

"That tickles."

"Sorry." JD works his hand down and around. "Does that tickle?" He squeezes until he feels the stiffening. And then he presses his own hardness into the warmth of the cleft. "How about that? Tickle now?"

"Not . . . a . . . bit," Tilly says through staccatoed inhales. And now that he's fully awake and erect, he shifts his position just a little, just enough to let JD in.

CABIN NUMBER TWENTY-EIGHT, RIVERTON, 2015

The man is startled by the knock. He's bent over in the process of ripping out the shower stall, and when he hears the aggressive rapping on the door, he rises too quickly, snagging his arm on a piece of jagged metal. It rips his shirt, and a line of blood blossoms through the fabric. He grabs for a paper towel and presses it to the wound, cursing his stupidity, as another more aggressive knock rattles the front door.

"Hold on. I'm coming." He climbs over pieces of metal and old piping—the carcasses of the cabin's ancient plumbing—still pressing the towel to his bleeding arm. He yanks open the door and starts to yell at the intruder but catches himself. "Oh. Hello, Sheriff. What can I do for you?"

Sheriff Tufts extends a hand but notices that Taylor's is occupied. "Hurt yourself?"

"Just a scratch. Can I help you with something?"

The sheriff doesn't wait for an invite. He edges past the man and into the chaos of the cabin. "Not wasting any time are you?"

"Excuse me?"

"You know something, Mr. Taylor, this cabin's part of an investigation. You shouldn't be ripping anything apart until we've had a chance to look it over."

"I wasn't told that. In fact, I was under the impression that the crime, if that's what it was, had taken place some time ago. You can't expect to find any evidence now, can you?"

"Had to be a crime. I mean, the victim, whoever it was, didn't slip on a banana peel and end up wrapped in plastic under the floorboards. Do ya think?"

"I suppose not. But still, you can't expect to find anything after all this time."

The sheriff moves through the main room as they speak, looking over the remains of what had been the kitchen and the bathroom. "You may be right, Mr. Taylor. Probably happened twenty or more years ago. But you never know. I figured I should take a look anyway for the report. Dot the i's, cross the t's, as they say. There's just this main room, the kitchenette, and a bathroom, right?"

"That's right."

"And why did you buy it again?"

"I bought it because I had this land, as you know, and I needed a cabin for it. I already told you all this."

"Why not just build one? You'll have to do a lot of work on it anyway." The sheriff pokes his head into the kitchen area. "You'll need to change all these appliances, get new wiring put in. That's gonna cost ya. Why not just start from scratch?" The kitchen is dark with no electricity, and the sheriff pulls his flashlight from his belt.

"Because I thought it would be interesting to have this old cabin and build onto it. They don't make these anymore, you know. It's a piece of Americana." The man follows the sheriff's beam as it moves like a bug over the walls, into the corners, under the appliances. "I had considered buying two and have them put together. But there weren't any left."

"Really? I was down at the Sunset yesterday talking to Mrs. Simpson. Boy that is one big woman, huh? Amazing she's lived this long. Gotta be in her late seventies, early eighties. Says something for genetics over lifestyle, doesn't it?"

"I suppose, but—"

"And she told me there's still a few of those cabins left. Couple of them are a lot nicer than this one."

"I guess I was misinformed."

"So why this cabin?" The sheriff pushes past the old man, across the narrow hall to the bathroom. Taylor wedges in behind him.

"Because I liked this one. It's cabin number twenty-eight, and that happens to be a lucky number for me."

"I see, I guess. I'm not much into that superstitious stuff." The bathroom is small, with large holes in the walls and the floor where the discarded plumbing used to live. The sheriff shines his light into the dark and moldy gaps. "You're from New York, you said. Why buy land in Riverton? It's gotta be a long drive from the city."

The old man lets out an exasperated sigh. "I bought this piece of land back in the mid-seventies from my sister-in-law after my brother Henry died. She sold the larger piece with the house and barns to someone else. I thought I'd build something here at some point, but I never got around to it until now." He leans further into the cramped room. "Sheriff, what are you looking for?"

"Just looking. That must be where you cut yourself, huh?" The beam illuminates a bent and jagged piece of metal at the top of the stall. "You should get that scratch looked at, maybe get a shot. The metal looks a little rusty." He runs the light down the stall to the floor. He pauses there. "Huh! What's that?"

The old man peers through the space between the sheriff's shoulder and the door frame. "What's what?"

"That piece of cardboard down there. Must have fallen from between the stall and the wall." The sheriff bends down and squeezes into the corner. "Can't . . . quite . . . reach it."

"Reach what? I don't see anything."

The sheriff pushes himself further. "Looks like there's some writing on it. Must have been hanging from the back of the shower with that piece of hanger. You're tearing this out, right?"

"Obviously. That's what I was doing when—"

"Then you won't mind if I help." Using both hands and placing a foot onto the wall, he pulls at the edge of the shower stall, slowly bending and folding it into itself. Then he grabs a rubber glove from a pocket, slips it on, and reaches down behind where the stall had been. He comes out with a piece of cardboard, about 3-by-5 inches, attached to a piece of hanger that's been bent into an S.

"What is it?" The man rises on tiptoe to get a better look.

"Dunno." It's nearly covered, on both sides, with dates and symbols. At the top, in heavy red marker, is printed **JD WUZ HERE**. Starting below the words, and onto the other side, are dates from 1970 to 1987. Beside each is a hastily drawn symbol. Some are hearts, others are broken hearts or circles with either smiles of frowns in their centers. A few of the broken hearts have drops coming from them while some of the whole ones are followed by exclamation points. "Isn't that something! Looks like someone had this hanging off the back of the shower, added to it every year. How funny is that? Somebody really liked this cabin. Must have been their lucky number, too."

"Can I see it?" The old man reaches, his fingers trembling just a little.

"Sorry, Mr. Taylor. We're going to have to take a good look at this. It might have nothing to do with that body, but we have to check it out." The sheriff blows into a plastic bag to expand it and then slips the card and hanger piece inside. "tell me something. Would you have brought this to us? You know, if I hadn't been here to see it?"

"Of course, I would have, Sheriff. Why wouldn't I?"

"Good. Then I'll expect to hear from you if you come across anything else."

"Absolutely."

"Great. Well, I'm going to get out of your way, Mr. Taylor, but please hold off on the redecorating for now. I might need to get the state involved in this. I'll be in touch. You have a good day and try to be more careful around rusty metal."

After the sheriff leaves, the man pours himself a short tequila. He had purchased the bottle in New Hampshire on his way up from New York the week before, assuming he would probably need it at some point considering the stress of the week ahead. His wife would not approve, but Martha has approved of very little over the years. And besides, Martha is nowhere around. He doesn't need ice; he only needs the medication. He raises his glass to the ceiling in the gesture of a toast.

"Here's to you, JD. I guess we're not done yet, are we?"

I knew what was going on. Maybe not the first year, but I got it eventually. I was cool with it. I got no problem with homos. But damn, what a waste of good man-flesh. They were hot, both of 'em. They'd go down to the pool every once in a while, and I'd watch from the office. Both of 'em were thin but real muscled, like they did sports or something. Eye candy, I used to call it. And pretty as girls. One dark haired, the other a blond. I'll admit it, I was a horny kid back then. I probably would have done both of 'em if they'd wanted. But then Mama would've killed me and kicked their sweet asses back to what-ever city they'd come from.

—Dorrie Simpson Foster, former employee at the Sunset Motor Lodge. Interview with Sheriff Wilfred Tufts, Franklin County. October 22, 2015

CHICAGO, 1968

"I'm starving. And the bourbon is gone."

"Call room service."

"I don't even know what time it is. Will they answer?"

"It's the Conrad Hilton. Of course, they'll answer."

JD goes to the window and opens the curtains a few inches. "It's dark. You think it's morning or night?"

"I'll say night. I think my watch is under the bed. Yup. Here it is. It's night, almost nine."

"What day do you think?"

Tilly laughs. "Well, we got here Sunday. And judging by the number of room service trays over there, and the two empty bottles over there, I'm guessing it's Tuesday night."

"What?" JD is standing in the middle of the floor, naked except for one black sock that he had put on when he'd considered leaving twelve hours earlier. "How could we have been here for two days?"

"How?" Tilly laughs again. "I'd say the how is pretty obvious."

JD remains in the center of the floor, but he starts to do a frantic spin. "I gotta go. Help me, Tilly. Help me find my clothes. Fuck! What the hell was I thinking?"

Tilly gets up and calmly goes to JD. He grabs one of the flailing arms and pulls him close. "Calm down. No one's missing you."

"Maybe no one's missing you, Tilly. You work for Humphrey. There's like a hundred of you guys. But McCarthy is definitely missing me right now, and I am in serious trouble. I should be on the floor talking to delegates." He tries to pull away but Tilly hangs on.

"Okay. Let's turn on the TV, see what's happening on the floor."

While Tilly is flipping through the channels, JD finds his other sock and is reaching for his underwear when he hears Tilly say, "Oh, my God."

The convention floor is chaos. The camera is focused on Dan Rather, who is in the middle of it, being pushed and crushed by the crowd. A man is grabbing him by the arm.

Dan Rather: "Take your hands off me, please. Take your hands off me unless you're planning to arrest me. Don't push me. Wait a minute." And then Dan is falling to the floor, surrounded by suits, some of them pushing, others reaching to help.

Walter Cronkite: "I don't know what is going on down there. There are obviously security people there, roughing up Dan."

Dan Rather is up again. "We were trying to talk to the man and got pushed down. This is the kind of thing that's gone on outside but it's the first time we've had it happen inside the hall. Sorry, I'm out of breath, but somebody punched me in the stomach."

"What's going on?" JD yells at the TV and then turns to Tilly. "What the hell is going on?" Before Tilly answers, JD is on the floor again, crawling around on all fours, finding the pants, a tie, a tee shirt. Then he's up again, grabbing at a dress shirt that's hanging off the corner of a picture frame. The shoes are in two opposite corners of the room, one of them is sticking out of a toppled lamp shade that now has a long crack in it. "Jacket. Jacket," he yells, doing another frantic spin.

Tilly is sitting on the bed again, still watching the TV. "Check over there." He points absently to where a mound of fabric is heaped in a corner near the door. "Guess I should go too. That looks like something I shouldn't miss." He gets up slowly, sighing as if he's annoyed at the prospect.

The sounds of chaos are getting louder, and both men go still in front of the TV. The picture shows the outside now. There's masses of people running, being pushed and clubbed by policemen in blue helmets. People are screaming. There's a shot of a woman with blood running down her face. She's dazed, and someone catches her as she falls or faints. More police with nightsticks are pounding on the backs and heads of people who've fallen. Two policemen are dragging a man down the street. They toss him into a waiting paddy wagon. He struggles at the door, and they beat on his fingers until he lets go. One of the cops pushes him into the wagon and then reaches in and clubs him before the door is closed. The camera turns, and now the National Guard are coming down the street. They're wearing gas masks. More people are screaming and running. There's a loud bang, and the horizon fills with smoke. There's a close-up of a guard with a gas mask and a rifle, a cloud of yellowish haze behind him.

JD is motionless as he watches. His jacket is clutched in one hand as he stands in the middle of the room, glued to the images that hardly seem real. Tilly is equally paralyzed. He stands in front of the TV naked. Then the scene changes and the visual is back to the floor of the convention.

"Let's go," JD says. He pulls on his jacket and throws some clothing in Tilly's direction.

"Are you kidding? I'm not going out there." He ignores the clothes that pile at his feet.

"We have to go, Tilly. It's our job. We should have been there already." JD checks for his room key, his wallet, his convention pass.

"Are you seeing this?" Tilly points at the video from the convention floor. Several blue helmeted policemen have entered and are making their way toward a struggle. "There's police on the floor now. It's like a fucking war down there. I didn't finagle out of one war to jump into the middle of another."

"No, Tilly. You're coming with me, goddammit! We agreed that we'd stick together this week. You're not staying in here and letting me go out into that mess by myself. Come on. Get your clothes on and let's go."

Tilly begins dressing slowly, reluctantly. "I'm scared, JD. Look at that."

They're showing more footage now from outside the International Amphitheater. The clashes between the police and the protesters are even more violent than before. The police are running after the receding crowd, beating on them as they seek the shelter of trees and parked cars and each other. It looks like a theatrical reenactment of some primitive inhumanity, something from an embarrassing history of man before he acquired sense.

"Don't be scared, Tilly. I'll be with you, and we have our convention passes. Nobody's gonna hurt us."

Tilly is not convinced. But in twenty minutes they're in the lobby and then they're out through the glass doors of the Conrad Hilton, directly into the flashpoint of chaos. JD grabs Tilly's arm, pulling him as they begin moving to the right where there seems to be more space, down South Michigan Avenue, pushing past groups of protesters.

"The whole world is watching! The whole world is watching!" they're chanting, and it's getting louder as the two find themselves in the middle of a parading crowd.

"Where are we going?" Tilly yells. The angry faces are getting closer and he feels hot spittle on his cheek.

JD turns and yells, "We'll get a cab at Roosevelt. Or we'll walk if we have to." He can see the fear on Tilly and he considers turning back. But in the next minute there's a wall of activity pressing down on them and the chanting changes to screaming. A half dozen blue helmets have muscled into the crowd. JD lets go of Tilly's arm just for a second to hold up his identification. And in that tiny fraction of time Tilly is swept away. The last images that he has of him are snapshots from between surges of protestors: a blue helmeted man, a descending black club, and Tilly's arms high over his head as he mouths the name of his lover. JD is still screaming for Tilly when he is pulled by an opposing stream of will, away and into a future that is without him for two years.

Yes, I remember those boys, the one named JD more than the other one, the blond. Nope, can't remember his name. It was a funny one, like something you'd call a dog. Sorry, it's not coming to me. The brain's not getting any younger, you know.

Anyway, we had a reservation for number twenty-eight every October, so we got to know JD a little. They were always in twenty-eight. The other one never talked. Kind of a snob, I figured. Always pulling JD out of a conversation as if he didn't like he was being so friendly. Sometimes JD would be up there by himself. That's when I got to talk to him a little more, when we'd be sitting around the pool, drinking beers and just chatting. Real sweet boy, but he was always so sad when the other one wasn't there, perking up every time a car pulled into the driveway. It would just break my heart the way he would wait, sometimes the whole two weeks. I remember telling my husband at the time that JD was probably the girl in the relationship. You know, the more caring of the two. 'Cause the other one seemed like a typical male jerk. Excuse me for saying it, Sheriff.

Last time I saw them? Probably '85 or '86. We'd already decided it was our last vacation there. The kids were getting sick of the place, and you know how kids are when they don't want to be somewhere. It was a miserable week. I didn't have the chance to talk to JD much. My soon-to-be-ex-husband wouldn't let any of us go into the pool when JD was there. It was an AIDS thing. I know, it was mean, but we didn't know any better then. Everyone was so afraid of catching it. My husband wouldn't even shake JD's hand. I was so embarrassed, but I was a little scared of being around the gays then too. Everyone was.

—From a phone interview by Sheriff Wilford Tufts with Millie Eastman, a seasonal patron of the Sunset Motor Lodge from 1976 to 1985/86. October 23, 2015

Johnson's General Store, Riverton, 2015

"Mr. Taylor. How are you?"

The old man spins too quickly and nearly falls. The sheriff steps up and grabs him by an arm before he topples into a display of keys.

"Woah. Didn't mean to scare you, sir. You okay?"

"Yes, thank you," he says, steadying himself and looking a little embarrassed. "I have a mild case of vertigo. It only acts up when I move too quickly."

"I guess you should avoid fast spins then, huh."

"Yes, I suppose that would be smart. But we don't always think before we act, do we? Did you need to speak with me, Sheriff?"

"Oh, no. Just thought I'd say hello. It's a day off for me. Just doing some home repairs. What about you? You're not planning to work on that cabin anymore, are you, Mr. Taylor? Do you mind if I call you Ben? It seems silly to call you Mr. Taylor when you're a part of our town now."

"I'm sorry, I'd rather you didn't. I've never liked my first name. Friends call me Tilly."

"Really? That's an unusual name, isn't it?"

"I suppose it is." The old man approaches the explanation as if he's needed to do it too often in his long life. "My middle name is Tilson. That was my mother's maiden name. I've always been called Tilly. Benjamin was my father."

The sheriff slaps the counter, and the sound startles several in line. "You're a Tilson? As in the French-Tilson House?"

"Yes, that's right. I believe it's the Historical Society now. My grandfather was Dr. Tilson, Dr. French was my great-grandfather."

"Well, now it makes sense, why you'd want to have that cabin here. It's like coming home, I guess."

Tilly sighs, clearly bored with the conversation. "Not really. It's just my history. My brother and I grew up in Bangor, actually, and I had very little connection to Riverton except for occasional visits. My brother settled here, I moved to New York City. And that is my story in a nutshell." He smiles apologetically at the sheriff. "I really should get back to the cabin. I just came here to get a few names of contractors." He waves a sheet of paper. "And now I have them. So, take care Sheriff Tufts. Good luck with your projects." He makes toward the exit, but the sheriff touches his arm.

"By the way, did you get my message?"

"What message is that?"

"About the State Police. They need to go through the cabin. Tomorrow. So you didn't get the message?"

"Whatever for? Why would the State Police need to ransack my home? I haven't found anything else that you'd be interested in."

"Of course not. You would have brought it to me, right? It's just that I'm getting assistance from Portland, and they'll need access tomorrow. I'm sure they'll be respectful."

"Tomorrow? But why? I just told you—"

"Fingerprints. Blood. All that stuff. Portland has equipment we don't have. Anyway, they'll need to get under the cabin where the body was, and then inside too, I'd assume. I'm glad I ran into you. See you tomorrow."

CABIN NUMBER TWENTY-EIGHT, SUNSET MOTOR LODGE, OCTOBER 1979

JD is nearly asleep when he hears the car door slam followed by three slow and heavy steps leading to the porch. There's no knock, just a rush of cold air as the door swings open and bangs against the armchair. There's a giggle and a "Woops."

"Tilly?"

"That's my name," he bellows. Another giggle. "Don't wear it out," he says to himself and bursts into a longer stream. "As if he won't."

JD grabs his glasses and turns on the bedside lamp. "Jesus, what time is it?" He looks at his watch and then at the disheveled man swaying at the foot of the bed. "Are you drunk?"

"So many questions before a proper hello." Tilly kicks off his shoes and stumbles to the bed. "Scoot over, honey bunny. All of a sudden, I am exceedingly exhausted."

"You didn't drive up from New York like this, did you?"

Tilly's words are slow and muffled. "I would never do that. I got drunk in Portland. Sweet little town. Very friendly people. Very friendly." He giggles.

"Perhaps you'd like to take a shower before bed?"

Tilly grunts an affirmation but doesn't move.

"Goddamnit. Tilly, I've been here for four days. Why didn't you call? Leave a message or something?" He's on an elbow now, looking down at the back of the man's blond head. "Tilly? Come on, we need to talk." But Tilly is beyond talking. For tonight, anyway.

The next day is rainy and cold, with nothing to do *but* talk. So they do, once Tilly has had several cups of coffee and a fistful of aspirin.

"I'm sorry," he says. "For the millionth fucking time, I am sorry. Sorry about being so late, sorry for that lovely boy in Portland—who I think you would have liked, by the way—and sorry about every fucking thing I've ever done. There. What else do you want?"

"How about an explanation? You must have one handy. You usually do when you stand me up."

"I'm here, obviously, so I didn't stand you up, did I? I was just a little late." He frowns at his empty cup, lifts it toward JD and whines, "Please, sir, may I have more?"

Tilly doesn't make an effort to get off the bed. JD is sitting at the kitchen counter and grabs his cup. "So, why were you four days late?" He stirs in cream and two sugars before handing it back. "Please entertain me with a clever story. I could use a laugh." His tone holds more sarcasm than humor.

After a long sip and an even longer sigh, Tilly says, "I will tell you, but you're not going to laugh. In fact, you're not going to like it at all."

"Okay," JD says as he lowers himself into the glider at the foot of the bed. From there he is at eye level with Tilly. "You're scaring me just a little."

"It's nothing terrible. I just know you're not going to approve, that's all. You can be a little self-righteous sometimes, a bit on your high horse."

JD doesn't respond. He waits.

"I've been offered a position in DC. It's temporary, but it could lead to something. I'll need to move there for a couple of years."

"That's great. Is it a campaign?" JD is getting excited. "Wait, are you going to be working on Carter's reelection? Why would you think I'd be upset? Sure, you'll be farther away, but we'll still have this cabin. Maybe we'll miss a year, but we'll be fine." JD is standing now. He's pacing as he thinks through the possibilities. "I'll come down to DC and help once in a while. I know we'd need to be careful but we know how to do that."

Tilly reaches out and grabs his arm. "Sit down, JD. It isn't what you think."

JD sits on a corner of the bed. "Well, what is it then? Are you seeing someone else?"

"No. It's not about us. You were right. I am working on a campaign. It's . . . it's just not the President's campaign."

"What? Whose then?"

"I got a call last week from Bill Casey."

"Casey?" JD works through the name. "You mean Nixon's Casey? Why in hell would he be calling you?"

"He wants me to work on the Reagan campaign. He's managing it."

JD stares at Tilly as he digests the concept. "Reagan? As in the governor of California? Republican Reagan?"

"The very one."

"You're not going to do it, are you? You're a Democrat, for Christ's sake."

"Well, actually, I'm not so sure that I am. I mean, Carter is not what I would call an inspiring leader. He's weak and easily manipulated. And he's not going to win, obviously."

"And that's what you base your work on now? Who the winner might be?"

"That's the new plan. I'm going to start working for winners. You should try doing that, JD. Instead of defending the hopeless and the powerless. That's a losing battle, honey."

JD is momentarily paralyzed. He stares at Tilly, his mouth agape. He's uncertain about what to do, working through his options—go, stay, argue, punch a wall. He finds his pants and shoes and starts there. Then he grabs his raincoat and heads for the door.

"Oh, come on, JD. Don't be like that. Big deal, I'm working for a Republican. It's not the end of the world."

JD stops. "It might be," he says into the rain. "At least it feels that way. You're considering working for the people who openly hate us."

"They all hate us, dear. The Republicans are just honest about it."

"I . . . I can't talk about it now." JD turns back to the man that in that moment he both loves and dislikes in equal parts. He takes in the tousled blond hair, the lopsided grin, the tan arm that rests casually on one knee as if they were having a conversation about where to go for dinner instead of the future of the country. He is torn in that moment, but only briefly. He leaves for several hours, and when he returns, Tilly is gone.

CABIN NUMBER TWENTY-EIGHT, RIVERTON, 2015

"When are you coming home, Tilly? What in God's name could you be doing up there for this long?"

Tilly has the phone pressed between his ear and his shoulder. He pulls the cord twice before the generator catches. "I'm working on the cabin, like I've told you a hundred times. My God, Martha, are you going senile?"

"Don't you talk to me like that, Benjamin Taylor. I—Oh, my lord, what is that horrible sound?"

"It's the generator. I need it for power tools, obviously." He plugs in the pressure washer and starts it up. The resulting noise is deafening. "I'm hanging up now, Martha. I'll call you tomorrow." There's a faint screaming from the other end as he clicks off.

He has just aimed the spray at the underside of the cabin when a vehicle enters the yard. Sheriff Tufts bolts from his SUV, waving his arms and screaming something Tilly can't hear above the racket of the two motors. The sound ceases when the sheriff switches off the generator.

"What are you doing, Mr. Taylor?" He has set aside the familiarity he'd established the day before.

"What am I doing? I would think it would be obvious. I'm attempting to remove the grime of sixty plus years so I can start painting tomorrow."

"I thought I'd made myself clear the last time. This is still a crime scene until the authorities say otherwise." The sheriff reaches for the wand and Tilly grudgingly hands it to him. "I'm not sure why you're not getting the severity of this, Mr. Taylor. Maybe you'd like to explain?"

Tilly removes his gloves slowly and tosses them in the direction of a lawn chair. He crosses his arms and stares back at the sheriff with the amused arrogance of a smarter man. "I can't help but be less than impressed by what you call the 'severity' of this. I happened to purchase a cabin where someone died and somehow ended underneath it. The 'hows' and the 'whys' are mysteries that I have no understanding of and no interest in. All I want is to get this cabin in some sort of livable condition so that I can enjoy it. The fact that you're not able to—"

His words are interrupted by the sound of another vehicle kicking up gravel and braking just behind the sheriff's car. A man leans from the open driver's door and calls out, "Sheriff Tufts?"

"That's me." The sheriff waves to the man and quickly leaves Tilly still standing with folded arms and a less pompous expression.

"Sorry I'm a little late. Had a hard time finding the place." The man extends a hand to the sheriff. He's a large man, well over six feet with a corresponding weight. "Sergeant Collins, State Police. Call me Tom."

"Will Tufts, Franklin County." He accepts the gesture. "No problem. I just got here. Been arguing with the owner of the cabin over there. He's not being very cooperative."

Collins chuckles. "I deal with assholes every day in Portland. I'd be happy to help."

"Be my guest."

The sergeant walks with a stride that speaks of confidence and authority. When he gets to Tilly, his size speaks even louder, dwarfing the thin older man by nearly a foot. After introducing himself, he says, "I'm afraid we need to ask you to leave us to our work for a few hours, Mr. Taylor. I have two other men coming, and I'm sure you don't want to be in the way."

"Well, no, but I don't understand what—"

"There's really nothing for you to understand, sir. Why don't you go over town, grab some lunch, do some shopping? Does the sheriff have your cell number?"

"Yes, but—"

"Great. We'll let you know when we're done. Go along now. Enjoy the day."

As Tilly is heading down Maple Street, another official-looking vehicle passes him. He slows and watches in the rearview as it turns into his drive. He glances at his watch. 1:30. The Hogpenny will be open, and what he needs more than lunch at this hour is a very strong drink.

"What's AIDS?" Speakes says. "I don't have anything on it."

"It's known as the 'gay plague,'" Kinsolving replies. "It's a pretty serious thing. One in every three people that get this has died. And I wonder if the president was aware of this."

"Well, I don't have it," Larry Speakes says. "Do you?"

"You don't have it? Well, I'm relieved to hear that. Larry."

"Do you, Lester?"

"No, I don't."

"How do you know?"

The press pool laughs.

"Does the president—in other words the White House— look at this as a great joke?" Kinsolving asks.
"No," Speakes says. "I just don't know anything about it."
—From a White House press briefing, Oct. 15, 1982. Reporter Lester Kinsolving had asked Press Secretary Larry Speakes about a new disease called AIDS that is ravaging the gay community

The Zodiac Restaurant, Neiman Marcus, Boston, 1985

"Why did you want to meet here?" JD says as he slides into the booth across from Tilly. A stick-thin model approaches, does a slow spin in front of them, and says something about the couture collection on the fourth floor. She holds Tilly's eyes for a few seconds and then smiles slightly before moving to the next table.

"Because I had some shopping to do and I thought I could kill two birds with one stone."

"Lovely thought, Tilly. Apparently I'm a bird to kill? I'd hate to put you out, so let's get to it. Why are you in Boston?" JD grabs a popover from the basket, splits it open, and lathers it in strawberry butter.

"Be careful with those. You know what they say, 'A moment on the lips, a lifetime—'"

"I'll worry about my own hips, thank you."

A waiter approaches, half-bows at their table, and asks, "Could I get you something to drink, gentlemen?" He is very tall and strikingly handsome, and Tilly gives him a full inspection.

"Is everyone incredibly beautiful here?" Tilly says, smiling up at the waiter with a grin that reveals an unnerving number of white teeth.

The waiter is without words, so JD rescues him. "My friend is obviously very hungry. I'll have a gin and tonic and the Cobb salad. Tilly?"

Tilly is at eye level with the waiter's crotch and has a difficult time pulling away. Finally, he says, "A beer. Nothing from California, obviously. They're warning against fluids from San Francisco, you know." He chuckles at his cleverness.

"How about Stella Artois?" the waiter says, offering no reaction to the comment.

"Perfect. And a nice piece of meat. Medium-rare. Your choice of cut. French fries. No vegetable." He hands the menu to the waiter who is quickly off to another table.

"Why would you say that?" JD is visibly annoyed.

"Say what? He's very attractive. Why shouldn't I tell him?"

"About the fluids from California. Why would you make a joke about that? Do you really think it's funny?"

Tilly snickers but stops when he notes the seriousness on JD's face. "It's just a stupid joke, for God's sake. Besides, if those San Francisco gays would use a little discretion, they wouldn't be in the situation they are now."

"You mean dead? If they were smarter, they wouldn't be so dead?"

"Well, I wouldn't put it as crudely as that, but yes. They should be more careful. Not so quick to shove their dicks into any available hole."

JD takes a long breath and lets it out slowly. "I see that your proximity to evil has increased your penchant for insensitivity. It's what I should have expected."

"Evil?"

"Yes, that's what I'd call a president who refuses to acknowledge a horrible condition that's killing thousands of people. Your people, if we're going to be honest here."

The waiter arrives with the drinks. JD notices that it's a different waiter, and he's amused, although Tilly is not. The latter takes a second look and makes a tsking sound, then raises his glass to his lips, pulling a long swallow while working through his next words.

"I didn't come here to argue, JD. Just the opposite. I've been thinking a lot about you lately. And about the cabin up north."

"You mean the one that you didn't come to last fall? The one where you haven't spent an entire two weeks for nearly ten years? The one where I've spent more time alone in recent years than with the man who claims to be in love with me? That cabin? Your lucky number twenty-eight?"

"Well, that sounded only slightly rehearsed. I see you've been holding on to some anger."

"Ha! You could say that. I've been trying to hold on to a bit of self-respect as well. That hasn't been easy."

After some silence, the waiter arrives with their food, and for a long while there is no talking, only the fretful clangor of silver on china. They each concentrate on their plates and their glasses, barely acknowledging the other. Tilly has nearly finished his steak when he says, barely audibly, "I've missed you, JD. There's no one in my life like you." He isn't addressing the man directly. It's as if his words have ventured out on their own. He's staring down at the remnants on his plate and the fork that is pierced through the last piece of meat. "I want it to be better between us. I want it to be good again. That's the real reason I've come."

"The real reason? Knowing you, Tilly, there's got to be another. Why are you in Boston? Really."

"Right to the point." Tilly pushes his plate to the side. "Okay, I'm doing a little favor for 'Evil', as you call him. It's the governor's race here. I'm helping with the Kariotis campaign, although I'm not sure I'll be much help. Dukakis is running a damn good one."

"Kariotis will surely be a write-in. Why would you waste your time? He doesn't have a chance."

"I'm fully aware of that. It's a test, I guess you'd call it. The White House knows he's a long shot, but they're watching me for future opportunities. It looks like Dukakis is a strong possibility for a presidential run in the near future, and this is a way for me to study his strategies and find his weaknesses. I'm apparently really good at that."

"No surprise there. You could even call it your forte."

Tilly studies JD for a moment before saying, "Yes, I guess you could. I'll choose to take that in the manner in which it was not intended, thank you." Then he raises his glass and says, "Could we not argue? Could we toast to a future of less friction and better times? Please, JD. May our differences never get in the way of our appreciation for our similarities." He clinks his glass to JD's which has remained on the table. "Let's enjoy the day, shall we? Let's not talk about things that drive a wedge between us." He smiles broadly, without the leer of earlier, and says, "Last we spoke you were considering a job at a school here. What happened?"

JD sighs resignedly. "Yes, that's right. I was and I took it. Poly-sci adjunct at Boston College. It's good. A lot of work, but good."

"I bet they love their handsome professor."

"I'm not a professor. Just an adjunct, but it's a step."

With effort on both sides, the tension relaxes. There is more talk of subjects that go beyond politics and the sufferings of gay men on the other coast. They reminisce about their good times on the campaign trails, their vacations in cabin number twenty-eight, and the possibility of a future that could bring them together again soon. JD is torn as he regards the man across from him. The physical properties that he fell for are still there. The hair is still as blond, the eyes as blue green as before. And the hand that rests on the table—as if to caress it—is that same hand that has always been blessed with an enviable tan and so many capabilities. His eyes move over the cuff of the white linen shirt. He follows to where it is unbuttoned just enough to reveal a few wisps of light brown hairs at his nape. It's at that point that JD recognizes the weakness rising up and filling him. He knows this feeling well and where it will lead. The check will be paid. The walk will be swift.

And tomorrow the hotel room will be left in the same disheveled condition as so many others have been left before.

Cabin Number Twenty-Eight, Sunset Motor Lodge, 1986

"Have you noticed?" JD says, standing at the window that faces the pool.

Tilly is lying on the bed, thumbing through an old magazine he found in the bathroom. It's a *Field and Stream* from 1966. "I never realized how hot hunters are. Must be the camouflage."

"Tilly, I'm talking to you. Haven't you noticed anything different?"

Tilly looks up. "I've noticed how good you look in that suit. Is that it?"

"Have you noticed that no one's using the pool this year?"

"Well, it's October. What's your point?"

"It's not cold, though. It's a beautiful day—mid-seventies with no clouds. Usually, they'd be a half dozen people out there."

"And this concerns you why?"

"Because I think it's about us. I think people know about us, and they're afraid. You know, because they think we may have AIDS."

"What are you talking about? You're being a bit paranoid, my love." Tilly rises from the bed and joins JD at the window. A couple with a small child are walking past. The parents look up and then away when they see the men looking out. The father shakes his head with an expression that could be either sadness or disgust.

"See? Everyone knows to stay away from the homos in twenty-eight. I wouldn't be surprised if they're warned when they check in." He turns to Tilly, but he's not beside him. He's at the bureau changing clothes. "What are you doing?"

"I'm putting on my bathing suit and then I'm joining you at the pool. If they're gonna talk, they might as well talk about how much fun those homos are having."

And people do talk, but mostly in whispers. Some just stare. Families walk past with towels slung over their shoulders, but they veer away when they catch sight of the two. Some of the children whine their frustration at not being able to swim. A quick slap puts the whining to rest. The pool is all theirs that beautiful day, and they make use of it until nearly sunset. Only once is there an exchange between them that could be volatile if pursued. It's JD who decides not to.

"I thought to call you last month, but I wasn't sure how you'd react," Tilly says. He's applying more lotion to his face and neck.

"React to what?"

"Well, I was wondering if you'd noticed that my evil leader mentioned AIDS in a press conference last month. I figured you'd be pleased to hear that."

"Pleased to hear that after more than ten thousand deaths, Reagan is finally able to say the word? No, I wasn't that pleased. The only reason he mentioning it now is because it's affecting kids. It's a heartstrings thing. He can't ignore a disease that's taking children. That would make him too obvious of a monster. At least now he won't have to acknowledge what's happening to the queers and the degenerates."

"Jesus, that's a bit cynical. At least he's doing something now. That's what you wanted, isn't it?"

JD considers how far he wants to go with this. He knows that the information and the numbers are on his side, but does he want there to be sides this time? There's another week of vacation and it would be best for both of them if it could be a good one all the way through, with no arguments that are so intense that one of them will need to leave. He opts to ignore all his facts and numbers and go for the easy answer.

"You're right. It's good that he's using the word now. Definitely a step in the right direction."

Tilly lifts his sunglasses and stares at his lover. "Wow, that is some impressive placating, my dear. Must be the beautiful weather. Whatever it is, I'll take it."

"As well you should. Who knows if there'll be any more of it." JD reaches across the span between their lounge chairs and lightly touches his fingertips to Tilly's. It's a subtle gesture, but even during that minor suggestion of intimacy a passing couple notices. The man mutters loud enough for them to hear, "Fruit-cakes!" The woman giggles and slaps the man's shoulder. Tilly and JD maintain their modest connection and do not react.

CABIN NUMBER TWENTY-EIGHT, RIVERTON, 2015

Tilly is sweating. He's been moving furniture all day, taking most of it out to the yard to make room for the deliveries of appliances, a new bed, and new light fixtures. All of the deliveries are scheduled for today, and he's been frantically at it since early morning. He found the campaign button when he moved the bed away from the wall. The pin part had lodged into the knotty pine and must have been stuck behind the headboard for twenty years. At first he doesn't recognize it, not until he pulls it from the wood and turns it over. The red letters against the white background weaken him enough that he needs to sit to avoid falling.

The words **NO MALARKY VOTE McCARTHY** punch him in his gut and in his brain and in the deepest crevices of his heart. It is such a strong punch that it pushes the air out of him, and he isn't able to move for most of the next hour. He sits on the edge of the old mattress that is now stripped of sheets and pillows—a decayed and stained remnant of vacations past—as he tries to pull in deep breaths to manage his palpitations. He grips the pin so hard that the point causes blood to drip from his hand and onto the mattress. He doesn't feel the prick, isn't even aware that he's holding the thing so tightly. He stares at it—into it, really. He sees visions of days and nights that he had forgotten or at least had packed away. But they are unpacking now in a steady stream of the good and the bad of all those years with and without JD.

It isn't until the knock on the door that he wakes and realizes he's weeping, and then he sees that he's bleeding. He grabs a towel on his way to the door. He wipes his face and then wraps the towel around his hand, still clutching the pin in his fist.

"Mr. Taylor," the sheriff says. He notices the towel and adds, "Oh, no. You seem to have a penchant for injuring yourself, don't you? Let me take a look."

Tilly pulls away from his reach. "It's just a small cut. Nothing that needs attention."

"All right, but I hope you'll get that shot I suggested." The sheriff moves through the door without invitation. "I need to talk to you. It won't take long."

Tilly moves aside, but says, "There's really nowhere to sit here except for the bed, and I wouldn't suggest it. Shall we go outside?"

"Getting some new furnishings?"

"It's a necessity if I'm going to spend time here. I hope it's not a problem. I'd assumed you were done with whatever you were doing the other day."

"Yes, we're done. That's why I need to talk to you."

Tilly leads the sheriff outside and motions toward the two chairs that he's discarding. "They're old, but they'll hold."

The sheriff takes the smaller of the two, a glider, and settles in with the back-and-forth. "You're throwing this out?"

"I am."

"Well, I might just take this off your hands, if that's okay."

"Of course. You're welcome to it." Tilly sits in the other, an old and tattered Queen Anne. "Now, aside from the furniture, there's something you'd like to talk about?"

"Actually, I'd like to schedule a meeting with you, if I could. But first, you seemed very upset when you came to the door just now. Is something wrong?"

Tilly considers the towel, but resists wiping it across his face again. "Not really. Just an unsettling conversation with my wife. She's not what you would call a reasonable person. She relishes in her ability to push every button as well as every emotion. It gives her a perverse pleasure, I think."

"I'm sorry to hear that. Will she be coming up here anytime soon?"

Tilly chuckles. "Not if there's a God. She doesn't do well with rustic, and she would surely make everyone in her path miserable."

"Wow! That doesn't sound like a healthy relationship."

Tilly squeezes the towel until he feels the pin driving into him again. "Anyway, you wanted to schedule a time with me? Whatever for? Have you learned something about the body?"

"No, we still haven't identified the bones. We know it's a man. And we have an estimate of his age, probably in his late thirties, early forties. There's no DNA on file, but we're hoping for something to come through one of the genealogy sites."

"I don't understand."

"Well, they're very popular sites these days, apparently. Mostly for people who want to discover their background. If someone's signed onto one of them, we might be able to make a family connection for the man. It's time-consuming and doesn't always come through."

"I've never heard of such a thing."

"Neither had I, but there's a lot of this world I don't know. The internet still baffles me."

"So, that's all you have? Then why do you need to schedule something? Why not just talk to me now?"

"We'd like to conduct a formal interview, if you don't mind. We really should have done this before, but now some evidence has surfaced and it's become more necessary. It should be at my office in Farmington so we can get everything down as it should be. At least you won't have to go all the way to Portland. What day works best for you?"

Tilly squeezes the towel so hard that the pin hits bone, and this time he winces.

Yeah, that's right. I completely forgot about that. There was a new rug in the cabin after they left that last time. I probably wouldn't even have noticed, but one of them left a note, something about spilling wine on it so they'd got us a new one, way better than the old piece of shit we'd had for a hundred years. I figure it was nice of them to do that. I mean, most people would have said "fuck it" and bolted. But not those two. They cleaned the place so good it smelled of bleach for a year. Didn't matter, 'cause business fell off and we stopped renting the twenties anyway. By the nineties, nobody wanted to stay in some smelly old cabin.

By the way, I had time to go through the old register books. My God, there was a ton of 'em. Ma said she threw some of the really old ones out and that musta been where JD's full name was. He started just writing "JD" in '75. We knew who he was by then, so I guess he figured—and Ma probably figured too—that a full name didn't matter. We didn't run a very tight ship, obviously. Sorry I couldn't help more.

Nope, couldn't tell you the other guy's name. He never registered. And that picture you faxed over doesn't help much. That guy looked pretty beat up. I showed it to Ma too, but neither of us could say for sure. Truth be told, I hadn't spent much time looking at his face. He may have been a fucking dick but he had one too. That's all I cared about back then. I remember he was real good looking but that's it. Sorry, Sheriff, you can

*take the girl outa the cesspool, but you can't get the shitstain
outa the girl.*

—Dorrie Simpson Foster, former employee
at the Sunset Motor Court.
Interview with Sheriff Wilfred Tufts,
Franklin County. November 2, 2015

Cabin Number Twenty-Eight, Sunset Motor Lodge, October 1988

When JD arrives, he slips the key in the cabin door and it
swings open, already unlocked. He steps in carefully and looks
around the room. Tilly is sitting in the Queen Anne, smiling
too broadly for JD's comfort. His legs are crossed and each hand
holds a martini. On the table next to him is a martini shaker and
a plate with a vividly orange ball of cheese surrounded by round
yellow crackers.

"Hello, my dear," Tilly says as he extends a glass toward JD.

"Well, this is a first—you getting here before me." He
examines the plate closely. "I don't think I've ever seen a cheese
quite that color."

Tilly laughs. "It's all I could get in town. Come on. Sit,
relax, drink."

JD tosses his bag on the bed, removes his jacket, and then
slides into the glider before taking the glass. "Thank you." He
takes a long sip and smiles. "Perfect. You do know how to make a
martini." He sips again and then adds, "So, what's going on, Tilly?"

"What's going on? What do you mean? I'm welcoming my
man to our vacation. Something wrong with that?"

JD studies his lover carefully, taking in the smile and the
overly casual way he's occupying the chair, as if he were born to
command from it. "Seems like something's up. You gotta admit

that all this—the martinis, the whatever-that-orange-things is, and the fact that you're here before me—is just a bit odd. I mean, it's a little out of character, don't you think?"

"Wow . . . you are not ready to be welcomed, are you? Bad day, hon?"

JD doesn't respond, only stares back, waiting for an answer.

"All right. I guess I'm apologizing. Sort of. I know I can be a little difficult. Very difficult, probably. And I haven't liked it, fucking hated myself for it sometimes. Not returning your calls, always late, and then not always amicable once we do meet. I've been thinking—seriously thinking—that I've taken you for granted and now is a good time to change. Maybe to a better person, a better friend, a better boyfriend. I mean, I am your boyfriend, right?"

JD stands and does an exaggerated examination of the room, squinting into corners, glancing under the bed. "So, who are you and what have you done with Tilly?"

Tilly grabs him and pulls him onto his lap. "I'm feeling good tonight. I'm feeling like I might be figuring things out." He's moving his tongue along the pulse of JD's neck. "Enjoy it, for fuck's sake." The last two words are mumbled into the corner of JD's nape.

He squirms and then stands, looking down at Tilly. "Figuring what out? What the fuck are you figuring out, Tilly? This, maybe? Are you finally trying to put a name to whatever this is? If you figure that out, buddy, I'd really like you to tell me." He glances toward the sink and sees the half-empty gin bottle. "Jesus, Tilly. Was that full? How long you been here?"

Tilly takes a breath and lets it out slowly before starting. "A couple of hours, I guess. I needed some thinking time. And what I've been thinking about is how to make everything, all the crazy parts of my life, work. You know, not get in the way of each other."

"No, I don't know. I'm assuming I'm one of those crazy parts?"

"Just one of them."

"Get to the point, Tilly. What the hell is going on?"

"Will you sit, please?"

JD flops back into the tattered glider and signals for Tilly to go on.

"Okay, this is kinda big. And I want you to hear me out before you go nuts."

"That's a shitty way to start." JD is deep in the chair's cushions. He resembles a child who is anticipating the worst.

"I know. I'm not good at this."

"You mean talking?"

Tilly refills both of their glasses from the shaker on the table between them. "Yes, talking . . . about difficult things. Like changes. So anyway, this is it, and you may have some difficulties with it. The thing is that it looks like Vice President Bush will be moving into the White House in January."

"Yeah. Sadly."

"Not fair! People are happy with what Reagan's done, and they want more." He holds up his palm to JD who appears to be ready with a comment. "Let me get this out, okay? Anyway, all the people in power there have been pretty impressed with the work I've been doing. They liked what I did with Dukakis."

"You mean making him look like an idiot? I figured that was your work."

"Please! Could you hold your fucking tongue for a couple of minutes?"

JD does a zipping gesture across his mouth.

"As I was saying, they like me and my methods, as disgusting as they may be to you. And Atwater has taken particular notice. He's invited me to join his team, primarily to work on strategies that will focus on the next Democratic candidate. Bill Clinton. Heard of him?"

JD nods.

"Well, I hadn't, but Atwater is a little concerned about his potential. When I get back to DC. I'll be studying the man. God, I love that shit."

"So, that's it? That's what you wanted to tell me, that you're continuing with the devil's work?"

"Jesus, JD. everything is not so black and white, good and evil. And this is about moving forward. You should be happy for me. Atwater thinks I have a future in DC. Maybe even a political position. Or an ambassadorship. Who knows? I could write my own ticket if I play it right. Why shouldn't I go for it?"

"Fine. Go for it. I won't stand in your way. I'm just thinking that this tidbit of yours is not the real news. You've gotten plenty of noxious jobs over the years, but you've never met me on time and with cocktails. You're usually late and irritable if you make it here at all. So, let's hear it. What's the rest? I'm not buying that you're a new man because of a possible job." JD pulls himself out of the hollow of the chair and goes to the bed where his bags are still packed. He rummages through until he finds the bottle of bourbon, pours himself a hefty shot, and makes no offer to Tilly.

"Will you sit back down please?"

"No, I'm fine right here." He leans against the counter with his arms folded, the glass of bourbon held tightly in his fist.

Tilly takes a swallow of his martini and stares back at JD, considering his words carefully. "You're right. There's more. You can always tell, can't you? I guess you know me better than anybody. But this isn't a second shoe dropping or anything like that. It's just an issue that I—that we—need to address." A breath and a sip. "You see, Atwater is concerned about the fact that I'm a forty-three-year-old man who's never been married."

"Oh, fuck. Here we go." JD tosses back the shot and pours another.

"And if I want to continue on this path—"

"Fuck you!"

"I'm going to need to make some changes. In my personal life."

"Fuck you all to hell!"

"At least in what people think of as my personal life. It won't change us, probably make us better. We'll still see each other.

We'll still come up here. It's just that I could do great things, I think, and I need to be a more respectable person out in public, someone people can identify with. You know what I mean?"

"Yeah, I fucking know what you mean." JD abandons the glass and drinks from the bottle, then turns his back to Tilly.

"Atwater is not a well man. He's thinking of me as a possible successor. Yeutter is in line, but Lee's tapping me as another option. Do you realize the honor attached to that?" Tilly eases out of his chair and slowly goes to JD. He tries to hug him from behind, but JD turns and pushes him away.

"I'm so damn sick of this," JD bellows, too loudly for the room.

"Jesus, keep your voice down, for God's sake."

"No, goddamnit, I won't. I don't give a shit who hears me. I've had it. I'm sick to death of this, all of it. And so fucking tired I could scream." And he does scream. Then he sweeps a hand over the counter, taking the bottles of gin and bourbon and whatever else is in his way across the room and crashing to the floor. "I am sick of being a goddamn secret. I'm sick of hiding myself and you from everybody, even people I don't give a shit about. I want to live like a normal person for a change, go to a restaurant, hold hands on a street, kiss a guy in public without being afraid of what people are going to say or, even worse, do to me and to him. No, goddamnit. I'm not doing it. Fuck this. I'm not going to be afraid to live a human life. They can beat me up, fire me, put me on some kind of blacklist, I don't give a shit anymore. No job, no approval, no cabin retreat—and yes—no lover, or whatever you're calling yourself, is worth any of this. Fuck it!"

Tilly looks around the room, at the broken glass and the puddles of bourbon and gin. There's a long slash of sugar running through it, soaking up the liquid and going dark. He turns back to JD. "What are you saying?"

"I'm saying, 'No more!' I'm saying I'm going to do the right thing for a change. I'm going to stop this, stop the hiding and the lying. You've been thinking? Well, I've been thinking too. I've been thinking about how cowardly and paranoid I've been our whole time together, just accepting it as how it had to be. But I'm not so sure about that anymore. I keep reading stuff about the movement, about the strong ones who are clearing the way for the weak. It's been making me worried that maybe I'm one of the weak ones. How fucking depressing is that, that I'm a forty-year-old coward, too weak to stand up for myself and counting on the younger ones to fight my battles." He throws his arms over his head and screams again—scaring Tilly back into the wall—and this time the sound is louder, emanating from deep in his gut. "But you know what? Fuck that. I'm not going to be that kinda queer. I never was until I met you. You're the one who made me hide, talking about careers and how it would look. You've made me think it's okay to be a secret, as if it's the natural way our kind should be living. So, I've made a decision, a really big one just like you have. It's been festering in me for a while, keeping me up, making me struggle with the idea of who I really am. And suddenly, right now this very night, it's clear. How funny is that? You come here with your big decision and it just solidifies mine." He tosses his head back and laughs so loudly that Tilly rushes to him and cups a hand over his mouth. JD bites into it until Tilly cries out.

"Have you gone off the deep end? What the fuck are you doing?" He pushes past JD to the sink. He runs cold water over the side of his palm, which is showing tooth marks but no blood.

"What am I doing? Damn good question, Tilly. You've got your solutions, and I've got mine. I've made a decision too. I'm going to tell everyone I know who I am, finally. Maybe even people I don't know. I guess I'm lucky that I don't have any family left. They say that's the hardest. So, I'll just tell everyone who cares to listen. And you know something else, Tilly? If you don't do it too, if you don't get off your comfortable, faux-straight ass and make a stance against all this bullshit, I'm going to do it for you."

"What?"

"Yeah. That's what I'm going to do. It just came to me. Just now. I suddenly remembered I've got friends, Tilly. What a shock, huh? Big surprise that I actually have a good life beyond you. And some of my friends are actually proud of who they are. They're the kind of friends who will be supportive of what I'm doing. Some might not be, but I'm okay with that, too. And then there's a few—just a couple—with sweet little jobs that allow them influence and a voice. Like at a little rag called the *Globe*. Heard of it? Those friends would love a story like this. They'll feast on it like it's All-You-Can-Eat night at Denny's. I can see it. REPUBLICAN POLITICO GOES QUEER. Try finding a woman to marry after that. But maybe your new friend Atwater will be able to help. He'll probably know a few loyal right-wing groupies who don't have the heavy baggage of a moral compass."

Tilly has gone white. His glass has fallen from his grip, adding more debris to the already ravaged floor. He starts pacing in circles, crunching shards under his shoes. It's a small and cramped cabin so his circles are the same. He finally stops on the opposite side of the room from JD. "You wouldn't do that."

"I wouldn't have thought so either, but I'm thinking now that I actually could."

The space between them is filled with emotions beyond memory. It's made up of desire and disappointment and betrayal, with very little of what Tilly had always counted on—forgiveness. Neither of them move. Their eyes are locked, welded together like a rod of rebar, for what could be anywhere between a minute and an hour. But then the tension is broken by a loud and aggressive knock.

The last time I saw them? Jesus, Sheriff, you're asking a lot from an old girl. Lucky for you, I got a brain like a fucking roach motel. Shit goes in and just stays there. It's a curse, really.

So . . . I'm guessing here . . . but it might have been that time I'd gotten complaints from a couple of cabins. I'm not saying it's the last time I saw them, but it's gotta be close. We didn't get complaints much at the Sunset, so it stands out. Got a call from a New York couple, number twenty-three or maybe twenty-four. They were typical New Yorkers, so I didn't pay it much mind. Hate those shitheads. But then the guy from thirty comes banging on the office door. I always closed at nine, so I was fully in the mind to say, "Fuck off." But he was a big guy—and really pissed—so I pulled my annoyance back a little.

Long story short, me and him went over to twenty-eight together. Probably took a bat with me just in case. Back then I didn't care if you were a bear or a moose or a fucking asshole, I would take your head off if you fucked with me. I may be fat, but I'm no marshmallow.

What happened? Ha! Nothin'. The blond guy came to the door, JD right behind him. I asked them what the hell was going on, told them folks were complaining. The blond apologized. JD piped in that they were fooling around and got carried away, which musta pissed off the blond 'cause he gave him a dirty look. Well, I didn't wanna hear any more about that. I know what fooling around means, and I don't need a play-by-play. I told them to keep it down and I left, sent that big guy back to his cabin and told him to close his windows.

That was it. I don't think I saw either one of them after. Folks usually just slipped the keys in the box and left, no need to stop in. I figured that's what they did. They bought me a nice rug, though. I guess whatever freaky thing they were up to got real messy.

—Natty Simpson, Owner of
the Sunset Motor Lodge.
Interview continued with Sheriff Wilfred
Tufts, Franklin County Police.
October 20, 2015

Franklin County Sheriff Station, Farmington, October 2015

"Thanks for coming down, Mr. Taylor. Could I get you something?"

"No thank you. What I could really use is an explanation. Why am I here?"

Sheriff Tufts smiles as he reaches for a folder. "Okay, let's get right to it. Take a seat." He flips through several pages.

Tilly lowers himself into the chair before he realizes it's the glider he had given the sheriff. He stays put but is not comfortable. "Were you able to identify the man? Did all that time I spent evicted from my cabin yield anything worthwhile?"

"Not what I hoped for. Apparently, that man isn't in our database, so fingerprints are useless. Still hoping for a DNA match, but that probably won't go anywhere either. However, we did find another match."

Tilly says nothing at first. He waits as the sheriff looks through his papers. Finally, he says, "My God, sir, don't keep me in suspense."

"Well, it's a little strange. You see, there was only one set of prints that had a match." Sheriff Tufts flips to the third page. "You were arrested in Chicago in 1968? Is that right?"

Tilly smiles. "Yes, I certainly was. And I'm damn proud of it. It's a sort of badge of honor if you will. I was working on the Humphrey campaign, and I was detained without cause during those horrific riots. They treated me like a criminal, even when I showed them my pass. It's an experience I both cherish and wish to forget."

"I see. I didn't realize you were in politics."

"It was my career for nearly forty years. For both parties. Now why would you be concerned that my fingerprints are in the cabin? I mean, I've been working on it for weeks. They must be everywhere."

"Of course, I understand that. But the prints we're concerned about are the ones we found on the remnants of rug backing and plastic. Could you explain how your prints would be there? You did claim never to have stayed at the Sunset, right?"

"That is exactly my claim, sir. The explanation is quite simple."

"Well, I do like simplicity. I guess it's the Mainer in me."

"Sheriff," Tilly says with blatant exasperation. "If you had bothered to ask me back in Riverton, you could have saved both of us some time."

"No time like the present, sir. Please, enlighten me."

"The fact is that when the cabin was moved, I followed it. I'd paid a decent price for the old girl, and I wanted to be sure she got to Riverton in one piece. It was nearly forty miles on that horrible excuse for a road, and, as I'm sure you're aware, bits of what I assumed to be insulation or something more structural kept coming off the bottom in transit. I honked several times to have them stop, but apparently the driver either couldn't hear or didn't want to hear. So when we arrived at my site, I examined the underneath. I pulled off pieces of plastic and, I suppose, pieces of rug. The driver was right there. I believe it was he who called the police when we realized what we were seeing."

"So, you had no idea that bone fragments were falling all over Route 16?"

"Of course not. You may be familiar with the effects of a decaying body, but I assure you I am not. To me, those bits looked like pieces of rotting building materials. I was more concerned about the integrity of my purchase than what might have been attached to it. By the way, were you able to recover any of those pieces?"

"Unfortunately, no. Animals must have found them before we could get back there."

"That is unfortunate. Sheriff, let's be candid, shall we? Are you under the impression that I may have had something to do with the death of whomever that body had been in life?"

"I never said that, sir."

"You didn't need to. It's been quite obvious. You've been questioning me for weeks now, and I'd like it to stop. Or you should arrest me, if that's what you consider to be appropriate. But if it's the latter, I'll need to speak to my lawyer. I find this constant badgering to be most annoying. And disruptive."

"I'm not badgering. Just questioning, which is what we do here."

"Whatever you call it, I think it's over now. I've explained everything from why I bought the cabin to why my fingerprints might be on certain surfaces. I've even explained my family connections, as if that was any of your concern. All that said, I see no reason for us to talk further."

Tilly rises quickly from the chair and, again, needs to steady himself before heading to the door.

"How old are you, Mr. Taylor?"

Tilly turns, hand on the doorknob. His expression doesn't mask his annoyance. "I'm seventy years old. Why in God's name would you care?"

"I was just thinking that you've taken very good care of yourself. I'm a little envious."

Tilly chuckles. "Thank you. Apparently, I was blessed with resilient genes. Now, if there is nothing else, I'll bid you a good afternoon, Sheriff. I hope this conversation will serve as an appropriate ending to our relationship."

CABIN NUMBER TWENTY-EIGHT, OCTOBER 1988

"Well, that's just great," Tilly says. "Now you've brought the owner down on us." He parts the shades just enough to see Natty peeling away on her golf cart.

"Good." JD kicks shards of glass aside as he goes to the bed and starts putting his bags back together. Underwear and socks had spilled out from when he'd grabbed the bourbon. "I have no intention of coming back here anyway."

"So, that's it? Twenty years and now you're giving up? Can't you see that what I'm suggesting will make everything better? We can still be together without people thinking anything. Like we're best friends or something. We can still come here. Hell, we can go anywhere you want." Tilly crosses to JD, but when he puts his hand on his shoulder JD spins around and slaps him hard across the face.

"No!" JD says. "Get the fuck off me. I'm done, Tilly. Why it's taken me this long, I have no idea. I'm ashamed of myself. Ashamed for being so afraid. But I was serious when I said I'm going to be honest with people now. They're calling it 'coming out,' but to me it's like shedding something. A mask, maybe. Or a whole identity that's got nothing to do with who I really am." He has his bags together, and he tries to push past Tilly.

"Wait," Tilly says. "Just wait, for fuck's sake. You're not going to walk out after everything we've been through, are you?"

"Watch me." JD pushes at Tilly without success. He tries to maneuver around him but he only slips on a puddle of gin and falls hard, fully splayed onto the carpet. Tilly offers a hand but JD slaps at it. "Get the fuck out of my way." He manages to get up to his knees and then his feet. He's nearly standing when he feels the pain. He looks down and sees the long shard of glass poking from his thigh. Without thinking, he pulls at it and at first the glass won't budge. It slides down his palm, parting the flesh from index finger to metacarpal. It comes out on the second try, and he holds his hand up to Tilly to show him the jagged shard and the slice it's given him. But Tilly isn't looking. He's staring down at JD's leg, and his expression is paled with so much horror that JD drops the piece of glass and follows Tilly's focus to the pant leg that's now soaked in thick red. He looks back up to Tilly, and then collapses.

Tilly is frozen for several seconds before he drops down next to JD, tears the fabric of the pants apart until he finds the wound that is now spurting fountains of crimson. With both hands he presses into JD's leg, but the bleeding isn't stopping; it squirts between Tilly's fingers and drenches his arms and even his face and chest. He repositions his hands and presses harder, but the liquid continues to pulse and finds new paths along the sides of Tilly's hands.

JD looks up at him. His eyes are wide and there is a fear there that Tilly has never seen in the man before. JD's lips move just a bit, and then he is able to form one word. "You . . ." he says, but that's all he can manage. The pulsing fades below Tilly's palms, and he watches as every evidence of life leaves his lover's face.

The scene that was so frantic a second ago has become still. Tilly's hands remain pressed against the leg. JD's eyes and mouth remain open. The streams of blood have pooled and paused. Cabin Number Twenty-Eight has gone quiet.

Tilly is soaked to his elbows. He slowly pulls himself to his feet and takes in everything: his hands and arms, the carpet that has lost any evidence of pattern, the broken fragments of glass that are now spotted and streaked. And the body. He regards what is now stretched out below him as if it's something he can't quite identify. All of it—the blood, the glass, the body—is too vivid to be real. The sight of everything, along with the quantities of gin he'd consumed, brings on a fatigue so strong that he feels incapable of fighting it. The room seems to darken and his vision goes wobbly. He lowers himself back to the floor, stretching out next to JD, and plunges into sleep.

When he awakes three hours later, it will take him three more to decide what to do. Three hours of pacing, crying, cursing himself and his new career—all the while taking large swigs of what's left of the gin. By seven in the morning, he will have a plan, or at least a direction. He'll find a hardware store where he'll get everything he needs: plastic, bleach, scrub brushes, a crowbar, a hammer and nails, a new rug, and, as an afterthought, a bag of quicklime. That last need will disgust him as he considers what it will do the body of his beautiful lover, but he will move beyond it in the same way that he has already moved beyond so much.

The process will take all day and most of the night. As he's nailing the final floorboard back into place, he will apologize one more time and add, "I'll be back for you, JD. I promise." It will take him nearly thirty years to keep his word.

RIVERSIDE CEMETERY, RIVERTON, 2015

Tilly is staring down into the newly dug grave at the top of the cemetery. His thoughts and his memories have so consumed him that he jumps a little and nearly tumbles into the hole when he hears the voice behind him. The sheriff rushes forward and grabs him by the arm before he falls.

"You should be careful around these open holes, sir. Especially considering that vertigo thing. You don't want to get into one before your time." He laughs a little, but Tilly does not.

"Cemeteries make me a bit introspective, it seems," Tilly says.

"I can understand that. Cemeteries can make us think about our lives. Our futures."

"And mostly our pasts." Tilly's voice is low, nearly a mumble, as he stares into the depths of the hole.

"I'm sorry, sir?"

"Nothing, Sheriff. Just the blatherings of an old man. What can I do for you?"

"I heard you were having the body buried this afternoon, and I thought you might want some company."

"That's kind of you, but a need for company is a rare condition for me. There's really no reason for you to be here. It's not as if there's a funeral or anything. I just came to make sure things were done properly. The stone should be here soon, if they ever get the damn hole filled in. I didn't realize long siestas were the practice this far north."

"You purchased a stone? For a man you never knew? That's very nice of you, sir."

"It's only a courtesy. I would certainly hope that if my body were found under a cabin, someone would give me a proper burial."

"Of course. Still, it's a kind gesture."

Tilly shrugs, His eyes remain on the casket. The sun is now angled in such a way that the polished oak seems to be illuminated. The reflective sheen is so bright that Tilly needs to shield his eyes, but still he squints into it.

"That's a lovely casket you've put him in. You could have gone for a less expensive one, I'm sure. It's not like anyone would judge."

"Everyone judges, Sheriff. But no one judges more than we do ourselves."

Each of them is quiet then. Tilly continues to look into the hole as the sheriff observes him.

"You know something, Tilly, if you ever need to talk through something, just man-to-man—" But the sheriff's words are cut off by the sounds of a truck ascending the hill. They turn to see four workmen riding in the back, supporting a tall, canvas-covered rectangle.

"Thank you, Sheriff, but I rather doubt that a conversation is in our future. Excuse me, please." Tilly waves to the driver and descends the mound. Sheriff Tufts follows.

"What did you have engraved?" he says when they reach the truck.

"See for yourself."

The sheriff goes to where the men are unloading their shovels, the cement, and the wooden form for the foundation. When they've removed everything but the headstone, the sheriff hops onto the bed and pulls back the canvas tarp.

JD WAS HERE
1948–1988

"It's what was printed on that card you found. I figured it to be appropriate."

"But you gave him a date of birth. How could you know that?"

"I went with your estimation. I had to put something there." When the sheriff hops out of the truck, Tilly extends a hand. "It was nice meeting you, Sheriff Tufts. We will hopefully have no reason to meet again."

The sheriff watches the man as he follows the workers back up the hill. He is walking very slowly now, exposing the fatigue of his seventy years.

Tilly will stay at the gravesite as the hole is filled with dark loam, topped with sod, and crowned by the stone that is mounted and cemented into place. The process will take hours, and he will remain there long after the workers have left. He will lower himself with difficulty to the ground beside the strip of bright green, and he will converse at length with the simple piece of granite, questioning his feelings of guilt and cowardice. He will consider the few words engraved there, and he will wish that he could have said more. He will wish that his guilt could have allowed him the courage to tell the world how much one man's life had meant to another's.

$\mathcal{W}ilma$

WILMA STODDARD FRENCH
1951-2020
"I'VE MISSED YOU TERRIBLY"

THE WELL WAS DEEPER THAN I WOULD HAVE THOUGHT, DEEP enough that I had time within my descent to consider my future, or rather the lack of one. And it was drier. Only a small puddle in the corner—most likely the result of a recent rain. That tiny splash of mud was the third to last thing I saw. The second was the red ball, still bright with its yellow specks, rolling into the darkness of the well's edge. Then there was the very last: my wife's face, pale and without expression, as she regarded me from above.

I can't say that I blame her even if she had done it intentionally, which is a reasonable assumption. I should take partial responsibility, at least. If I had done what I knew very well that I should, we would not have been in the situation that we were. If I had put an end to our miseries on the multiple occasions when I had the opportunity, we would never have made it that far. But I didn't, and we did, and now I am where I am.

Relationships can be unpredictably volcanic. There were years of livable cohabitation, decades of peace between the eruptions. But the length of passivity only intensified the explosions. We each would pass our days during those stretches of quiet in the way that one waits for the inevitable storm. The longer the calm, the more certain we were of the downpour.

The first time Wilma tried to kill me was on an ordinary Sunday in May, thirty years before she finally succeeded. We were doing the *New York Times* crossword puzzle as we always did on Sunday mornings: tangled around each other on the soft couch that we had purchased shortly after our marriage the year before. She was wearing a wine-colored robe that was made of fabric so soft and fluffy it brought to mind memories of teddy bears and baby blankets. It was loosely tied at her waist, exposing the curve of one pale breast. Each time she reached across to consider a word, it slipped out and rested on my shoulder as she counted the spaces. I was in my usual Sunday attire: boxer shorts and a tee shirt. We rarely dressed on Sundays unless company was expected, which we did not encourage. Our Sundays were special and full of intense lovemaking followed by long, replenishing naps.

The eruption was ignited by a word. Two words, actually. *Languor* and *malaise*. The horizontal word was *frantic*, and the clue for the intersecting word was *despondency*.

Wilma leaned over me, allowing her breast to do as it was accustomed, and began to pencil her word without discussion. We'd generally say the word aloud, testing it for approval before assuming its legitimacy. But this time she was so sure of herself that she ignored our process. She got to the third letter when I pushed at her pencil.

"What are you doing?" I said, ignoring the nipple that gazed up as if to challenge.

"It's obviously *malaise*," she said. "It fits and it makes perfect sense." She tried to continue her entry, but I pulled the paper aside.

"Not necessarily. It could be . . . *languor*, possibly? Yes, that makes much more sense to me. We should work on 34-down before we decide."

"Don't be so gutless. Crossword puzzles are about certainty and risk."

"What are you talking about? Risk of what?" Since she was oblivious to her exposure, I closed her robe for her.

"The risk of being wrong, a condition with which you should be quite familiar." With a defiant gesture, she tore open the top of her robe, airing both of her neatly composed breasts. Now there were two pink nipples judging me.

"My dear," I said with as much condescension as I could muster under the gaze of those perfect orbs, "If risk were an asset in crossword puzzles, I surely would be a master. I've risked quite a lot, don't you think?"

The insinuation was clear. When I had ignored my parents' disapproval and had gone ahead with the marriage, I had lost a lot of financial backing. Wilma was not of what my mother referred to as "the right stock." They didn't disown me exactly, only secured the purse strings.

"The risk has been all mine, my dear." She reached for the pencil sharpener and slowly turned it over the lead. "The only risk that you have suffered has been that I might get bored with your lack of it."

And there she had a point. Wilma's adventurous and sometimes devil-may-care lifestyle was what had attracted this riskless moth to her fire.

"Are you bored?" I asked.

"Not at the moment."

"Well, I am," I said, attempting for the upper hand. "Your flagrancy is boring me to death. Cover yourself for God's sake." I will admit that I pulled the sides of her robe together a bit too violently.

There is smoke before flame, and smoke is what I saw the second before Wilma thrust her pencil into me. I drove to the nearest hospital with three inches of Yellow No. 2 jutting from my chest.

The sex that night was careful but satisfying.

You may think that an incident such as a stabbing would be a stepping stone to divorce or at least separation. Not for Wilma and me. We rise from our ashes, nearly as good as new. At least until the next eruption. And that one, I must admit, was all my doing.

It was a celebration of our third anniversary. Per tradition, we spent it at our cottage on Pinnacle Pond in Riverton. It was where Wilma had lived out her impoverished youth, and her parents had willed her the dilapidated cottage and several acres. Once we had made it livable, it became the getaway where all of our most important occasions were enjoyed, or at least happened. This particular occasion held less enjoyment than happenstance.

Our anniversary was in late June, and during our drive up from Manhattan, the natural evidence of the season changed from sweltering summer to spring. The private road to the cottage was inspiring in multiples: lush greenery, the purple and pink lupine that lined the drive, and the hydrangea bushes that banked the entrance to our summer home. It was a joy to be there, at least initially.

The conflict rose too quickly to avoid. I had unloaded the car and set everything in the appropriate rooms: liquor in the bar, food in the kitchen, clothes in our bedroom, sex toys in the special room in the basement. It was the latter accoutrement that started this eruption. I had no idea how much my toys meant to me until they were not there. If I had packed or if I had set Wilma's needs aside to be sure that mine had made it to our summer destination, what happened later could have been avoided. Yes, it is all my fault. But still, my wife of several years should have known. What else is a bond such as marriage if not a mutual understanding of our specific needs?

We had dinner. I cooked. It was a recipe I had learned from a chef in the city: angel-hair pasta with shrimp, tomatoes, basil, red bell peppers, fiddlehead ferns (which we had purchased in the town's center), and a plethora of garlic. It was delicious, and we ate it with a bottle of luscious Chianti. After small glasses of Fernet and a reasonable digestive period, we went to the basement.

"Where is my toy?" I said, as I rummaged through the massive bag of objects that held promises of dubious pleasures, at least for me.

"What toy?" She fumbled with a mechanism that seemed to have lost its power. "I packed it all."

I scanned the floor that was now littered with everything from small-and-supple to ridiculously rigid. "It's not here!" I screamed. "My special toy is not here!"

"Yay," she said. "It was just a button problem. Now, what's wrong?"

"Where is my fucking toy?" My volume was louder than it should have been. For that I also take responsibility. But it was my favorite toy, and it was Wilma who was responsible for the packing. She surely shares the blame for what happened next.

"We have plenty of toys," she said. She sighed and gestured to the array of objects strewn across the shag rug. There was so much dismissiveness in her tone that I could not control my rage.

"YOU have plenty!" I couldn't believe how little she cared for my needs. Our years of marriage flashed before me, a sequence of giving and taking with me on the worst end of it all. I scanned the floor again, taking in all of Wilma's pleasures, all of those objects that had satisfied her in ways that I could never. My eyes landed on one. It was my nemesis. I hoisted it, feeling the familiar heft in my palm, and aimed it at her. The weight couldn't have been more than a pound, but its flexibility surely made it stronger.

She countered with a riding crop we had only used once. We had both agreed that it was more painful than we'd been in the market for. But there she was, brandishing the thing like an épée complete with lunging stance. So I returned her challenge with my vein-riddled, ten-inch weapon. We circled each other, lunging and connecting, often with satisfactory results. We battled like that for nearly an hour until the blood and the bruising became too painful.

There was no sex that night, with or without embellishment. We agreed to return to New York the next day after we were released from the hospital.

It was many years before the well incident when we had one of the most satisfying battles of our lives. It was a silly disagreement, although in retrospect I can see that they all were. This one had to do with macaroni and cheese, a dish that I revered and considered to be the perfect and most comforting of all foods. My recipe, gifted to me by my late mother, combined all the ingredients that made me happy on many levels. And on that particular evening I certainly needed comfort and happiness.

I should mention here that Wilma and I were both in the advertising business. We were not the idea people, but rather the minions who wrote the copy after the idea was approved. It was a lucrative business for us, although the stress that accompanied it had been challenging. Generally, we were supportive of one another, although on that workday we were not.

We rarely worked on the same concepts since the firm preferred to use our individual talents on projects that required one senior associate in charge of a small team. But with a staff shortage that year, it became necessary to work together on this one, without subordinates to minionize.

The task involved a feminine hygiene product, something that addressed a supposed problem which I had never heard of. Vaginal farting made no sense to me or to Wilma. Still, it was our assignment so we faced it head-on. Our first step, per usual, was to name the product. It needed to be both inoffensive and enticing.

"How about "Fem-ex?" I quickly tossed to Wilma. She smirked.

"You want to ex-out women? I'm not surprised, but I don't think that will sell, do you?"

"Of course I don't want to eliminate women, just the condition. I'm playing off Gas-X, you know, the gas-problem pill."

"Yes, I get it. But it's not very clever, I think." She twirled her pen and stared into the air. I hadn't allowed her to use pencils in many years for obvious reasons.

"Well. you're the woman here. Any better ideas?"

"Nice of you to recognize that." She wrote several words on her pad but did not share them. I was already disliking our working relationship. I was accustomed to being the smart one in the room. This situation brought my favored position into question. "Let's discuss what they're trying to do with these pills." She was taking charge and I hated it.

"Fine. Apparently, some women discharge a gas while in the throes of coitus. Have you ever had that experience?" It was an attempt at acknowledging her status.

"You should know. Have I ever farted on you?"

It didn't require much thought. It seemed I would have remembered such a thing. "No, I can't say that you have."

"Well then. I guess we're on a level playing field."

The box with no name and very little information sat on the conference table between us. I snatched it up and read what little it offered. There was no clue as to how it did as it professed or even why the condition existed in the first place.

"I think we need to address this without considering the actual product," I said. "We just need a catchy name. It doesn't need to give away its function. My God, the concept is disturbingly obvious."

"You find vaginal noise disturbing?"

"No," I said emphatically. I sensed I was being baited. Or at least toyed with. I was in no mood. "My point is that the name can simply attract the shopper without pointing at her vagina."

"Any ideas? Any at all?"

I considered. She stared toward nothing. Eventually, I said it.

"A Quieter Love." My jaw was jutted and firm as if it were the only possible answer. She looked at me with no expression at all for a full minute. Her mind was working but she showed nothing. Then she burst into hysterical laughter. Tears poured down her cheeks, dragging streams of mascara with them. The outburst made me angry, but I held it close.

When she had contained herself, she said dryly, "You have got to be kidding. Are we writing romantic fiction or are we taking this seriously?" She scanned the words on her pad. "How about 'Shushhh'! I like all the h's at the end. It has a marketing ring. Or maybe 'Silencio'? It would certainly appeal to the European wannabes."

I hated both, of course, but I just wanted to get out of that room. I thought, *eenie, meenie* . . . and chose the latter.

For the next three hours we worked on the text that would be used in print and possibly television. Those hours were as peaceful as the name we had given the product. It wasn't until later, during the creation of a most magnificent baked macaroni and cheese that all hell erupted.

My recipe was very specific. I only used the finest pasta. It had to be of the elbow variety and it needed to be of the best durum wheat. Never whole wheat. I was partial to the darker pasta but it had no place in this dish. I bought my special ingredients in one store: Citarella Gourmet Market on the Upper West Side. While Wilma exited the subway and turned left toward our condo, I turned right to do my shopping.

The cheese sauce was made of equal portions of Gruyère, sharp cheddar, and Gouda. In a double boiler I mixed in a half-cup of plain organic yogurt. It had to be full fat and Greek. Whole milk was required but only conservatively. While the sauce was melting to a homogeneous consistency, I sliced the very ripe cherry tomatoes into halves. The reason I did this was so they would be small enough to nearly melt in the oven, marrying with the cheeses, creating a zest that would be subtle on the tongue while creating a balanced note to the yogurt.

The pasta was nearly done—which, by the way, needed to be two minutes' shy of al dente—when Wilma entered the kitchen, showered and smelling of lavender. It was a scent that immediately put me and my recipe off. It did not go well with the cheese sauce.

"What are you doing?" she said as she toweled her thinning hair. She had removed her fall hairpiece and it always caught me by surprise to recognize how little of the real Wilma was left.

Her question was ludicrous, but since I was feeling better while in the action of cooking, I simply replied, "Making dinner. Is there a problem?"

"I mean, what are you doing with those tomatoes?" She said that last word with a soft "a" as if she were British royalty. I had grown to hate that affectation.

"I'm prepping them for the dish. I always put tomatoes (said with a hard "a") in my mac and cheese. It's my mother's recipe."

"No, you don't."

"Yes, I do."

It was a cadence of childish back-and-forth which had never ended well.

"I'm allergic to tomatoes. You know that."

I went still, working through our past and wondering if her assertion could possibly be true. It wasn't unlike Wilma to throw out something like that in an effort to confuse and humble me. My Victorinox paring blade seemed to squirm in my fist as if to suggest another target. I released it to the counter.

"Since when do you have an allergy to tomatoes?"

"Since forever. Have you never noticed that I set them aside? And still you insist on putting them in everything. It's as if you want me to die from eating one."

"Die? Are you that allergic?"

"That's generally what dying from eating something means. It's a serious allergy. Do you want me to die, Arthur? Do you?"

My brain flashed back to the dozens of moments when I had, but on that night it was nearly the last thing on my mind. I only wanted a comforting dinner. I gathered the cutting board with those very expensive tomatoes and brought it to the garbage. With the Victorinox once again firmly in my fist, I scraped the red and yellow beauties into the bin.

The dish was lovely when I pulled it from the oven. Italian bread crumbs and butter gave it a golden sheen with light brown crispness at the edges. I stared at it with pride as if it had been born of my loins. Wilma regarded it with a less appreciative eye.

"Well," she said. "I suppose I should set the table if we plan on eating that."

The dinner was dismal. Without the backing of tomatoes, the yogurt screamed for company. And the cheeses, recognizing an unfamiliar vacancy, seemed to fight for attention. One taste, and I lost my appetite in a rush of disappointment. The only salvation was the wine. I had picked up two bottles of Saint-Émilion merlot assuming it would pair well with the tomatoes. But since that ship had sailed, I was afraid even the wine would fall short. It did not. By the second bottle I had forgotten all about my pathetic attempt.

Until Wilma brought it up again.

"I suppose you expect me to do the dishes," she said as she swirled a finger through her negroni. She always chose something strong with a digestif after dinner. She made it clear while mixing this one that although she had only indulged lightly, a hefty stomach-calmer was in order.

"That's how we usual do it. One of us cooks, the other cleans."

"Usually, the dinner is edible. I'll only have to make something later if I'm going to sleep through the night. I don't think this counts as your turn."

"You're suggesting it wasn't edible?"

"My God, Arthur, examine the evidence. Neither of us managed more than a few forkfuls. I'm sure if you would do the dishes it would help with your shame."

It was that last word that got me. How dare she. As if a recipe passed down from my mother could ever inspire anything other than satisfaction and a desire for more. The only reason it hadn't this time was Wilma's absurd protest of the tomatoes. She'd eaten them before; I was certain she had. Yes, I could even picture her in the act: in salads, on pizza, sliced with mozzarella drizzled and with olive oil. Even—I remembered with rage—even in my mother's macaroni and cheese. She had always enjoyed tomatoes, no doubt. Her sudden allergy was her reaction to our work that day. She had taken charge and this was her way of maintaining it.

I went to the trash bin and pulled out a large handful. Wilma was turned away from me, smoking a cigarette and flipping through the most recent *Vogue*. With my left hand cupped against the back of her head, I pressed the tomatoes into her face. I smashed them, getting as many as I could into her mouth, and then I closed it for her to swallow. The magazine connected with my face almost immediately.

"You are trying to kill me, aren't you?" She continued to swat me as she spat out remnants of the fruit.

I did my best to avoid her painful strikes but she managed to land most of them. "You're not allergic to tomatoes, are you? Tell me the truth, damn you!"

She tossed the magazine across the room, knocking over a vase of Casa Blanca lilies, then went to the sink where she gulped fistfuls of water. "Fine," she said when she turned back to me. "I'm not allergic to tomatoes, you idiot. The fact that you believed me is only proof of your incredible stupidity and lack of awareness. I hate your mother's macaroni and cheese. I always have. And your mother wasn't exactly on my favorite list either."

The knife was close but not close enough. I reached but she noticed. My thought as the entire casserole was ground into my face was how much better the experience would have been if it had only included that one missing ingredient.

Our lovemaking that night was volcanic.

We discovered the old well years later on a hike into the mountains behind the cottage in Riverton. It was October, and the colors were as vibrant as I'd ever seen. The maples especially, the way they blazed against a sky of deepest Azure blue. It was a breathtaking day, and we started out at noon in order to get the best of it. But also, to be back for cocktails at five. It was a tradition we never ignored.

Approximately two hours up the mountain we came across an abandoned farmhouse. It seemed to grow out of the landscape which must have included a cleared field and garden at one time but had given itself over to scrub brush and saplings. The structure had gone the way of all old and abandoned things: gray and barren. It brought to mind a carcass.

"Let's explore this one," Wilma said. "Who knows what treasures these deserted farms may hold."

"Don't you think it might be dangerous?" I put my hand to her elbow, but she yanked it free and moved toward the door. I followed more out of a need to gloat—in case she was hurt—than anything akin to a treasure-hunter's curiosity.

But once inside, I was intrigued. It had been a home, a place where people had lived and then left. It was a dying memorial to a family and the things they had loved. We split and went in directions that called to us. Wilma explored the kitchen and its pantry, which was still stocked with cans and jars. I moved to the bedrooms and found myself in what must have been a child's room. There were toys strewn across a floor that showed evidence of animal infestation and decades of exposure to the elements. Dolls and stuffed animals had been torn open, toy trains and guns that surely had been whittled from soft wood by a caring parent were now dark with mold. Every item was covered by a layer of grime that mocked the lives of the children who must have treasured them. I was overwhelmed by my imagination, and I sat on what seemed like the only piece of furniture in the room that still was capable of holding weight. It was a mother's rocker, sturdily constructed and apparently shaped by hand. I could hear Wilma in the other room, rummaging with little regard for the souls that had inhabited it. An image welled up in me. It was of a family, parents and children—possibly a child of each sex—who had left their home in such a rush that they needed to leave all of this behind. And in dramatic opposition to whatever that tragedy entailed was Wilma in the kitchen, treating it like a day at Goodwill. I couldn't help but compare that imagined family's scenario to my own. The effects of the juxtaposition poured out of me in sobs.

Wilma must have heard me. She came into the room holding a cast iron pan of considerable size. "What are you doing?"

I hung my head as if to inspect something on the floor, hoping to hide my absurd outburst. There was a bright red ball resting directly beneath my chair. It did not hold the grime of the other toys, possibly due to its protected location. I picked it up and bounced it in my palm. It was heavier than it looked.

"Why do you suppose these people left?" I said.

"Farm life," she said disdainfully. "And possibly hostile weather. Who knows? Shall we go?" Her spirits had lifted now that she had found her treasure. "A little cleaning and this will be a lovely addition to the cottage."

We left the house, and it wasn't until we were halfway across what had been the yard that I realized I was still clutching the ball. For whatever reason, I did not bring it to Wilma's attention. It was several more yards when we came to the well. Wilma spotted it rising up from a cluster of wild roses: a round, two-foot-high construction of mossy rock with the remnants of a trestle that had fallen to the side. I led us to it, still needing a moment to sit and collect.

"Why are we pausing here?" she said. "We should get back. It's getting close to the hour, and this damn pan is getting heavy."

"Let's take a minute here. And then we'll start down." I tested the sturdiness of the stonework and sat.

Wilma made a frustrated grunt and sat beside me. "Just for a minute. I could use a martini."

We were quiet for a while, each of us examining our finds. I started tossing the ball up lightly and catching it. The sun was getting low, and it captured the color which made it even brighter. "This must have belonged to a child," I said, still tossing and catching. I was mesmerized by how bright the red was getting, as if life had been brought back to it. "I think it was a boy's."

Wilma shifted on the well and stared hard at me. "What in hell are you going on about?"

"Have you ever thought that we should have had children?"

Her laughter was a howl. "Are you crazy? Us—you and me—with children? Oh my lord, darling, have you had a stroke?" She reached across and tested my forehead and then my wrist. "I think we should get you home. You're worrying me."

I examined the ball, noting the tiny specks of yellow like stars amid a blazing universe. "I could have been a good parent."

"We're too selfish to have had children. You know that as well as I. We discussed this years ago and we agreed. In fact, if I remember correctly, we laughed at the idea of us as Ma and Pa. It was ludicrous then and even more so now."

I was listening but not fully. I continued to toss the ball, higher and higher, captivated by the red and the yellow and the universe of what might have been. I was so engaged on that perfect twirling sphere that I didn't see her hand as it reached up and grabbed it.

"That's quite enough," she said. Then she carelessly tossed it over her shoulder, lobbing it high but close enough that it arced and paused several feet above the well.

There was no thought in my next action. It came out of instinct and possibly a desire for something I couldn't name. I leaped up and leaned out, watching the glowing arc as it peaked and then headed down toward the hole's center. Whether it was to assist or to stop me or something less helpful, I do not know, but I felt Wilma's palm on my back. And then I was following the ball on its long drop to the well's bottom.

Wilma comes to the well often when the seasons allow.

"I miss you terribly," she calls down to me.

If I were not still so angry and still so dead, I would call back to her. "I miss you too," I would say. "I miss you terribly, too." And I would mean it.

Gertie

GERTRUDE O'SHAY LAMPERT
1923-1998
WIFE AND MOTHER
IN HEAVEN WITH HIM

RICK'S DREAM HAS COME IN THREE PARTS, EACH EXACTLY AS THE one before but just a little longer and with more information.

They all begin the same—with a car, his old car, the VW Bug his dad had bought him for graduation in 1971, an occasion his parents had missed due to the cost of a flight from Maine to Georgia. He loved that car—powder blue with rust and dent accents.

In the dreams he's driving up a hill, and the Bug is reacting as it always had. It chugs and groans and slows to a crawl as the hill gets steeper. "Come on, Ladybug," he says, affectionately patting the dashboard. Later, he'll remember the feel of that, the grain of the fake leather embedded with bits of Georgian sand that he could never get out completely. Even in the dream it annoys him.

That's when he looks out the window and realizes where he is. He's in Riverton, a place where this old VW has never been. But now, she's struggling up Winter's Hill, heading toward Riverside Cemetery. And as she sputters and then stalls, he senses that he's not alone. He slowly turns to the right and sees that he has a passenger. It's his father.

It's not unusual for a father to work his way into the dreams of his children. But what Rick recognizes in those first seconds is that the man beside him is not as he remembers. This is his father as he is now: dead. There are no worms exiting his eye sockets. His skin isn't rotting and peeling like in a horror movie. But there is a deathlike pallor about him. And when he puts his hand on Rick's, the chill pours up the younger man's shoulder.

"There's something important I need to tell you," The dead Reverend Morty says. It's his voice as Rick remembers, but now its hoarse and dry.

This first dream, if that's what we're calling it, ends there. It dissolves around him. The other two will go further. By the end, after that third night, Rick will question whether they've been dreams at all.

Rick Lampert—once known as Ricky and now as Reverend Rick—has come back to Riverton. There's no joy in his return to the place he's rarely visited in thirty-five years. He's here to help his mother die and then to bury her next to her husband. It's an obligation that's been left for the youngest and only surviving child. The plan is that he'll do his duty for his mother, pack up the remains of their home, and then leave Riverton behind for good.

He stays in his old room in his old house, still decorated with the longings of a ten-year-old boy. His mother, with tubes and a monitor, is in the next. There's care workers who come in daily, managing the more difficult and less attractive tasks. But Rick will do the rest: cooking, cleaning, and talking to the woman who is more and more difficult to talk to. Gertie Lampert has become, in the past two years, a vessel that is slightly cracked and losing its contents. She remembers little, and when she is alert enough to greet Rick in the mornings, it's her husband Morty that she sees.

It's the day after Rick's third dream that he runs into Mavi in Johnson's General. They haven't seen each other since they were kids, not since Rick's parents sent him to the evangelical school in Georgia hoping to save him from the "evil" that was growing in Riverton. It's Mavi's wild orange hair, now duller and striped with white, that catches his eye. Still, he's not completely sure. It's been thirty-five years, after all. She's a few people ahead of him in a long line at the one register. Old Mrs. Johnson is slowly working the machine, and when Rick hears someone mumble—low but loud enough for the line to hear—"Jesus H. Christ, could we get someone with opposable thumbs back there?"—he knows it's her. He laughs too loudly, and since he's the only one to do so, Mavi turns.

"Hello, Mavi. Still acting the boss, I see."

He watches as her mind tours her past and then settles.

"No fucking way! Ricky?" She pushes back through the line, leaving sneers and angry mutterings behind her.

"Yup. But I'm more of a Rick now."

"What the hell are you doing back in this place?"

An older woman turns and angrily jabs a finger at Mavi. "You need to learn some manners, missy."

Mavi ignores her. "Wait till Sam sees you. He's gonna flip."

"Heard you guys were married. How's that going?"

"Oh, you know, ups and downs." She takes Rick's few groceries without asking, puts them in her basket, and then shoves it into a corner on the floor. "Come on, mister. Screw this line. You're coming home with me."

Mavi takes his hand and pushes through the line toward the door. As they pass, the older woman mutters her disgust with girls these days.

"What the fuck!" Mavi is incredulous. "That's no dream, Rick. More like a fucking vision, don't you think?"

Sam isn't saying anything. He's been quietly absorbing every detail that Rick has sketched for them. He's been so attentive that he can see it all: the car, the hill, Rick's dad and the chill that he emanates, and even the embedded sand in the dash. By the end he agrees with Mavi. It seems to be more than a dream.

Rick hadn't planned on telling them. In fact, he'd only wanted to stop by and say hello to Sam, maybe catch up a bit. But it had always been hard to say no to Mavi, and once he gets there he doesn't want to leave. There's no reason to. His mother was having a bad morning, and the caregivers had suggested he get out for a while. So he stays with his old friends and talks, like he hasn't talked in a long time.

Mavi sets out beers and a bowl of pretzels that they absently pick at. They go through the highlights of their years. Mavi bemoans her limited success as an artist, Sam minimalizes his own as a writer, and Rick admits, to his astonishment, that he's been questioning his life as a divorced and childless preacher who is lately unsure of his faith. They've only mentioned the death of Donnie Hickey briefly, although it had been the secret that had torn them apart in '63, as well as the real reason why Rick's parents had sent him to Georgia. They acknowledge it and then move on, as if to dwell could only bring back the nightmares of that summer. One subject leads to another—three old friends filling in time—and then Rick, despite his fear of what they might think, tells them of the dreams. There are no other people in his life that he would trust. Even after so much time apart, Sam and Mavi are the two best friends he's ever had.

By the end of the second dream, Sam is as stunned as Mavi, perhaps because it's such a detailed replay of the other. It is, according to Rick, exactly the same as the first, right down to the physical sensations. Even though he's anticipating the cold from his father's hand, the frigidity of it shocks him again. Instead of ending there, the second dream moves forward.

"There's something important I need to tell you," Old Reverend Lampert says, with the same gravity as before. "It's about your mother."

"She's dying, you know," Rick says. "Of course, you know."

"Yes, I know. That's why I'm here." He's not looking at his son. He's staring up the hill toward the cemetery. "She doesn't have much time."

"I know that."

"I have something to give you. You need to keep it safe until your mother's funeral." The dead man reaches into a pocket, removing something in his clenched fist. He extends it to Rick. "Take this," he says, as he slowly relaxes his fingers.

Rick can see an object cradled in the palm of the dead man's hand, but it's not registering in his brain.

"You need to take it, Ricky. It's important."

But just as Rick begins to understand what he's seeing, the scene dissolves around him again. He wakes to a call from the next room.

"Morty? Where are you? I need you, Morty." It's his mother.

"Coming." Rick shakes off what's left of the dream and goes to her.

"Wow," Sam says as he heads to the fridge for another beer. "You want one, Rick?"

"Got anything stronger?"

Mavi laughs. "You're asking the wrong guy, Reverend." She reaches deep into a cabinet and pulls out a bottle of something brown. "I keep this for emergencies. There's been a few of those lately and I think this might qualify."

Sam gives Mavi a look but says nothing as he pops the top of his beer and sits. Mavi pours Rick and herself a healthy shot.

"Do you get dreams like this often? Like Mavi said, it's more like some kind of vision. I suppose preachers get those more than normal people, huh?"

"Not me," Rick says.

"So, there's one more?" Mavi's doing her best to hide her impatience.

"There is." Rick tosses back the shot and winces. "I needed that."

Mavi grins and pours him another.

"Thanks."

"What do you think your pa wants to tell you?" Mavi says.

"I already know, 'cause he did in the third dream, the one I had last night."

"Exactly the same?" Sam asks.

"Yup. Longer, but exactly the same up to where the last one ended. And when I tell you, Sam, you might be needing a shot too."

His father is next to him, pale as before. Rick notices his clothes this time. He recognizes the shirt-and-tie combo. It's the one he bought for him on Father's Day a few years before he'd had the fall that killed him. It's what he was buried in: pale green shirt with a darker damask tie. It was handsome on him when he was alive, but now the vivid green makes him look paler and—the thought makes Rick shiver—deader.

"I have something to give you," old Reverend Lampert says from the passenger seat, exactly as he had the first two times. And again, there is that chill that crawls to Rick's shoulder as his father rests his hand on his. There's an intense desire to run, but even within the dream he knows he can't. He needs to stay to learn what's so important. The old man pulls his fist from his pocket and slowly unfurls his fingers. Rick can see the object clearly this time. When the dead man's palm is fully opened, there is a large and ornate key filling it.

Rick describes what it feels like when he takes it, how heavy it is and cold from his father's grip. He looks closely at the bow and sees there's a symbol there, created by decorative swirls. And in the center is a bright red stone.

"Why are you giving this to me?" Rick can feel the metal warming from the heat of his own palm.

"Because you have to give it to your mother. She'll need it. Not now. After she's passed. You'll slip it into her hand before they close the casket."

"What? Why?"

Old Reverend Lampert looks out the windshield, up the hill toward the cemetery. "I need you to know that if you don't give this key to your mother, she'll be stuck in a state of confusion. Ricky, look at me."

Rick does as he's told, even though looking at this version of his father is painful.

"You're the only one left in the family. There's no one else I can ask. What do you see in your hand right now?"

Rick studies the thing before answering. "A key. A large and beautiful key."

"And what does a key mean to you?"

"Well, I guess I think of a key as opening things. Doors. Boxes. Private places, I suppose."

"Exactly. A key unlocks things. Your mother will need to unlock parts of herself in order to transition."

"Transition to what, Dad? I don't understand."

The old man gives his son a look that the younger man knows well. It expresses annoyance, disappointment, and expectation. "You're a man of faith, or at least you were. Everybody needs that. It doesn't have to be in God, but it has to be in something. So, I need you to have some faith now. Trust that I know things that you can't know yet, and do this for me. Muster up enough faith to do it. Promise me."

Rick withers under that look as he always had when his father lived. "Okay. I promise," he says, and the dream dissolves around him as it had twice before.

"And that was it," Rick says as he takes in the slack jaws and wide eyes. "Except for one thing. When I woke up this morning, I was clutching this." He reaches into his coat pocket and slowly unfolds his fingers, revealing a small black key with minor decorative swirls that resemble a three-leaf clover. Sam recognizes it as a key that's used to wind clocks, similar to those that his father used on the old chiming clocks at the farm.

Mavi slaps the table, toppling Sam's beer. "What the fuck?"

"Jesus, Mavi!" Sam grabs a sponge from the sink and sops up the spill. "Rick, are you telling us that you woke up holding the key from the dream?"

"It's not the same key. That one was large and heavy. And it was really ornate. I have no idea where this came from. All I know for sure is that I had a dream about a key and then I woke up with this in my fist."

"Jesus H.," Mavi says.

"Seriously," Sam agrees.

All three stare down at the object that now rests in the center of the table, as if they are expecting it to explain.

Gertie has a rare alertness the next day. She recognizes Rick when he comes to her room in the morning. She sees her son and not her husband for the first time since he's been home.

"How are you, Ricky?" she says with a big grin when he enters. "I've missed you." She reaches one thin arm toward him.

The innocent comment stabs at him and unearths fresh guilt over his lengthy absences.

"I'm doing okay, Ma. I'm glad I'm here." He squeezes her hand then checks her pulse and the monitor. "What can I get for you? Some breakfast? Cup of tea?"

"Not yet. Sit for a minute."

Rick pulls a chair to the side of her bed. Gertie takes his hand in hers. It's cold. Not as cold as his dead father's, but it brings on a similar sensation, reminding him of how close she is to death.

"How are you feeling today? You look better."

"Don't lie to your mother. I look terrible. But I do feel a little more alive today."

"That's good. And how did you sleep? You called out last night."

"I think I slept pretty well. I dreamed, which is odd, 'cause I haven't dreamed in a long time. I can still feel it in me. It's not going away like dreams usually do."

Rick is a little afraid to ask, considering the dreams he's been having, but he does anyway. "Would you like to tell me about it?"

"I think I would. Maybe that's why it's still there, so clear, waiting to be told. It was a simple dream, just a slice of an ordinary Lampert morning, like so many we'd had in this house." Her eyes close to see it better. "I'm sitting at the kitchen table—that same old table your grandmother gave us—but the cloth on it is bright yellow, like the one we had when your father and I first got married. I'm sipping coffee and I look up and your dad is there sipping coffee too. He doesn't look good, Ricky. Not good at all. Real pale and thin. He's wearing what we buried him in, and the green makes him look so pale, as if every bit of color's been sucked out of him. We're just talking about ordinary things—the church, you kids, a car he's thinking of buying for you—and he suddenly touches me with a hand that's as cold as a morning stove. I can still feel the chill." She pauses and shivers. Rick rubs her hand to put some warmth into it. "Then he tells me he'll be seeing me soon. I smile and nod like it's the most ordinary thing for him to be saying to me at the kitchen table. We go on sipping our coffee and talking about nothing of any importance. Isn't that the oddest dream? And it's so clear, as if it really happened just yesterday."

"It's a strange dream, Ma. How did it make you feel?"

Gertie smiles. "It made me feel good, if you can believe it. Made me feel like maybe I'm ready. I'm looking forward to being with him again and finally knowing what's on the other side of this life."

"Really? I'd figure you'd be pretty sure of what that is."

His mother chuckles, which causes a mild coughing fit. Rick offers her a sip of water but she refuses.

"You mean Heaven?" she chuckles again. "I'll tell you a little secret, Ricky. Don't you be telling your dad." She holds a thin finger up to her lips and then whispers, "The truth is, Heaven never seemed right to me. Not right at all. Of course, I never woulda said that to your father, but it seemed to me all that Heaven and Hell stuff made for some good stories for kids, something to keep them in line. But they made no sense to me. What I've been thinking—and I don't know if it's just now and maybe I've always thought this way—that whatever is out there is so much bigger than any story we mortals could ever come up with. It must be something so amazing that our simple brains couldn't possibly understand it, 'cause it's just too big. Does that make any sense to you?"

Rick is too astounded to speak at first. His mother—a woman who has always stood by her preacher husband and has never said anything deeper to him than what he should and should not do with a girl—has just floored him with one of his own doubts. She's looking at him now, her eyes darting between each of his. She's waiting, possibly for some kind of confirmation or understanding. She's been thinking deeply, and to her son it doesn't seem like her at all. To Rick, she's always been a woman who has judged with one eye and been blind to life's mysteries with the other.

"Ma, where is this coming from? I had no idea you questioned anything."

"I know, you kids always thought I was empty-headed." Rick starts to protest but she holds up a hand. "Don't correct me, it's true. Your dad got to be the smart one, and it wasn't my place to make you think otherwise. I guess I'm not as dumb as you thought, huh?" She squints at him and shakes her head with feigned admonishment. "But you haven't answered my question, Ricky. Does what I said make any sense to you? What do you believe in?"

Again, she searches his face, which makes her son want to pull away. But he can't. If there has ever been a time for honesty and real communication, it's now. He's been given an opportunity that would be cruel to avoid.

"That's a pretty big question, Ma, and it's one I've been pondering a lot. But I do agree that whatever comes next is way bigger than anything we've come up with and told folks as if we know. Nobody knows. Whatever it is will be . . ." He searches for the right word, ". . . wondrous, I think."

"Yes, wondrous. That's surely what it'll be. And I'm looking forward to it." Her eyes widen as if she's hoping for a glimpse, and then she adds, "I nearly forgot one part of the dream. Your father said something else that was a little strange. He said you'd have something for me when I needed it. What do you think that could be?"

Rick watches his mother's hand move across the back of his. He's struck by how thin and bruised her skin has become. He can see nearly every vein and the many blotches of purplish bruising caused by too many needles. He's uncertain how much he should say about his dreams, if anything at all. But it's been so long since they've been able to talk and he wants this connection to keep going.

"I've been having some strange dreams, too, Ma. And Dad's been in them."

Gertie's eyes brighten and she grips his hand with more strength than he thought she was capable. "Really? Tell me."

He decides to lie and reveal just a little. "I don't remember most of it. But it was definitely Dad, and he told me that I had to—without fail or question—give you something. A key."

She laughs, and the sound is the prettiest thing Rick has heard in a long time. "Why would I need a key?"

"I don't know. But he was adamant."

"You know, your father always had a thing for keys. You probably don't remember, but there's a drawer in the kitchen still full of all kinds. I couldn't get rid of them. You'll probably have to after I'm gone."

"I do remember." But what Rick can't remember is the last time he saw that drawer and if he might have found it at some point in the night. His hand goes to his pants' pocket involuntarily, and he can feel the shape of it through the fabric.

"Well, if your dad says I need it, you better give it to me. He isn't one to give orders idly." She laughs again, and the sound makes Rick tear.

"I will. I promise."

That is the last conversation they have. By the next day, Gertie is worse than she's been since Rick's arrival. She no longer sees him as Morty. She doesn't see him at all. In just three days, on the advice of the caregivers, she is moved to a hospice, where she lies quietly until her death two weeks later. Arrangements are made, and the funeral is at the church where her husband had preached for so many years. Mavi and Sam sit with him in the first row, and each is reminded of another funeral they had attended together many years ago, although no one speaks of it.

After the service, folks line up to say goodbye to Gertie. Rick waits until everyone has passed the casket. Then he approaches, still gripping the object in his pocket. She looks better than she had toward the end, but nothing like the mother he grew under. Her once-full frame has been whittled down by half, and the dark hair that had always been an unruly annoyance to her is neatly brushed and set. He leans close and whispers, "Safe trip, Ma. I don't know what this means, but I promised." He kisses her on the forehead and subtly slips the key between her right palm and the back of her left. It starts to slip and he tries again. This time it stays, and later he will decide to believe that the slight movement in her hand was real, that his mother's will had reached beyond death, and that she had accepted the key that her husband had meant for her.

Mavi and Sammy

THE TOBOGGAN WAS AN AFTERTHOUGHT, OR AT LEAST I THINK IT was. There was no plan that I was aware of, no decision that we'd discussed or even mentioned in passing. Still, we were certainly motivated to do something that would move us beyond the darkness that had clouded us since Mavi's diagnosis. So, when I grabbed the toboggan's rope and headed toward the path, the one that leads through woods and field and along the river, Mavi smile and nodded as if a an understanding had been reached. And I suppose, considering how long we'd known each other, there had been. I read somewhere that hope comes with wings. We had lost our hope over the recent months, but we were still in search of our wings.

I led the way and Mavi followed, crunching along the trail we'd been using every winter for over thirty years, but not at all recently. There was no need for headlamps; the night was that bright. The moonlight made tiny diamonds on the snow-covered branches, and the shadows it created were deep purple across waves of fresh white. It seemed like something from a painting or a snow globe.

"The cold feels good," Mavi called up to me. "I'm feeling better."

And hearing that made me feel better too. It was as if the moon entered us as well.

I didn't tell Mavi where we were going and she didn't ask. She knew, of course. The toboggan was a giveaway. We'd been inside for too long dealing with pills and needles. But on that night, she was feeling better than she had in months. And when the moon had shone in at us, we both knew we had to get out and into it. I helped her into her layers, strapped the snowshoes to her boots, and then we were off, the toboggan hissing between us as if it were as excited as we were to finally be active again after an entire winter of inertia.

We hadn't been up Trenholm's Hill for years. During our winters in Riverton, we'd mostly just snowshoed along the river or sledded down the smaller hills closer to home. The big hill had been an important destination when we were kids, and I was hoping to rekindle some of that old thrill. Ricky, Mavi, and I used to sled there all winter, stargaze and catch fireflies all summer. From the crest, the whole town is spread out below with the river snaking through it and the mountains cupping it like a pair of hands. The sky is so massive from the top that you feel a part of it, as if you could jump up and sweep a hand through all those sparkling bits. The joy I'd had as a kid roiled in my belly as we left the path along the river and started up.

I kept looking back to make sure Mavi was okay. As the hill got steeper, I could hear her breathing become more labored, so we'd pause for a while until she'd give me a smile and a thumbs-up. I was afraid the hike might be too much for her—the snow wasn't heavy, but still it was a good distance—but she seemed okay, like her old self. I think it had to do with a plan that we'd silently agreed to at some point but had never addressed. That happens sometimes with people who have shared so much.

By the time we got to the top, the moon was still low enough that the Milky Way stood out against the blackness like a spiraling spill of salt. It bowed from one horizon to the other, disappearing into the mountains on each side. We both stood there for a while, staring up at the vastness of it as if we hadn't seen it a thousand times before. I took off my snowshoes and helped Mavi with hers. I positioned the toboggan and adjusted the two brakes so it wouldn't take off without us. I asked her where she wanted to sit. Up front with the brakes or behind to do the steering? Just like when we were kids, she chose the front. Back then Ricky would pick the middle, probably so he wouldn't be responsible if something went wrong. I'd always been the one to steer. I suppose I'd always been the one most afraid to die. And that night was no different.

Before she got in, she did something that was so true to the old Mavi that my heart filled right up. With a grin that nearly took up her whole face, she dropped to the soft ground and stretched out in all directions. For a few minutes she stayed like that, looking up at the sky and pointing out the few constellations she could remember. And then she told me a story about when she was in art school, a Mavi story I'd never heard. Every time I'd figured I'd heard all her history; she'd surprise me with a new tale she'd decided to free from her well-guarded repository.

In art school, she'd written an essay on the Mona Lisa. She'd covered all the usual crap, as Mavi called it, and then she'd offered her theory about that unusual smile. It was her premise that the celebrated grin was actually inspired by the face in the full moon. Her theory was that da Vinci had spent a long time looking up at the heavens, possibly influenced by some mind-altering drug. And when he was finishing the painting that would become his most famous, he chose to use the smile of the moon instead of the less pleasing one on Lisa Gherardini. Mavi's teacher hadn't thought much of her bizarre theory and in the end had given her a shitty grade. But I thought it was a beautiful idea. As she spoke, I looked up at the moon that was then full and slowly rising, and I could actually see it. That intriguing smile was surely there—Mona Lisa's—and I wondered at how amazing Mavi's brain must be to be able to see something only she and one of the world's greatest artists had ever considered.

Then she waved her arms and legs, making a perfect angel with huge wings and a full skirt. So I dropped down and did the same. How could I not? It was Mavi and me, and we were kids again at the top of Trenholm's Hill. I'm not sure how long those angels will last, but I'd like to think they'll be there for a long time: Two perfect angels side by side, frozen in place and connected by the tips of their outstretched wings.

"Okay, let's do this," she said as she jumped up, flung off her hat—just threw it aside into the snow—and folded herself into the curve at the front of the sled. Her hair, white now as opposed the bright orange of the girl, spiraled out like a wad of springs that'd been set free. She hunkered down, preparing for the speed of the hill and the power of cold wind that would push up against us. She released the brakes, and that wind hit us hard when I kicked off. I pushed and ran beside the sled for several steps and then crumpled into it, feeling the ache of knees and back that hadn't been pushed into those positions for too long. The pain faded as we picked up speed.

At first it was just a giggle. Bubbly and far too girlish to be coming from Mavi. Then it grew into a full-on laugh like I hadn't heard from her in years. It went on in waves of rich, exuberant howls as we barreled down the hill, getting pelted by sprays of icy crystals. And then, as we hit the steepest part, her laugh changed to something strange. It became a long and loud exhaling sigh, nearly a groan, that seemed to come from somewhere deep inside of her, in her belly or in her heart. It was like the release of something, maybe of her pain or her worry, I don't know, but I feel there might have been some resignation in there too. As if she were resigning herself to a plan we had silently agreed to.

When we got to the bottom of where the open hill narrows toward a winding path, the place where she'd always done what the kid in front was supposed to do: pull those two pieces of wood on each side of her knees that would dig into the snow and slow us enough so we could get out feet out to stop us fully. But she didn't do that this night. Instead, she did what I fully expected her to. She screamed, "Let's keep going!" When the three of us were kids, we'd sworn we were going to do it someday, but we'd never dared. "Too narrow," Mavi would yell as we'd get closer, and then she'd pull on the brakes. We'd never gone any farther than that first hill. We'd been too scared. It was crazy that we'd do it now, at our age. Crazy that we would finally do something we'd never dared to do when we were young and closer to immortal. But it was a crazy night with nothing to lose, so I yelled back, "Yes!" and I gave her shoulders a squeeze that told her I was right behind her, like I'd always been. With that decision made and with the speed from the long hill behind us, we flew on.

I leaned to the left to enter the path and Mavi leaned too. It was like we were all one: the toboggan, Mavi, and me. The path was darker than the hill with those dark purple shadows slicing across the white and making everything—the rocks, the trees, the mounds and the dips—harder to see. There'd be splashes of moonlight through the trees and then the trail would go nearly black. Large pines were suddenly bearing down on us from the left. I yelled, "Lean right," and we did it together, Mavi still hunkered down so I could see over her head. Occasionally, her hair would fly up and I'd have to reach out and pat it down. The sled nearly toppled as we skidded along a tree's edge. "Lean hard left," I yelled over the sound of peeling bark. Miraculously, we did it and kept going.

I couldn't believe we weren't crashing. I steered by dragging a hand, sometimes so hard my glove nearly tore off. Bearing left, barely missing a tree, then bearing right around a boulder that scraped against my knee. Slaloming through a five-foot-wide track so fast that I could barely see an obstacle before it was on us. There was a spot where a tree must have fallen across the path and had been covered by snow. We hit it straight-on and soared off the other side. Mavi whooped and I laughed even harder when we crashed down and kept going.

Mavi was screaming at that point—a high-pitched cackle that was so full of excitement that I screamed with her. Years were peeling away and we were ten years old again, laughing at danger as if nothing could hurt us. It felt like that, the way the trees and rocks seemed to cooperate. The farther we went, the more it seemed like we were invincible, like we were being guided along, helped by a whim of nature. I swear it felt that perfect, as if the universe understood our need and was helping us to accomplish it.

We were getting close to what I figured must be the end of the path, but I couldn't see past Mavi's hair. She'd lifted her head and had shaken it, suddenly blocking my view completely. I was trying to steer but I couldn't see anything except a patch of light directly ahead. I suppose I didn't need to see. I knew where we were going, but we were so close, and I wanted to be as much in that moment as Mavi. She was screaming then and I think I was screaming too. But hers were so loud I could barely hear my own. They were filled with anticipation and joy and an excitement neither one of us had felt in years. They were the screams of two lives that had been joined for more than sixty years and would not accept a life that wouldn't include the other.

We were moving so fast at that point that I couldn't feel my face or my hands. The snow crystals and the cold press of the wind had numbed everything except my brain. It flashed on a question I hadn't considered. *What now?* I thought. *What will happen to us now?* And as quick as it had come to me the question was gone, as if it didn't matter anymore because there was so much thrill to acknowledge in that moment. We launched off the edge of the riverbank, soaring nearly as high as the trees, and into the stark brightness of moon and snow.

It's strange how time can sometimes stretch. While we were blasting through bitter cold air and bright moonlight, there were so many thoughts and memories packed into a few spacious seconds. One memory that filled me the longest was of a moment from way back. It was more of a feeling, really. Of catapulting off a bank into a favorite swimming hole with Mavi and Ricky behind me. I could almost hear Ricky laughing and Mavi swearing as I screamed up at the sky that I would be the boss for the summer.

And as it had on that day nearly sixty years before, my heart seemed to seize up when I looked down to see what was below me. It wasn't the body of a poor dead boy this time. There was nothing down there except the frozen expansiveness of an unforgiving river.

We slapped it hard, so hard that the toboggan splintered beneath us. There was a series of wooden cracks and then—oh God, that sound—an even larger crack as the river opened and swallowed us. All my bones seemed to shift. It felt like everything—our bones, the wood, the ice, even the sky—was shattering. I think I only let out one yelp before we went under.

The sound when it opened was like thunder. There was a crack and then the roar of rushing water when it took us, deep and resonant like an avalanche. It pulled us down and moved us fast below the thick ice. I can remember looking up at the shimmering blueish-green and thinking how beautiful the world was from down there. And it surely would have been beautiful if it were not so terrifying. We had made our choice and there would be no going back.

I reached for Mavi who was just ahead of me. I could see her hair, white against the black of the water. It was like seaweed or marsh grass the way it swayed in the current. I almost touched her, had one hand nearly to her hair, when a boulder or something spun me around and my boot connected hard against something that gave in a little. I knew immediately it was her head. I screamed her name and felt the river fill my lungs. Then, quick as that, it was all over.

But not quite, it seems.

It could be a dream, a memory, or some trick of the expiring mind, but whatever it is it feels real. Mavi is ahead of me still, but not under the ice now. It's summer and I can feel the heat and that excitement of longer and warmer days rippling through me. She's running fast and her orange curls—yes, they're orange again—are vibrating when she turns to laugh at me.

Stubs of ryegrass are stabbing at my feet and catching in the clefts of my toes, but it doesn't hurt a bit. My skinny legs are pumping, but I can't catch up to Mavi. I'd forgotten how fast she can run. Without pausing, she peels off her shirt, jumps out of her shorts—barely missing a stride—and yells something back to me. All I catch through the wind is the word *dummy*. I'm laughing because it makes me so happy.

I can see where we're heading. She'll get there first this time, and I'm okay with that. She'll catch the edge of the bank with the toes of her right foot, cannonball through the summer air, and scream with full voice, "I'm the Boss." Her arms will be stretched out as if to embrace the sky before she plunges into the frigidity of our favorite swimming hole. And I'll yell back that she surely is.

Mavi will be the Boss forever, and there could be no better ending.

MAVIS GOFF TAYLOR
1953–2019
SAMUEL WINSLOW TAYLOR
1953–2019
IN DEATH AS IN LIFE